PENGUIN CRIME FICTION

THE JUDAS PAIR

Jonathan Gash is the pen name of a distinguished English doctor. His "Lovejoy" series, including *The Sleepers of Erin, Moonspender, Spend Game, The Vatican Rip, The Gondola Scam, Firefly Gadroon, Pearlhanger,* and *The Tartan Sell* (all available from Penguin), is among the most original and consistently entertaining currently being written. A television series based on the Lovejoy character recently aired on the Arts and Entertainment channel.

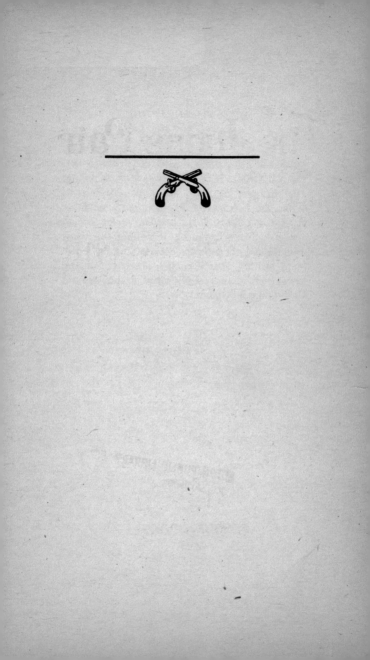

The Judas Pair

by

JONATHAN GASH

PENGUIN BOOKS

PENGUIN BOOKS
Viking Penguin Inc., 40 West 23rd Street,
New York, New York 10010, U.S.A.
Penguin Books Ltd, 27 Wrights Lane, London W8 5TZ
(Publishing & Editorial) and Harmondsworth,
Middlesex, England (Distribution & Warehouse)
Penguin Books Australia Ltd, Ringwood,
Victoria, Australia
Penguin Books Canada Limited, 2801 John Street,
Markham, Ontario, Canada L3R 1B4
Penguin Books (N.Z.) Ltd, 182–190 Wairau Road,
Auckland 10, New Zealand

First published in the United States of America by
Harper & Row, Publishers, Inc. 1977
Reprinted by arrangement with Harper & Row, Publishers, Inc.
Published in Penguin Books 1988

LIBRARY OF CONGRESS CATALOGING IN PUBLICATION DATA
Gash, Jonathan.
The judas pair.
Originally published: New York: Harper & Row, 1977
I. Title.
PR6057.A728J8   1987   823'.914   87-19683
ISBN 0 14 01.0646 4

Printed in the United States of America by
Offset Paperback Mfrs., Inc., Dallas, Pennsylvania
Set in Caledonia

This book is dedicated, with respect
and humility, to the Chinese god Wei Dt'o,
protector of books against fire, pillaging,
decay, and dishonest borrowers.

LOVEJOY

1

This story's about greed, desire, love, and death—in the world of antiques you get them all.

Just when I was in paradise the phone rang. Knowing it would be Tinker Dill, I pushed her into the bathroom, turned all the taps on, and switched the radio on.

"What the hell's that noise?" Tinker sounded half sloshed as usual.

"You interrupted again, Tinker," I said wearily.

"How am I to know you're on the nest?" he said, peeved.

In the White Hart they only had one record that worked, and it was notching up the decibels in a background muddle of voices.

"What is it?"

"Got somebody for you," he said.

I was all ears. You know that tingling a sexy promise gives? Double it for religion. Treble it for collecting. And for antique dealers like me hearing of a customer, multiply by infinity to get somewhere near the drive that forces a man over every conceivable boundary of propriety, common sense, reason—oh, and law. I almost forgot law. I'd been on the nest two days with

Sheila (was she Sheila, or was that last Thursday? I couldn't remember) and here I was quivering like a selling plater at its first race. All because one of my scouts was phoning in with a bite.

Scouts? We call them barkers in the trade. An antique dealer has scouts, people who will pass information his way. Tinker Dill was one of mine. I have three or four, depending on how rich I'm feeling at the time, paid on commission. Tinker was the best. Not because he was much good, but because he was loyal. And he was loyal because he judged every deal in terms of whisky. Or gin. Or rum.

"Buying or selling?" I said, quite casual. Twenty years dealing antiques, and my hands sweating because a barker rings in. It's a right game.

"Buying."

"Big or little?"

"Big."

"You having me on, Tinker?" That stupid bird was banging on the bathroom door wanting to be let out.

"Straight up, Lovejoy," he said. All right, all right. I was born with the name. Still, you can't forget Lovejoy Antiques, Inc., can you? The "Inc." bit was pure invention, brilliance. It sounds posh, reeks of dollars and high-flying American firms backing that knowledgeable antique wizard Lovejoy.

"Got enough copper in case the bleeps go?" I asked.

"Eh? Oh, sure."

"Hang on, then."

I dropped the receiver, crossed to open the bathroom door. There she was, trying to push past me into the room, blazing.

"What the hell do you mean—?" she was starting to say when I gave her a shove. Down she went on the loo amid the steam.

"Now," I explained carefully, "silence. Si-lence. Got it, love?"

She rubbed her arm, her eyes glazed at the enormity of these events.

I patted her cheek. "I'm waiting," I said. "Got it, love?"

2

"Yes." Her voice barely made it.

"I've got a deal coming in. So shut your teeth. Sit there and listen to all my lovely hot water going to waste."

I slammed the door on her, locked it again, and found Tinker hanging on by the skin of his alcohol-soaked teeth.

"Big? How big?" I demanded.

"Well . . ."

"Come on."

"S and four D's," he said shakily.

My scalp, already prickling and crawling, gave up as the magic code homed in.

"Give over, Dill."

"Honest, Lovejoy. God's truth."

"In this day and age?"

"Large as life, Lovejoy. Look, this bloke's real. He's here now."

"Where?"

"White Hart."

My mind took off. Computers aren't in it. Speed they've got and memory too, so people say. I have both those attributes and a bell. This bell's in my chest. Put me within a hundred feet of a genuine antique and it chimes, only gently at first, then a clamor as I get nearer the real thing. By the time I'm touching it I can hardly breathe because my bell's clanging like a fire engine. It's never been wrong yet. Don't misunderstand—I've sold some rubbish in my time. And lies come as natural to me as blinking in a gale. After all, that's life, really, isn't it? A little half-truth here and there, with a faint hint of profit thrown in for good measure, does no harm. And I make a living mainly from greed. Not my greed, you understand. *Your* greed, his greed, everybody's greed. And I want no criticism from self-righteous members of the indignant honest old public, because they're the biggest school of sharks on this planet. No? Listen:

Say you're at home relaxing in your old rocking chair. In comes a stranger. He's heard of your old—or indeed your *new*

3

—rocking chair. Could it be, he gasps, that it's the one and only rocking chair last used by Lord Nelson on his flagship the *Golden Hind?* Good heavens, he cries, clapping his eyes on it in ecstasy. *It is!*

Now, you put your pipe down, astonished. What the hell's going on? you demand. And who the hell is this stranger butting into your house? And what's he babbling about? And—*take your hands off my old rocking chair!*

With me so far? Good.

The stranger, confronted with your indignation, turns sincere and trusting eyes to you. I've searched all my life, he explains. For what? you demand suspiciously. For Lord Nelson's famous old rocking chair, he confides. And here it is, at last. It's beautiful. My lifelong search is over.

See what I'm getting at? At everybody's dishonesty. At mine. And at yours. No? *Yes!* Read on.

Now, if I were a trusting soul, I'd leave you to complete the story, give it a proper ending, so to speak. How you smile at the stranger, explain that the chair's only a secondhand mock-up your cousin Harry's lad did at night school, and how in any case Nelson, who is pretty famous for rocking on the cradle of the deep for years on end, was the last bloke on earth ever to need a rocking chair, and how you kindly proceed to put the misguided stranger right over a cup of tea with gay amusing chat. But you can't be trusted to end the story the way it really would happen! And why? Because the stranger, with the light of crusading fervor burning in his eyes, reaches for his wallet and says those glorious magic words—*How much?*

Now what's the *real* ending of the story? I'll tell you. You leap off your—*no, Lord Nelson's!*—rocking chair, brush it down, bring out the Australian sherry left over from Christmas, and cod on you're the hero's last living descendant. And you just manage to stifle your poor little innocent daughter as she looks up from her history homework and tries to tell the visitor that Nelson missed sailing on the *Golden Hind* by a good couple of centuries, and send her packing to bed so she won't see her honest old dad shingling this stupid bum for every quid he can.

Convinced? No? *Then why are you thinking of that old chair in your attic?*

Everybody's got a special gift. Some are psychic, some have an extra dress sense, beauty, a musical talent, or have green fingers. Some folk are just lucky, or have the knack of throwing a discus. But nobody's been missed out. We've all got one special gift. The only trouble is learning which it is we've got.

I had this pal who knew horses—they used to come to him even when he'd no sugar. He and I once collected a Chippendale from near a training stables and we paused to watch these nags running about like they do. "Quid on the big one," I said, bored. "The funny little chap," he said, and blow me if it didn't leave the rest standing. It was called Arkle, a champion, they told us. See what I mean? To me that tiny, gawky, ungainly brute breathing all wrong was horrible. To my pal it was clearly the best of the lot. Now, to him a Turner painting—screaming genius over every inch of canvas—would look like a nasty spillage. Not to me. I've only to see an eighty-eight bus labeled "Tate Gallery" and my bell goes like the clappers. Like I say, a gift.

Once I brought this dirty old monstrosity for ten quid. It looked for all the world like a little doll's house with a couple of round windows stuck on, and a great sloping piece of broken tin fixed to the back. The boys at the auction gave me an ironic cheer, making my face red as fire. But my bell was bonging. My find was eventually the only original Congreve clock ever to be exhibited within living memory—a clock worked on a spring controlled by a little ball rolling down a groove cut in an inclined plane, designed and made by the great inventor William Congreve almost two hundred years ago.

If you've got the courage, find out what your own particular knack is, then trust it. Obey your bells, folks. They're telling you about cold stone certainties.

Where was I?

Tinker Dill. S and four D's, and he'd sounded frantic. Ten thousand.

S and D's? Look in any antique shop. Casually, you'll find yourself wanting some lovely little trinket, say a twist-stem drinking glass. The more you look the more you want it. So you search it for the price and find a little ticket tied on marked HA/-, or some such.

We use codes, all very simple. One of the most elementary is that based on a letter-number transposition. Each code has a key word—for example, SUTHERLAND. Note that it has ten letters. For S read 1, for U read 2, and so on to N, which is 9. For D read not 10 but nought, because you already have a letter to denote 1. So the glass goblet you fancied is priced at forty-eight quid. There are several ten-letter codes. A quick look around tips you off.

One further point. X is often used to denote the pound sign —£—or zero. That way, the customer thinks the ticket is something mysterious to do with bookkeeping or identification. Not on your life. When in doubt, it's money. The code price marked is often what the dealer paid for the glass in the first place, so naturally he'll stick about fifty per cent on, if not more. And remember you may actually look a mug. In antiques you pay for appearances—yours, the antiques themselves, and the antique dealer's wife's fur coat. So my tip is: Argue. Even though it goes against the grain in polite old Britain, never pay the marked price, not even if the dealer offers an immediate discount. Hum and ha, take your time, look doubtful. Spin it out and then, as gently and sincerely as you possibly can, barter.

Listen to me, giving away my next year's profit.

"Look, Tinker," I said, not daring to believe him.

"I know what you're going to say, Lovejoy," he said, desperate now.

"You do?"

"Trade's bad. Profits are bad. Finds are bad. Everything's bad."

Like I said, some are psychic.

"Who's got ten thousand these days?" I snapped.

"It's right up your street, Lovejoy."

"Where's the mark?"

"In the saloon bar."

Yet something was not quite right. It was too good to be true.

"How did he know you?"

"Came in looking for barkers and dealers. Somebody in the Lane told him we used this pub. He's done a few pubs at the Lane and on the Belly."

Petticoat Lane and Portobello Road, the London street markets. To ask after reliable dealers—and I'm the most reliable of all known dealers, honest—was reasonable and sounded open enough.

"He spoke to you first?"

"No." Tinker was obviously proud from the way his voice rose eagerly. "I was at the bar. I heard him ask Ted." Ted is the barman. "He asked if any antique dealers were in the bar. I chipped in." He paused. "I was in like a flash, Lovejoy," he added, pained.

"Good lad, Tinker," I said. "Well done."

"I told him I was your runner. He wants to see you. He's got your name in a notebook."

"Look, Tinker," I said, suddenly uneasy, but he protested.

"No, no, he's not Old Bill. Honest. He's straight."

"Old Bill" was the law—police. I had licenses to worry about. And taxes, paid and unpaid. And account books. And some account books I hadn't got at all.

"What's he after?"

"Locks. Right up your street."

My heart almost stopped.

"Locks locks, or just locks?" I stuttered.

"Locks," Tinker said happily. "Flinters."

"If you're kaylied," I threatened.

"Sober as ever was," the phone said. That'll be the day, I thought. I'd never seen Tinker Dill vertical in twenty years. Horizontal or listing, yes.

"Any particular ones?"

"See him first, Lovejoy. I'll keep him here."

"All right." I suddenly decided. A chance was a chance. And buyers were what it was all about. "Hang on to him, Tinker. Can you hear a car?"

He thought for a second.

"Yes. One just pulling into the car park," he said, sounding surprised. "Why?"

"It's me," I said, and shut off, grinning.

To my surprise the bath taps were running and the bathroom door was shut. I opened up and there was this blonde, somewhat sodden, sulking in steam.

"What on earth—?" I began, having forgotten.

"You pig," she said, cutting loose with the language.

"Oh, I remember." She'd been making a racket while I was on the phone. "You're Sheila."

She retorted, "You pig."

"I'm sorry," I told her, "but I have to go out. Can I drop you somewhere?"

"You already have," she snapped, flouncing past and snatching up her things.

"It's just that there's a buyer turned up."

She took a swing at me.

I retreated. "Have you seen my car keys?"

"Have I hell!" she screamed, rummaging under the divan for her shoes.

"Keep your hair on." I tried to reason with her, but women can be very insensitive to the real problems of existence.

She gave me a burst of tears, a few more flashes of temper,

and finally the way women will began an illogical assault on my perfectly logical reasons for making her go. "Who is she?"

"That 'she' is a hairy bloke," I told her. "A buyer."

"And you prefer a buyer to me. Is that it?" she blazed.

"Yes," I said, puzzled at her extraordinary mentality.

She went for me, firing handbag, a shoe, and a pillow as she came, claws at the ready. I gave her a backhander to calm the issue somewhat, at which she settled weeping while I found a coat. I'm all for sex equality.

"Look, help me to find my keys," I said. "If I don't find them I'll be late." Women seem to have no sense sometimes.

"You hit me," she sobbed.

"He's been recommended to me by London dealers," I said proudly, ransacking the bureau where my sales and purchase records are kept—occasionally and partly, that is.

"All you think of is antiques," she whimpered.

"It isn't!" I said indignantly. "I asked you about your holidays yesterday."

"In bed," she cut back viciously. "When you wanted me."

"Look for keys. They were here the day before, when I brought you back."

I found them at last under a Thai temple woodcut and rushed her outside the cottage, remembering to leave a light on and the door alarm switched over to our one vigilant hawkeye at the village constabulary station, in case the British Museum decided to come on a marauding break-in for my latest acquisition, a broken Meissen white I'd have a hard time giving away to a church jumble.

My elderly Armstrong-Siddeley waited, rusting audibly in the Essex night air between the untidy trees. It started first push, to my delight, and we were off.

"Antiques are a sickness with you, Lovejoy." She sniffed. I turned on the gravel and the old banger—I mean the car—coughed out onto the dark tree-lined road.

"Nothing but," I replied happily.

"I think you're mad. What are antiques for anyway? What's the point?"

That's women for you. Anything except themselves is a waste of time. Very self-centered, women are.

"Let me explain, honey."

"You're like a child playing games."

She sat back in the seat staring poutishly at the nearing village lights. I pushed the accelerator pedal down hard. The speedometer needle crept up to the thirty mark as the engine pulsed into maximum thrust. With a following southwesterly I'd once notched forty on the Cambridge Road.

"He might be a collector," I said. She snorted in an unladylike manner.

"Collector," she said scornfully.

"The collector's the world's greatest and only remaining fanatic," I preached fervently. "Who else would sell his wife, wreck his marriage, lose his job, go broke, gamble, rob and cheat, mortgage himself to the hilt a dozen times, throw all security out of the window, for a scattering of objects as diverse as matchboxes, teacups, postcards of music-hall comedians, old bicycles, steam engines, pens, old fans, railway-station lanterns, Japanese sword decorations, and seventeenth-century corsets? Who else but collectors?" I looked rapturously into her eyes. "It's greater than sex, Sheila."

"Nonsense," she snapped, the wind from the car's speed almost ruffling her hair.

"It's greater than religion. Greater love hath no man," I said piously, "than that he gives up his life for his collection."

I wish now I hadn't said that.

"And *you* make money out of them. You prey on them."

"I serve them." There were almost tears in my eyes. "I need to make the odd copper from them, of course I do. But not for profit's sake. Only so I can keep going, sort of make money to maintain the service."

"Liar," she said, and slapped my face.

As I was driving I couldn't clock her one by way of return, so I resorted to persuasion. "Nobody regrets us having to split more than me" was the best I could manage, but she stayed mad.

She kept up a steady flow of recrimination as I drove into the village, the way women will. It must have been nine o'clock when I reached the White Hart. The Armstrong was wheezing badly by then. Its back wheels were smoking again. I wished I knew what made it do that. I pulled into the forecourt and pushed a couple of quid into her hand.

"Look, darling," I said hastily. "See you soon."

"What am I to do now?" she complained, coming after me.

"Ring for a taxi, there's a good girl," I told her. "To the station."

"You pig, Lovejoy," she wailed.

"There's a train soon—probably."

"When will I see you?" she called after me as I trotted toward the pub.

"I'll give you a ring," I said over my shoulder.

"Promise?"

"Honestly."

I heard her shout something else after me, but by then I was through the door and into the saloon bar.

Women have no sense of priorities. Ever noticed that?

2

The saloon bar was crowded. I labeled everybody in there with one swift glance. A dozen locals, including this bird of about thirty-six sitting stylishly on a barstool and showing thighs to the assembled multitude. We had been friends once—twice, to be truthful. Now I just lusted across the heads of her admirers and grinned a lazaroid greeting, to which she returned a cool smoke-laden stare. Three dealers were already in: Jimmo, stout, balding, and Staffordshire pottery; Jane Felsham, thirtyish, shapely—would have been desirable if she hadn't been an antique dealer—blond, Georgian silver and early watercolors; and finally Adrian, sex unknown, elegant, pricey, and mainly Regency furniture and household wares. Four strangers, thinly distributed, and a barker or two chatting them up and trying to interest them in antique Scandinavian brass plaques made last April. Well, you can only try. They can always say no.

Tinker Dill was in the far corner by the fireplace with this middle-aged chap. I forged my way over.

"Oh," Tinker said, acting like the ninth-rate Olivier he is. "Oh. And here's my friend Lovejoy I was telling you about."

"Evening, Tinker." I nodded at the stranger and we shook hands.

He seemed fairly ordinary, neat, nothing new about his clothes but not tatty. He could have saved up ten thousand all right. But a genuine collector . . .? Not really.

"Mr. Field, meet Lovejoy." Tinker was really overdoing it, almost wagging like a dog. We said how do and sat.

"My turn, Tinker, from last time," I said, giving him a note to shut him up. He was off to the bar like a rocket.

"Mr. Dill said you are a specialist dealer, Mr. Lovejoy." Field's accent was anonymous southern.

"Yes," I admitted.

"Very specialized, I believe?"

"Yes. Of course," I hedged as casually as I could manage, "from the way the trade has progressed in the past few years, I maintain a pretty active interest in several other aspects."

"Naturally," he said, all serious.

"But I expect Dill's told you where my principal interest lies."

"Yes."

This guy was no dealer. In fact, if he knew a Regency snuffbox from a Rolls-Royce it was lucky guesswork.

Barkers like Tinker are creatures of form. They have to be, if you think about it. They find possible buyers who are interested, say, in picking up a William IV dining set. Now, a barker's job is to get clients: buyers or sellers, but preferably the former. He's no right to go saying, Oh, sorry, sir, but my particular dealer's only interested in buying or selling oil paintings of the Flemish School, so you've had it from me. If a barker did that he'd get the push smartish. So whatever the mark—sorry, buyer —wants, a barker will agree his particular dealer's got it, and not only that, but he will also swear blind that his dealer's certainly the world's most expert expert on William IV dining sets or whatever, and throw in a few choice remarks about how crooked other dealers are, just for good measure.

Now a dealer coming strolling in at this point only showing interest in penny-farthing bicycles would ruin all the careful groundwork. The customer will realize he's been sadly misled and depart in a huff for the National Gallery or some other inexperienced amateur outfit. Also, and just as bad, the barker (if he's any good) pushes off to serve another dealer, because clearly the first dealer's going to starve to death, and barkers don't find loyalty the most indispensable of all virtues. The dealer then starves, goes out of business, and those of us remaining say a brief prayer for the repose of his soul—while racing after the customer as fast as we can go because we all know where we can get a mint William IV dining set at very short notice.

"He has a very high opinion of your qualities," Field informed me.

"That's very kind." If Field got the irony it didn't show.

"You made a collection for the Victoria and Albert Museum, I understand, Mr. Lovejoy."

"Oh, well." I winced inwardly, trying to seem all modest. I determined to throttle Tinker. Even innocent customers know how to check that sort of tale.

"Wasn't it last year?"

"You must understand," I said hesitantly, putting on as much embarrassment as I dared.

"Understand?"

"I'm not saying I have, and I'm not saying I haven't," I went on. "It's a client's business, not mine. Even if South Kensington *did* ask me to build up their terracotta Roman statuary, it's not for Dill or myself to disclose their interests." May I be forgiven.

"Ah. Confidentiality." His brow cleared.

"It's a matter of proper business, Mr. Field," I said with innocent seriousness.

"I do see," he said earnestly, lapping it up. "A most responsible attitude."

"There are standards." I shrugged to show I was positively weighed down with conscience. "Ordinary fair play," I said. Maybe I was overdoing it, because he went all broody. He was coming to the main decision when Tinker came back with a rum for me and a pale ale for Field.

I gave Tinker the bent eye and he instantly pushed off.

"Are you an . . . individual dealer, Mr. Lovejoy?" he asked, taking the plunge.

"If you mean do I work alone, yes."

"No partners?"

"None." I thought a bit, then decided I should be straight—almost—with this chap. He looked as innocent as a new policeman. I don't know where they keep them till they're grown up, honest I don't. "I ought to qualify that, Mr. Field."

"Yes?" He came alert over his glass.

"There are occasions when an outlay, or a risk, is so large that for a particular antique it becomes necessary to take an . . . extra dealer, pair up so to speak, in order to complete a sale." I'd almost said "accomplice." You know what I mean.

"In what way?" he said guardedly.

"Supposing somebody offered me the Elgin Marbles for a million," I said, observing his expression ease at the light banter. "I'd have to get another dealer to make up the other half million before I could buy them."

"I see." He was smiling.

"For that sale, we would be equal partners."

"But not after?"

"No. As I said, Mr. Field," I said, all pious, "I work alone because, well, my own standards may not be those of other dealers."

"Of course, of course." For some reason he was relieved I was a loner. "Any arrangements between us—supposing we came to one—would concern . . .?" He waited.

"Just us," I confirmed.

"And Dill?"

"He's free lance. He wouldn't know anything, unless you said."

15

"And other employees?"

"I hire as the needs arise."

"So it *is* possible," he mused.

"What is, Mr. Field?"

"You can have a confidential agreement with an antique dealer."

"Certainly." I should have told him that money can buy silence nearly as effectively as it can buy talk. Note the "nearly," please.

"Then I would like to talk to you—in a confidential place, if that can be arranged."

"Now?" I asked.

"Please."

I glanced around the bar. There were two people I had business with. "I have a cottage not far away. We can chat there."

"Fine."

I crossed to Jimmo and briefly quizzed him about his Chinese porcelain *blanc de Chine* lions—white pot dogs to the uninitiated. He told me in glowing terms of his miraculous find.

"Cost me the earth," he said fervently. "Both identical. Even the balls are identically matched."

For the sake of politeness (and in case I needed to do business with him fairly soon) I kept my end up, but I'd lost interest. The "lions" are in fact Dogs of Fo. The point is that even if they are K'ang-hsi period, as Jimmo said, and 1720 A.D. would do fine, they should *not* match exactly to be a real matched pair. The male dog rests one paw on a sphere, the female on a pup. Jimmo had somehow got hold of two halves of two distinct pairs. I eased away as best I could.

Adrian—handbag, curls, and all—was next. He and Jane Felsham were bickering amiably over a percentage cut over some crummy "patch-and-comfit" boxes. "Real Bilston enamel," Adrian was telling her. "Pinks genuine as that. Oh." He saw me at his elbow and stamped his foot in temper. "Why won't the silly bitch listen, Lovejoy? *Tell* her."

"How many?" I asked.

"He's got six," Jane said evenly. "Hello, Lovejoy."

"Hi. It sounds a good collection."

"There you are, dearie!" Adrian screamed.

"Only two are named." Jane shook her head. "Place names are all the go."

These little boxes, often only an inch across, were used in the eighteenth century for holding those minute artificial black beauty patches fashionable gentry of the time stuck on their faces to contrast with the powdered pallor of their skins. Filthy habit.

"Any blues?"

"One," Adrian squeaked. "I keep begging her to take them. She can't see a bargain, Lovejoy."

"Any mirrors in the lids?"

"Two."

"Four hundred's still no bargain, Adrian dear," Jane said firmly.

"Show us," I said, wanting to get away. Field was still patient by the fireplace.

Adrian brought out six small enameled boxes on his palm. One was lumpy, less shiny than the rest. I felt odd for a second. My bell.

"I agree with Jane," I lied, shrugging. "But they are nice."

"Three-eighty, then," Adrian offered, sensing my reaction.

"Done." I lifted the little boxes from his hand and fought my way free, saying "Come around tomorrow."

Adrian swung around to the surprised Jane. "See? Serves you right, silly cow!"

I left them to fight it out and found Field. "My car's just outside."

I gave the nod to Tinker that he'd finished on a good note. He beamed and toasted to me over a treble gin.

The cottage was in a hell of a mess. I have this downstairs divan for, so to speak, communal use. It looked almost as if somebody had been shacked up there for a couple of days with a bird. I smiled weakly at my customer.

"Sorry about this. I had a, er, cousin staying for a while."

He made polite noises as I hid a few of Sheila's underclothes under cushions and folded the divan aside. With only the table lamp, the room didn't look too much of a shambles. I pulled the kitchen door to in case he thought a hurricane was coming his way and sat him by my one-bar fire.

"A very pleasant cottage, Mr. Lovejoy," he said.

"Thanks." I could see he was wondering at the absence of antiques in an antique dealer's home. "I keep my stock of antiques dispersed in safe places," I explained. "After all, I'm in the phone book, and robbery's not unknown nowadays."

Stock. That's a laugh. I had six enameled boxes I'd not properly examined, for which I owed a mint payable by dawn.

"True, true," he agreed, and I knew I had again struck oil.

In his estimation I was now careful, safe, trustworthy, reliable, an expert, and the very soul of discretion. I drove home my advantage by apologizing for not having too much booze.

"I don't drink much myself," I confessed. "Will coffee do you?"

"Please."

"Everybody just calls me Lovejoy, Mr. Field," I informed him. "My trademark."

"Right." He smiled. "I'll remember."

I brewed up, quite liking him and wondering how to approach his money—I mean, requirements. So far he hadn't mentioned flinters. On the drive back in my jet-propelled Armstrong-Siddeley we had made social chitchat that got us no nearer. He seemed a simple chap, unaware of the somewhat horrible niceties of my trade. Yet he appeared, from what Tinker had said, to have gone to a lot of trouble to find a dealer known to have a prime interest in flinters.

"How long have you lived here?"

"Since I started dealing. I got it from a friend."

She was a widow, thirty-seven. I'd lived with her two years, then she'd gone unreasonable like they do and off she pushed. She wrote later from Siena, married to an Italian. I replied in a flash saying how I longed for her, but she replied saying her husband hadn't an antique in the place, preferring new Danish planks of yellow wood to furniture, so I didn't write again except to ask for the cottage deeds.

"Instead of London?"

"Oh, I go up to the Smoke maybe once a week on average." And do the rest of the Kingdom as well, inch by bloody inch, once every quarter. On my knees mostly, sniffing and listening for my bell. I didn't tell him that, seeing I was supposed to be temporarily the big wheeler-dealer.

"To the markets?" he persisted.

"Yes. And some, er, private dealers that I know."

He nodded and drew breath. Here it comes, I thought. And it did.

"I'm interested in a certain collector's item," he said, as if he'd saved the words for a rainy day. "I'm starting a collection."

"Hmmm." The Lovejoy gambit.

"I want to know if you can help."

He sipped and waited. And I sipped and waited. Like a couple of those drinking ostriches, we dipped in silence.

"Er, can you?" he asked.

"If I can," I countered cagily. For an innocent novice he wasn't doing too badly, and I was becoming distinctly edgy.

"Do you mean Dill didn't explain?"

"He explained you were interested in purchasing flintlocks," I said.

"Nothing else?"

"And that you had, er, sufficient funds."

"But not what it is I'm seeking?"

"No." I put down my cup because my hands were quivering slightly. If it turned dud I'd wring Tinker's neck. "Perhaps," I said evenly, "you'd better tell me."

"Dueling pistols."

"I guessed that." Flintlock duelers are the P. & O. line of weapons men.

"A very special pair."

"That too." I cleared my throat. "Which pair, Mr. Field?"

He stared at me across the darkened room. "I want the Judas pair," he said.

My heart sank. With luck, I could catch Tinker before Ted called time at the pub, and annihilate him on the spot for sending me a dummy. No wonder he'd been evasive when I asked him on the phone.

I gazed back at the poor misguided customer. "Did you say the Judas pair?" I said, still hoping I'd misheard.

"The Judas pair," he affirmed.

Digression time, folks.

Flintlocks are sprung iron gadgets which flip a piece of flint onto a steel so as to create a spark. This spark, at its most innocent, can be used to ignite a piece of old rope or other tinder and set it smoldering to be blown into a flame for lighting a fire, candles, your pipe. This is the standard tinder lighter of history. You'd be surprised how many sorts of tinder lighters there are, many incredibly ingenious. But these instruments are the humdrum end of the trade, interesting and desirable though they are. You see, mankind made this pleasant little system into the business bit of weapons for killing each other.

About the time of our Civil War, the posh firing weapon was a wheel lock. This delectable weaponry consisted of a sprung wheel spinning at the touch of a trigger and rubbing on a flint as it did so. (The very same mechanism is used in a gas-fueled cigarette lighter of today, believe it or not.) They were beautiful things, mostly made in Germany, where there were clock-and-lock makers aplenty. A ball-butted German wheel lock costs the earth nowadays. And remember, the less marked the better. None of this stupid business of boring holes and chipping the walnut stock to prove it's old. Never try to improve *any* antique. Leave well alone. Sheraton and Constable knew what they were doing, and chances are that you are as ignorant as I am. Stick to wiping your antiques with a dry duster. Better still, don't even do that.

These wheel locks were rifled for accuracy. Prince Rupert, leader of his dad's Cavaliers, had a destructive habit of shooting weathercocks off steeples as he rode through captured towns. However, they were somewhat slow, clumsy, heavy, and took time to fire. The reason was the spark. It plopped into a little pan where you had thoughtfully sprinkled black gunpowder. This ignited and burned through a small hole into *your* end of the barrel, where you'd placed a larger quantity of gunpowder, a small lead bullet about the size of a marble, and a piece of old wadding to keep it all in. Bang! If you knew the delay to a millisec, the shift of the wind, could control your horse, pointed it right, and kept everything crossed for luck, you were one more weathercock short. It asked to be improved.

The culmination in weapons was the true flintlock—faster, and quicker to fire again should you miss. This may not be important, but only if your enemies are all weathercocks. Once the idea caught on, the wheel lock was replaced and the true flintlock came onto the historical scene.

The French had a crack at making them, and wonderful attempts they were. Some superb examples exist. I've had many with knobs on, gold inlay, silver escutcheons, Damascus-barreled beauties with delicate carving on precision locks that would melt your heart. And some beautiful Spanish miquelet pistols—a Mediterranean fancy of a strangely bulky style—are decorated to perfection. I admit that tears come to my eyes writing this, mostly because everybody else has them, not me. And Dutch too, though their taste for carving ugly ivory heads and figurines on the grips gives me the willies. All nations did their stuff on the flintlock, from the early snaphances and English doglocks to the final great explosion of exquisite functional murderous perfection in—you've guessed it—dear old peaceful Britain.

Came the industrial boom days and an outburst of inventive genius which was to catapult these islands into wealth, prominence, and power. Don't think our armies won by unaided valor, though they had it in plenty. They used an improved flintlock, standardized by a thoughtful young English squire, Oliver Cromwell by name. And it fired faster, surer, and noisier than anyone else's, which was a blessing in war.

From then the flintlock didn't look back. Inventors added devices you would hardly believe: flintlocks that fired under water (work it out), flintlock repeating rifles, flintlock revolvers, flintlock machine guns, ingenious safety catches that actually worked even if you forgot to slip them on, breech-loading flintlocks by the score, all the time edging toward a shorter firing time between pulling the trigger and sending regrets to your opponent's widow.

And ladies were at it too—no more than you'd expect—in subtle little ways having a charm all their own. Muff pistols, made for folding away in their hot little hands, were their scene, but they also liked tiny collapsible guns built into their prayerbooks—presumably in the Exodus bit. Church was more exciting in those days.

By the 1770s dueling was in, and here comes the Judas pair. Or, rather, here they don't come.

Be careful, O ye innocent purchaser of these valuable—I mean, and repeat, *valuable*—weapons. They should be Damascus-barreled (i.e., spiral-welded barrels) and, at their best, *brown* because of a veneer of faint rust skillfully applied to the metal by makers of genius. They should have walnut stocks, and usually be rifle-grooved. But if the barrel measures less than nine inches, utter a loud derisory snort and mentally divide the asking price by three, if not four, because you are being had by some dealer who is trying to pass off a pair of officer's holster pistols as genuine duelers. A sneer is useful at this stage. On the other hand, if, say, they have ten-inch barrels, try to keep cool and go on to the next step, which is to look for decoration. Almost *any* metallic decoration on the barrels or on the locks disqualifies, because dueling, remember, was naughty, and silver squiggles and gold inlays tended to catch the first gleam of light on Wandsworth Common and reflect it unerringly into the eagle eyes of London's annoyed watchmen. You are allowed one silver escutcheon plate on the butt. And even this displeases you, because the real flintlock geniuses of Regency London knew their onions. Somber perfection was their aim. They achieved it.

Pick up a genuine Regency dueler. Hold it with your arm straight down. Now lift as if about to aim. Its weight makes it wobble in the strongest fist as it rises. Up it comes, wobbling and waggling, and you begin to wonder how they managed to hit anything with the long barrel waving in the breeze. Then, just about on level with your bottom rib, something so remarkable happens you won't believe me, but it's the truth—a genuine flintlock dueler *begins to lift itself!* Honestly. Try it. The weight evaporates. The wobble disappears. Up it goes, seemingly of its own accord, and all you need to do is point it right. Its perfect balance, its meticulous design, and the love and joy expended in its making have achieved the seemingly impossible. That's the genuine dueler—grim, somber, almost dull of appearance, lying with its identically matched partner in a wooden case with powder flask, bullet molds, flints, separate ramrod, and screwdrivers. It reeks of class. It screams of perfection.

A pair of mint—that is, perfectly preserved—cased flintlock

duelers would buy you a couple of new cars nowadays, minimum. A mint pair of them with a pedigree—belonging, say, to some hero, a famous dandy of the time, or perhaps some pal of Beau Brummell's or a member of the then royalty—will virtually buy you anything. If you discover such a pair of old pistols in a dirty old box upstairs, rush to the nearest church and light a candle in thanks to your Maker—Bate, Monlong, Murdoch, Pauly, whoever it turns out to be. *Then retire for life in affluence.*

Finally, one point more. Just like Queen Anne silver, each weapon is, or should be, named on the lock. Don't throw value away. Your famous silversmith's monogram can double or treble the value of your fruit bowl. So your famous maker's name can send your find ever upward in value. The names are too many to give here, but Joseph Manton; John Manton; Wogden, who gave his name as a nickname to dueling (a "Wogden affair"); the brilliant Joseph Egg; Henry Nock the Great and his younger relative Sam that he had a terrible row with; Mortimer; Tatham, who blew himself to pieces on a cannon for reasons best not gone into; Freeman; the fashionable Rigby; the Reverend Alexander Forsyth, who invented the percussion system, which did away with flintlocks altogether and doubled the killing speed—they are some you should not lose on your way home.

And last but not least, one "Durs" (nearly as bad as Lovejoy) Egg, flintlock maker to kings and princes, genius extraordinaire, maker—so they say—of the one and only Judas pair of flintlock duelers. Well.

This young man came to London about 1770 to seek his fortune. With another Swiss, Pauly, he became interested in the science of pneumatics and air propulsion, and between them they produced a variety of odd but lethal air guns. In later years he lost a fortune by inventing a flying machine, the *Flying Dolphin,* which he kept in a hangar down Knightsbridge way, to London society's huge delight and derision. A genius whose habit it was to pattern the walnut stocks of his flintlocks with a curiously stippled star design, to aid in the grip. He signed himself always by his nickname, Durs.

The legend is that he made twelve—only twelve—pairs of dueling pistols. The legend goes on to say that he privately made a thirteenth pair, when something terrible happened. What it was the legend fails to explain.

That thirteenth pair, sinister weapons of ill-omen, were his last. They were never found or heard of except as obscure rumors. Any antique dealer worth his salt will laugh till he falls down if you ask after them. They don't exist, and everybody knows it.

That thirteenth pair of flintlock duelers is the Judas pair.

I drew breath.

"I've bad news, Mr. Field," I managed to get out.

"Bad news?"

"The Judas pair. They don't exist," I said firmly, and rose to get my emergency beer. "They're a myth, a legend. The antique trade's riddled with myths."

"Is it really?" He was oddly calm for somebody who'd just been put down.

"Really," I told him. No use mucking about.

He watched me splash the ale as I drove the truth savagely home. "Michelangelo's *Goliath* to match his *David*. Turner's mysterious set of portraits and industrial paintings. Napoleon's woodcuts done by his very own lily-white hands. Sir Francis Drake's poetry in two breathtaking volumes. Bill Shakespeare's latest play, *King Penda*. Robin Hood's diary. Czar Alexander's secret will. The Grail. Excalibur. Prince John's necklace from the Wash. Friar Bacon's perpetual clock. Leonardo's jeweled casket of secrets. Cleopatra's ruby ring. The Kohinoor's partner diamond, even bigger and better. Nazi treasure chests in those tiresome bloody lakes. Rembrandt's French landscapes. Chippendale's missing design books. All myths. Like," I added harshly, "the Judas pair."

"Did Dill tell you how much I was willing to pay?" he asked.

"Ten thousand," I said bitterly. "Just my luck."

"Now I believe you, Lovejoy," he said, calm as you please.

"Look," I said slowly. "Maybe I'm not getting through to you. Can't you understand what I'm saying? Ten thousand's too little. So is ten million. You can't get something if it doesn't exist."

"Before," he continued evenly, "I thought you were leading me on, perhaps pretending to be more honest than you really were. That is a common deception in all forms of business." I took a mouthful of ale to stop myself gaping too obviously. "Now I believe you are an honest man. A dishonest dealer, seeing I know little about the subject, would have exploited my ignorance."

"It happens," I admitted weakly.

"I accepted that risk when I came to you." Field stared thoughtfully at me.

"So you knew about the Judas pair being legendary?"

"From various sources."

"And it was a try-on, then."

"Yes."

"Well, Mr. Field." I rose. "You've had your fun. Now, before you leave, is it worth your while to tell me what you *do* want?" I stood over him. To my surprise he remained unabashed. In fact, he seemed more cool as the chat wore on.

"Certainly."

"Right. Give." I sat, exuding aggression.

"I want you to do a job."

"Legal?"

"Legal. Right up your street, as Dill would say." So he'd listened in on Tinker's phone call as I'd guessed. "You'll accept? It will be very lucrative."

"What is it?"

"Find me," he said carefully, "the Judas pair."

I sighed wearily. The guy was a nutter. "Haven't I just explained—?"

"Wrongly." Field leaned forward. "Lovejoy, the Judas pair exist. They killed my brother."

It was becoming one of those days. I should have stayed on the nest with Sheila, somewhere safe and warm.

3

Elizabethan ladies—the First, I hasten to add—had fleas. And lice. And gentleman suitors who came courting also suffered. If these heroes were especially favored, they were allowed to chat up the object of their desire. If they were really fancied, though, matters progressed to poetry, music, even handclasps and sighs. And eventually the great flea-picking ceremony. You've seen baboons do it on those unspeakable nature programs. Yes, our ancestors did the same, uttering rapturous sighs at all that contact.

What I am getting at is this: If you see a little (one and a half inches maximum) antique box, dirty as hell, that *should* be neat and enameled to be a proper patch-and-comfit box and somehow isn't quite right, it can be only one of two things. The first is a battered nineteenth-century trinket or snuffbox, in which case you can generally forget it. The second—oh, dear, the second—is an Elizabethan flea and louse box. Don't shudder. Don't boil it to kill any remaining creepy-crawlies. Lock it carefully in the biggest safest safe you can find, swallow the key, and then scream with ecstasy. These little jeweled boxes were used by lovers for holding fleas and lice that they captured on their paramours' lovely chalk-powdered skin. It was an exquisitely charming pastime of those days. We don't advertise them as such, these boxes. We call them anything: "Early antique sixteenth-century lady's minute toiletry box, heavily inlaid, made by . . ." and so on.

Remember Adrian? I spent part of the night cleaning the lumpy box—it was a genuine flea box. I kissed it reverently, drew all the curtains, doused my lamp, and rolled up the carpet. Underneath was the hinged paving stone. Down I went, eight wooden steps underground into my secret cave. Eight feet by eight, cold as charity, dry as a tinderbox, safer than any bank vault on earth. I laid the box on a shelf and climbed out, replacing the stone flag and making sure the iron ring lay in its groove. It wouldn't do to have a visitor tripping up over an unexpected bump in the carpet, would it? I smoked a Dutch cigar to celebrate, though they make me sleep badly, and went to bed. It was four o'clock.

Field's brother was a collector, apparently. One of the indiscriminate kind. To his wife's dismay he filled the house with assorted antiques and semi-antiques and modern junk, a mixture of rubbish and desirable stuff. In short, a collector after my own heart.

Somewhere, somehow, Field's brother found the Judas pair, so Field told me, not realizing they were anything more special than a pair of supreme antique flintlock duelers made by any old passing genius. He seems to have mentioned to all and sundry about his luck and I daresay let interested callers click the triggers—knocking guineas off their value at every click. Tender-hearted as I am, by this point in Field's narrative I was getting the feeling his brother might have got the same fate from me, but I suppressed it.

Anyway, one night several months ago Field had a phone call from his brother, who told him very excitedly that the flintlocks were very special, unique in fact, if not world-shattering. He would bring them over next day, it being Saturday, and show him.

"He never came, Lovejoy," Field told me.

He was found by Field himself, at noon. Field drove over to see why he hadn't turned up. He was in his living room among all his clutter. Blood seemed to be everywhere. He seemed to have been shot through his eye, but the bullet was never found not even at the post-mortem.

"Sorry about this," I said, "but did the pathologist say what bore?"

"About twelve, but he wasn't sure."

"Could be."

Take a pound of lead. Divide it into twelve equal balls. They are then twelve-bore bullets for flintlock or percussion weapons. No cartridges, remember, for the period we're talking about. The impetus comes from your dollop of gunpowder and the spark. Flintlock weapons range from two-bore, or even one-bore monsters which throw a bullet as big as a carrot, to narrow efforts like the eighteen-bore or less. Duelers went with fashions, but twelve-bores were not unusual.

"Where did he buy them?"

"He never said." Wise man.

"Nor how much he paid?"

"No." Wiser still.

"Were they cased?"

"Cased?"

"In a special box, the size of a small cutlery box, maybe up to two feet by one, maybe four inches deep."

"There was a box that went with them."

I stirred from desire. "And the accessories?"

"As far as I remember, there were some small screwdrivers and a couple of metal bottles, and pliers," he said slowly, "but that's as much as I can recall." He meant a flask and mold.

"So you actually saw them?"

He looked surprised. "Oh, yes."

"And . . . you didn't notice if they were of any extra quality?"

"To me they were just, well, antiques."

I eyed him coldly. You can go off people. "Did you notice the maker?"

"Eric—my brother—told me. It's such an unusual name, isn't it? Durs. And Egg. I remarked on it." He grinned. "I said, I'll bet his mates pulled his leg at school."

"Quite," I said, knowing the feeling well. "And of course you searched for them?"

"The police did."

"No luck?"

"Not only that. They didn't believe me about them."

No good looking for a gun—of any sort—if there's no bullet.

"They said he'd been stabbed with a metal object."

"Through the eye?" It sounded unlikely.

"It's hopeless, as you no doubt see."

"What theories did they have?"

"Very few. They're still searching for the weapon."

"Without knowing what sort of weapon it was?" I snorted in derision.

He leaned forward, pulling out an envelope. "Here's five hundred," he said. "It's on account."

"For . . . ?" I tried to keep my eyes on his, but they kept wandering toward the money in his hand.

"For finding that weapon." He chucked the envelope and I caught it, so the notes inside wouldn't bruise. Not to keep, you understand. "My brother was shot by one of the Judas weapons."

"The Judas pair don't exist." My voice sounds weak sometimes.

"They do." For somebody so hopeless at pretending to be a collector he was persistent. "I've seen them."

"They don't," I squeaked at the third try. It's funny how heavy a few pound notes can be.

"Then give me the money back," he said calmly, "and tell me to go."

"I could get you a reasonable pair for this," I said weakly. "Maybe no great shakes, not cased, and certainly not mint, but—"

"Yes or no?" he asked. Some of these quiet little chaps are the worst. Never give up no matter how straight you are. Ever noticed that?

"Well," I said gamely, feeling all noble, "if you really insist . . ."

"If you've got a pen and paper," he said, smiling in a rather disagreeable way, "I'll give you all available details."

I'd tried, hadn't I?

Adrian brought Jane Felsham along. I handed him a check.

"You're flush!" he exclaimed. "Come across a Barraud?" Barraud, a London watchmaker, about 1815 made some delicious flat-looking watches. Only the central sun decoration and the astounding nineteen-line movement and the sexy gold and enamel surface and the beady surround (pearls) tell you it's somewhat above average. The highest artistic imagination crystallized in a luscious context of brilliant science. I smiled, I think. People shouldn't make jokes. I'd once missed a Barraud by five minutes, late for an auction.

"Steady progress," I replied.

"Will it bounce?" He draped himself elegantly across a chair. Both he and Jane couldn't help glancing sharply around in case any of my recent finds were on display.

"Don't you want it?" I brewed up to show we were still friends.

"I must confess little Janesy and I were discussing whether you'd have the wherewithal, dear boy."

"It was touch and go."

"Business going a bit slow, Lovejoy?" Jane lit one of her long cigarettes and rotated her fag holder. "Not much about for the casual visitor to see."

"I have these two warehouses . . ." They laughed.

"That chap last night," Jane pressed. "A client?"

"Trying to be," I said casually.

"After anything we could help with?" from Adrian.

"I doubt it." I rattled a few pieces of crockery to show I was being offhand.

"A furniture man, I suppose." Jane waggled her fag holder again. A psychiatrist I sold a warming pan once told me something odd about women who habitually sucked fag holders. For the life of me I can't remember what it was.

"Asking the impossible as usual." I hoped that would shut them up. "Wanting something for nothing."

"Don't they all?" Adrian groaned.

"Did you risk him in your car?" Jane was smiling.

"Of course. Why not? I gave him a lift to the station."

"Did he survive?" She's always pulling my leg about my old bus.

"He said it was unusual."

"A death trap," Adrian interposed. "All those switches for nothing. Trade it in for a little Morris."

This sort of talk offends me, not that I'm sentimental about a heap of old iron. After all, though it's a common enough banger, it does give off a low-level bell or two.

"He didn't buy, then?"

"Not even place an order." I carried in their cups and offered sugar. "I got a faint tickle, though. Bring in any tassies you find. We'll split."

"I might have a few," Jane said, and they were satisfied.

Tassies—intaglios, really—are the dealers' nickname for an in-carved stone, usually a semiprecious one. You know a cameo brooch? The figure—a bust silhouette or whatever—stands in relief above the main brooch's surface. Imagine the same figure carved inward, grooving out the design. That's an intaglio. Mostly oval, about the size of a pea and as high, with a shallow carving. Watch for copies, modern ones you can't even give

33

away except to some mug who can't tell bottle glass from the Star of India, though the way things are going, by the time you read this . . .

"Harry Bateman phoned in," Adrian said, pulling a face at my foul coffee.

"On the cadge?"

"Offering."

"Good?"

"Wordsworth's stuff. Genuine."

"Really?" I was interested, but Harry Bateman didn't know his bum from his elbow, which when you think of it is pretty vital information.

"His original chair and a shaving case given to him by his daughter Dora, 1839."

"Oh."

Jane looked up sharply. It must have been how I said it.

"Chair's a straight Chippendale—" Adrian was starting off, but I took pity.

"—And he's even got the date wrong as well. Trust Harry."

"No good?"

"How come he doesn't starve?" I demanded. "He'll catch it one day. For heaven's sake, tell him before he gets picked up. Wordsworth's chair was always a diamond-seater because of his habit of sitting with a hand in his jacket, Napoleon-style. And the National Trust will be narked if he's really got Dora's case. It should still be at Dove Cottage, on show with the rest of his clobber."

"That's what I like about Lovejoy," Adrian said to Jane. "He's abusive without actually giving offense."

"I'm pretty good value," I retorted.

We had a few similar rapierlike exchanges of witty repartee and then they left in Adrian's new Jaguar. A shower of gravel clattered the Armstrong-Siddeley as he spun down my path. I could hear the stones pattering into the bushes all the way through the copse onto the road. Jane had blown me an apologetic kiss.

I phoned Tinker to come over.

I had all the Wallis and Wallis auction catalogues out—Knight, Frank and Rutley's, Christie's, Sotheby's, and Weller and Dufty's of Birmingham—plus every reference book just as a check. My real filing system was below in the priest hole. There wasn't time to open up before Tinker showed, and he wasn't that close a confidant. Nobody was, not even Sheila.

"Watcher, Lovejoy."

"Come in, Tinker."

He was grinning. "Did a deal?"

"Not so's you'd notice," I said, narked.

"He told me to be sure and mention the money."

"All right, all right."

"Did he cough up?" He brought out the Black Label from where I hid it and poured a glug.

"No. All we've got is promises."

"Ah well." He smacked his lips. "You can't have everything."

"I thought he was a nutter at first." I gave him a glare. "Especially as you hadn't tipped me off what he was after."

"Do you blame me? Would you have come if I had?"

"No," I admitted. "Anyway, I talked him out of it. I ask you—the Judas pair. At my age."

"What's the job then?"

"He's decided to become the big collector," I improvised. "So he casts about for a real bingo, and hears of the Judas guns. He decides that's what he'll start with. I told him I'll get going after a pedigree pair that'll be just as good. He bought it."

"What'll we give him?" Tinker asked. Already I could see his ferret mind sniffing out possibilities.

"The best-named pedigree ones we can get."

"Same name?"

"Yeah—Durs."

"Some good Mantons might be on the move soon, word is."

"From where?"

"Suffolk, so people are saying."

"Well . . ." I pretended indecision. "Keep it in mind, but Durs for preference. I was just pinning them down."

"Three in Germany. Four in the States. Four here, and that Aussie." He ticked his fingers. "Twelve. That's the lot."

I nodded agreement. "I'll make sure none's come through the auctions lately."

"You'd have noticed, Lovejoy."

"It'll save you legwork."

"Right."

He sat and swilled my hooch while I sussed the auctions. In a dozen auctions three sets of Durs guns had been sold, two pairs of holster weapons, one by Joseph of Piccadilly and one by Durs, and one blunderbuss by Durs.

"Run-of-the-mill stuff," I said, forcing back the tears.

"Where do we go from here?"

"Out into the wide world." I watched his face cloud with misery. "I go to work writing and whizzing around the collectors. You get down among the dealers and listen. You don't ask anything, got it? You just listen."

"Right, Lovejoy. Only . . ."

I gave him some notes. "This comes out of your commission," I warned. He would expect that.

"I'll go careful."

"Do," I warned. "If you go shouting the odds—"

"I know better than go putting the price up." He winked. "Cheerio, Lovejoy."

"See you, Tinker."

I'd had to do it. If Tinker—who looked as if he hadn't two coppers to rub together—suddenly appeared, asking after high-priced stuff, it would be the talking point of the antique world within minutes and any trace of the Judas pair would vanish.

I caught myself in time. I should have to remember they

didn't exist. What I was really going after was a pair of unusual *real* weapons, which *did* exist.

I put the catalogues away and sat outside the front door on my stone alcove seat. The day was fine, dry. Birds were knocking around in the haphazard way they do. A squirrel raced up a tree, stopping now and again for nothing. It was all pretty average. I could hear a few cars on the road. When I was settled enough I let my mind flow toward the job.

A pair of guns existed. They had been bought by Eric Field, who'd got excited. They were certainly by the great Regency maker, and therefore not cheap. Said to be flint duelers, but were possibly not. The other possibility was that the weapons had been mere holster pistols, and Eric Field, not knowing much for all his collecting enthusiasm, mistook them as valuable duelers.

Yet, if they *were* only officer's guns, who killed Eric that Friday night just to get hold of them? Nobody would murder for a couple of antiques you could buy at open auction, however expensive.

But a hell of a lot of people would murder over and over again for the Judas pair—if they existed. The day took on a sudden chill.

I shook myself and planned action. First, locate for certain all sets over the past twelve months. Assuming they were all where they ought to be, I would have to think again.

I went indoors to warm up a cheese-and-onion pie. That, two slices of bread, and a pint of tea, and I would start.

4

It was about three that afternoon. I walked down to my gate, a hundred yards, and latched it as an added precaution. To come in you had to lift the latch and push hard. It screeched and groaned and rattled like the Tower dungeons. Better than any watchdog. My doors were locked, all my curtains were drawn, and I was in my priest hole.

Every weekend, while other dealers ginned it up at the local and eyed the talent, I cross-indexed sales. Newspapers, auctions, gossip, cheap adverts I'd seen on postcards in village shop windows, anything and everything to do with antiques. Those little cards and two hard-backed books may be no match for IBM, but my skills are second to none, powered as they are by the most human of all mixtures—greed and love. Let a computer get those.

As I checked mechanically back for Durs items in my records I occasionally glanced at the shelves about me, wondering if there was *anything* the Fields could have mistaken for the Judases. I had a pair of lovely mint double-barreled percussion Barratts cased and complete with all accessories. No goon could mistake percussion for flints, which narrowed the field considerably. There were other relatives of Joseph and Durs, one being

38

Charles, but he came later and in any case was only a pale shadow of the two older craftsmen. Then came Augustus Leopold, no less. Only, to see his masterpieces you have to go to the London art galleries, for he was the famous oil painter pal of Charles Dickens and Wilkie Collins. To read the scathing comments these writers left about him, he'd have run a mile on even seeing a pistol, flintlock or otherwise. No. It all pointed to Durs weapons. My own Durs flinters were holsters. The duelers I owned were a late large-bore pair by Henry Nock. All the rest, carefully wrapped and laid on dry sponges, were unmistakably non-Durs.

The more I thought about it, the more unlikely it was that Eric had got it wrong. His pair probably were duelers, and perhaps even Durs. If a master craftsman can make a dozen pairs, what's to stop him making one more set? Nothing.

But what made them so special that Eric would babble eagerly over the phone about them to his bored brother?

There was no other alternative. I would have to make the assumption that the Judas pair had been found and bought by Eric Field, that they were used to kill him by some unknown person, and that the motive for Eric's death was possession of the unique antiques. How they'd managed to kill Eric without bullets was a problem only possession of the weapons themselves could solve. I put my cards away, switched off the light, and climbed out.

It took only a couple of minutes to have the living-room carpet back in place. I opened the curtains and phoned Field.

"Lovejoy," I told him. "Tell me one thing. How long before his death did Eric have them?"

"I'm not sure. Maybe a few months."

"Months?"

"Why, yes," he said, surprised. "I'm almost certain he mentioned he'd found a pair of good-quality flintlocks quite some time ago."

"Who would know for certain?"

"Well, nobody." He cleared his throat. "You *could* try his wife, Muriel, my sister-in-law."

"Same address?"

"She still lives in the house. Only, Lovejoy." He was warning me.

"Yes?"

"Please go carefully. She's not very . . . strong."

"I will," I assured him and hung up.

So Eric had bought them, and only months later had he discovered their unique nature. I was justified, then, in searching for duelers which looked like most other flints.

This was a clear case for Dandy Jack over at the antique mart, the world's best gossip and worst antique dealer. I could do him a favor, as he'd recently bought a small Chinese collection and would be in a state about it. He always needed help.

I locked up and examined the weather. It would stay fine, with hardly a breeze. The nearby town was about ten miles with only one shallow hill to go up. My monster motor would make it.

I patted the Armstrong-Siddeley's hood. "Let's risk it, love," I said, set it rolling with the outside handbrake dropped forward, and jumped in.

Mercifully, it coughed into action just as it reached the gate. The engine kept grinding away while I swung the gate open, and we trundled grandly out onto the metaled road, all its remaining arthritic twenty cc's throbbing with power. I pushed the throttle flat, and the speedo sailed majestically upward from walking pace into double figures. The jet age.

Practically every town nowadays has an antique market, mart, arcade, call it what you will. Our town has an arcade of maybe ten antique shops. Imagine Billy Bunter's idea of the Sun King's palace, built by our town council, who'd run out of money before finishing the foyer, and you've got our shopping arcade. It's given to seasonal fluctuations, because people from holiday resorts along the coast push up summer sales, and the dearth of winter visitors whittles the arcade's shops—stalls included—down to five or six. They throw in a cafe to entice the unwary. Dandy Jack never closes.

I parked the Armstrong illegally, sticking the card on the windshield saying "Delivering," which could be anything from a doctor to a florist. It often worked. The cafe had a handful of customers swilling tea and grappling with Chorley cakes. I got the cleanest cake and a plastic cup. Within five minutes they were popping in.

"Hello, Lovejoy. Slumming?" Harry Bateman, no less, of Wordsworth fame.

"Hiyer, Harry."

"Hear about my—?"

"Remember the Trades Descriptions Act, that's all."

He gave me a grin and shrugged. "I thought I'd done me homework that time. Bloody encyclopedia you are, Lovejoy. See you later."

"It's Lovejoy. Going straight yet?" came a second later.

Margaret Dainty was perhaps a useful thirty-five, tinted hair, plump, and prematurely matronly of figure. She was cool, usually reasonably griffed up on her wares, and tended to be highly priced. There was a husband lurking somewhere in her background, but he never materialized. An unfortunate childhood injury gave her a slight limp, well disguised.

"Hiyer, Margaret. How's business?"

"Not good." This means anything from bad to splendid.

"Same all around."

"Interested in anything—besides Jane Felsham?" She sat opposite and brushed crumbs away for her elbows.

I raised eyebrows. "What's she done wrong?"

"One of your late-night visitors, I hear."

"Word gets around—wrong as usual. Daytime. Accompanied."

"I'm glad to hear it, Lovejoy," she said, smiling.

We had been good friends, once and briefly. I'd assumed that was to be it and that she'd developed other interests.

"Now, now, young Dainty," I chided. "You don't want an aging, disheveled, poverty-stricken bum like me cramping your style."

"You *are* hard work," she agreed coolly. "But never dull."

"Poor's dull," I corrected her. "Failure's dull. That's me."

"You're determined not to risk another Cissie." Cissie, my erstwhile lady wife.

"There couldn't be another. It's one per galaxy."

"You're safe, then." She eyed me as I finished that terrible tea. "Coming to see my stock?"

I rose, bringing my unfinished Chorley cake with me. Frankly, I could have gone for Margaret badly, too deeply for my own good. But women are funny, you know. They keep changing, ever so slightly, from the time you first meet them. There's a gradual hardening and tightening, until finally they're behaving all about you, unmasked and vigilant, not a little fierce. It's all made worse by the crippling need for them that one has. There's an absolute demand, and women have the only supply. I prefer them before their shutters and masks come down. Not, you understand, at a distance.

She had a *bonheur de jour*—lady's writing desk—eighteenth century.

"Sheraton?" Margaret asked.

"No. His style, though."

"Why not?"

I shrugged in answer. I couldn't tell her about my bell's condemnatory silence. "Doesn't seem quite right."

Tip: look for neat fire-gilt handles, that lovely satinwood, tulipwood, and ebony, and never buy until you've had out the wooden runners which support the hinged writing surface. You'll be lucky if the baize is original. Look at it edge-on to see if it's standing high or not. High: modern replacement. Low: possibly original. Forget whether it's faded or not, because we can do that on a clothesline, washing and sun-drying repeatedly, day in, day out for a week. It's only stuck on.

"Good or not?" she pressed.

"Pretty good." Which satisfied her.

She showed me two pottery birds, all bright colors, and asked if I liked them.

"Horrible."

"Genuine?" They looked like Chelsea.

I touched one. Ding-dong. "As ever was."

"You haven't looked for the gold anchor mark underneath yet," she said, vexed.

"It'll be there," I said.

"Seeing you're on form," she asked, "what are these?"

There were four of them, shell cases of various sizes, cut and decorated. A small cross, also brass, had been drilled into each. I picked one up. The crosspiece of each was loose and came free.

"Table bells," I told her. "Prisoners of war, probably Boer War. You signaled for the next course by combinations of these four bells. Not valuable."

"Thanks." I cast an eye for flinters, but they weren't in Margaret's line.

In he tore, alcoholic and worried, eagerly trying to judge if we were just browsing or up to something, stained of teeth, unshaven of chin, bleary of eye, shoddy of gear, Dandy Jack.

"Come and see my jades, Lovejoy," he said.

I tried to grin while backing from his evil breath. A customer was showing interest, so Margaret stayed put, making a smiling gesture for me to look in before I left.

I let Dandy tell me how clever he'd been to do the deal. A retired colonel's widow, Far East wars and all that. I would have to be careful asking about flinters, but so far my approach had been casual in the extreme. Out came the jade collection. I sat on his visiting stool while he showed me. By hook or by crook I would have to do him a good turn.

Jades are odd things. There are all sorts of daft ideas in people's minds about antiques of all kinds—that *all* antiques if genuine are priceless, for example, a clear piece of lunacy. Nothing is truly beyond price if you think about it. All you can say is that prices vary. Everything's always for sale. Another daftness is that anything is an antique, even if it's as little as five years old. Remember the golden date, 1836. This side equals modern. That side equals antique. The most extreme of all daftnesses, though, is the idea that if something looks mint and beautifully preserved, it shouldn't, and therefore needs false wood-worm holes bored into it, scratches and dents made in unscathed surfaces, and splinters worked from corners. Wrong. Moral: the better preserved, the costlier. *Keep things mint.*

Jades attract more daftness than any antiques. And Dandy Jack had every possible misconception, displaying them all to anyone who called.

"It's a pity some aren't proper green," he was saying, fetching the small carved pieces out. "They must be some sort of stone. But here are some deep green ones . . ." and so on. I tell you, it's bloody painful. You'd think these people can't read a reference book between them. "I played it cool," he kept on. "Maybe I'll let them go for auction. Do you think Christie's would—?"

I picked one up—a black-and-white dragonfly, beautifully carved. Not painted, but pure jade through and through. To tell real jade—though not its age, however—from anything else, feel it. *Never leave jade untouched.* Hold it, stroke it, touch it —that's what it's for, and what it loves. But never touch it with freshly washed hands. If you've just washed your hands clean, come back in an hour when your natural oils have returned to your fingers. Then pick up and feel the jade's surface. You know how oil gets when it's been rubbed partly dry, like, say, linseed oil on a wooden surround? Faintly tacky and slightly stiff? If the object you hold gives that *immediate* impression, it's jade all right. To confirm it, look at the object in direct light, *not* hooded like posh lamps. The surface mustn't gleam with a brilliant reflection. It must appear slightly matt. Remember what the early experts used to say of jade: "Soapy to look at, soapy to feel." It's not too far out.

Now, there are many sorts of jade. Green jades are fairly common, but less so than you might think. "Orange-peel" is one of my favorites, a brilliant orange with white, not a fleck of green. Then there's "black-ink" jade, in fact perhaps nearer blue-black, usually mixed with white streaks, as in the dragonfly I was holding. One of the most valuable is "mutton-fat" jade, a fat-white jade of virtually no translucency despite its nickname.

Of course, nowadays the common green jade comes from damn near anywhere except China—Burma, New Zealand, you name it. And it's blasted out of hills in a new and unweathered state, which gives a massive yield but of a weak, scratchable quality. Most of these wretched carvings of fishes or horses you see now are done in China, of jade imported there. Green, fresh, soapy, mechanical travesties they are too. Get one (they should be *very* cheap) to teach yourself the feel, texture, and appearance of the stuff, but if your favorite little nephew shatters it to pieces one day, don't lose any sleep. China's exporting them by the shipload. "New Mountain Jade" they call it in Canton, Kwantung, China.

But. That only goes for the new modern mine-blasted green jade. The ancients were much more discriminating. To satisfy them, a piece of jade had to be weathered. The raw pieces were found exposed on hillsides and were taken to a craftsman carver, an artist who loved such a rare material. With adulation he would observe where the flaws ran, what colors were hidden beneath the surface. And then, after maybe a whole year of feeling, stroking the magic stone, and imagining the core of beauty within, he would begin to carve. New Mountain Jade (i.e., modern) is soft. The antique stuff is hard, *hard,* and to carve it took time. This means that a dragonfly such as I was holding took about six months. The craftsman had left the dragonfly's wings, head, and body black, and the underbelly had been skillfully carved through so it was mutton-fat jade, white like the spindly legs. The dragonfly was on a white mutton-fat jade lotus leaf—all less than two inches long, the detail exquisite, all from one piece of antique hard jade. And not a trace of green. Lovely. An artistic miracle.

I did my own private test—put it down a minute, my hands stretched out to cool, then picked it up again. Yes, cold as ice, even after being held in a hot, greedy hand. That's jade for you. The miracle stone. The ancient Chinese mandarins had one for each hand, a "finger jade" just for fiddling with, to comfort themselves. It was regarded as a very human need and not at all unmanly to want dispassionate solace as well as human comfort in that civilization, and what's wrong with either?

Dandy Jack fetched out about thirty pieces. About half were agate, and of the rest some six were modern ugly deep leaf-green new jade pieces, carved with one eye on the clock and some productivity man whining about output. I found nine, including an orange-peel piece, of old jade—exquisitely carved foxes, hearts, lotus plants, bats, the dragonfly, fungi. It really was a desirable cluster.

"You've got some good stuff here, Dandy," I said. It hurt to tell the truth.

"You having me on, Lovejoy?" He had the sense to be suspicious.

"Those over there aren't jade at all. Agate."

"The bastard!" he exclaimed. "You mean I've been done?"

"No. You've got some stuff here worth half your business, Dandy."

"Straight up?"

"Yes. Those dark green things are modern—for heaven's sake don't scratch them. It's a dead giveaway and you'll never sell them. These, though, are rare. Price them high."

I gave him the inky dragonfly, though my hand tried to cling hold and lies sprang to my lips screaming to be let out so as to make Dandy give it me back for nothing. I hate truth. Honest. I'm partial to a good old lie now and again, especially if it's well done and serves a good honest purpose. Being in antiques, I can't go about telling unsophisticated, inexpert lies. They have to be nudges, hints, clever oblique untruths that sow the seed of deception, rather than naive blunt efforts. Done well, a lie can be an attractive, even beautiful, thing. A good clever lie doesn't go against truth. It just bends it a little around awkward corners.

"You having me on?"

"Price them high, Dandy. My life."

The enormity hit him. "Do you think they're worth what I paid?"

"Whatever it was, it was too little." I rose to go.

He caught my arm. "Will you date and price them for me, Lovejoy?"

"Look," I told him, "if I do, promise me one thing."

"What?"

"You won't sell *me* that bloody inky dragonfly. It's worth its weight in gold four times over. If I put a price of two hundred quid on it, then offer to buy it from you, don't sell."

"You're a pal, Lovejoy," he said, grinning all over his bleary face.

I pulled off my coat and set to work. I saw Margaret make a thumbs-up sign across the arcade to Dandy, who had to rush across and give her the news. Morosely, I blamed Field's mad search. If I hadn't needed Dandy's gossip, I could have tricked most of the old jades out of him for less than twenty quid and scored by maybe a thousand. Bloody charity, that's me, I thought. I slapped a higher price on the dragonfly than even I'd intended. Give it another month, I said sardonically to myself, the way things are going and it would be cheap at the price.

I eventually had three leads from Dandy Jack, casual as you like. I think I was reasonably casual, and he was keen to tell me anything he knew. Lead one was a sale in Yorkshire. Jack told me a small group—about seven items is a small group—of weapons were going there. The next was a sale the previous week I'd missed hearing of, in Suffolk. Third was a dealer called Brad. He deserved to be first.

I loaded up with gasoline at Henry's garage.

"Still running, is it?" he said, grinning. "I'll trade you."

"For one that'll last till Thursday?" I snarled, thinking of the cost of gasoline. "You can't afford it."

"Beats me how it runs," he said, shaking his head. "Never seen a crate like it."

"Don't," I said, paying enough to cancel the national debt. "It does six—gallons to the mile, that is."

I drove over to the estuary, maybe ten miles. Less than a hundred houses sloped down to the mud flats where those snooty birds rummage at low water and get all mucky. A colony of artists making pots live in converted boathouses along the quayside and hang about the three pubs there groaning about lack of government money. Money for what, I'm unsure.

Brad was cleaning an Adams, a dragoon revolver of style and grace.

"Not buying, Brad," I announced. He laughed, knowing I was joking.

"Thank heavens for that," he came back. "I'm not selling."

We chatted over the latest turns. He knew all about Dandy's jades and guessed I'd been there.

"He has the devil's luck," he said. I don't like to give too much away, but I wanted Dandy to learn from Brad how impressed I'd been, just in case he'd missed the message and felt less indebted. So I dwelled lovingly on some of the jades until Brad changed the subject.

"Who's this geezer on about Durs guns?"

You must realize that antique collecting is a lifetime religion. And dealing is that, plus a love affair, plus a job. Dealers know who is buying what at any time of day or night, even though we may seem to live a relatively sheltered and innocent life. And where, and when, and how.

This makes us sound a nasty, crummy, suspicious lot. Nothing of the kind. We are dedicated, and don't snigger at that either. Who else can be trusted but those with absolute convictions? We want antiques, genuine lustrous perfection, as objects of worship, and nothing else. All other events come second. In my book that makes us trustworthy, with everything on earth— except antiques. So Brad had heard.

"Oh, some bloke starting up," I said.

"Oh?"

I thought a second, then accepted. "An innocent. No idea. I took him on."

"They're saying flinters."

"Yes."

"Difficult."

I told him part of the tale I'd selected for public consumption. "I thought maybe duelers, a flash cased set."

"I'll let you have a few pair he can choose from."

I grinned at the joke. "I'm hardly flush," I said. "That's why I was around Dandy's, on the prod. He said you might have word of a pair. Have to be mint."

He looked up from replacing the Adams in its case. "I'm in the Midlands next Monday. I'm onto five pieces, but they might turn out relics."

I whistled. Five possible miracles. A relic is any antique defaced and worn beyond virtual recognition, but you never think of that. The desire for the wonderment of a sensational discovery is always your first hope. Some people say it's ridiculous to hope that way, but doesn't everyone in one way or another? A man always hopes to meet a luscious, seductive woman; a woman always hopes to meet a handsome, passionate man. They don't go around hoping for less, do they? We dealers are just more specialized.

"Keep me in mind," I said, swallowing. "The cash is there."

"Where exactly?" he rejoined smoothly, and we laughed.

We chatted a bit more, then I throbbed away in my fiery racer. I made a holiday maker curse by swinging out into the main road without stopping, but my asthmatic old scrap heap just can't start on a hill, whereas his brand-new Austin can start any time, even after an emergency stop. People ought to learn they have obligations.

Muriel's house turned out to be my sort of house. Set back from the road, not because it never quite made it like my cottage, but from an obvious snooty choice not to mob with the hoi polloi. I imagined banisters gleaming with dark satin-brown depths, candelabras glittering on mahogany tables long as football fields, and dusty paintings clamoring on the walls. My sort of house, with a frail old widow lady wanting a kindly generous soul like myself to bowl in and help her to sell up. My throat was dry. I eagerly coaxed the banger to a slow turn and it cranked to a standstill, coughing explosively. I knocked with the door's early nineteenth-century insurance company knocker. (They come expensive now, as emblems of a defunct habit of marking houses with these insignia of private fire insurance companies.) It had shiny new screws holding it firmly onto the door, though the thought honestly never crossed my mind. The door opened. The frail old widow lady appeared.

She was timid, hesitant, and not yet thirty.

"Good day," I said, wishing I was less shabby.

I've never quite made it, the way some men do. I always look shoddy about the feet, my trousers seem less than sharp, my coats go bulbous as soon as they're bought. I have a great shock of hair that won't lie down. I'm really a mess.

"Yes?" She stared from around the door. I could hear somebody else clattering things in the background.

"Look, I'll be frank," I said, feeling out of my depth. "My name is Lovejoy. I've called about . . . about your late husband, Mr. Field."

"Oh."

"Er, I'm sorry if it seems inopportune, Mrs. Field . . ." I paused for a denial, but no. "I'm an antique collector, and . . ." Never say dealer except to another dealer.

"I'm sorry, Mr. Lovejoy," she said, getting a glow of animosity from somewhere. "I don't discuss—"

"No," I said, fishing for some good useful lie. "I'm not after buying anything, please." The door stayed where it was. I watched it for the first sign of closing. "It's . . . it's the matter of Mr. Field's purchases."

"Purchases?" She went cautious, the way they do. "Did my husband buy things from you?"

"Well, not exactly."

"Then what?"

"Well," I said desperately, "I don't really know how to put it." She eyed me doubtfully for a moment, then pulled back the door. "Perhaps you should come in."

In the large hall she stood tall, elegant, the sort of woman who always seems warm. Cissie spent her time hunting drafts to extinction. This woman would be immune. She looked deeply at you, not simply in your direction the way some of them will, and you could tell she was listening and sensing. In addition she had style.

Now, every woman has some style, as far as I'm concerned. They are fetchingly shaped to start with, pleasant to look at, and desirable to, er, encounter, so to speak. And all women have that attraction. Any man that says he can remain celibate for yonks on end is not quite telling the truth. It's physically impossible. What astonishes me is that very few women seem to see this obvious terrifying fact, that we are completely dependent on their favors. Ah, well.

I had no plan of action, trusting simply to my innate instinct for deception and falsehood. Mrs. Field dithered a bit, then asked me into a lounge, where we sank into nasty new leather armchairs. There was a rosewood desk, Eastern, modern, and one tatty cavalry saber on the wall. On the desk I could see a chatelaine which looked like Louis XIV from where I was sitting but I couldn't be sure.

"You mentioned you and my husband were fellow collectors, Mr. Lovejoy."

A chatelaine is a small (six to eight inches or so) case, often shaped in outline like a rounded crucifix. It opens to show scissors, toothpick, manicure set, and sometimes small pendants for powders and pills, that sort of thing, for people to carry about. Quite desirable, increasing in value—

"Mr. Lovejoy?" she said.

"Eh? Oh, yes. Mr. Field." I dragged my mind back.

"You mentioned . . ."

In the better light she was quite striking. Pale hair, pale features, lovely mouth, and stylish arms. She fidgeted with her hands. The whole impression was of somebody lost, certainly not in her own territory.

"Poor Mr. Field," I hedged. "I heard of the . . . accident, but didn't like to call sooner."

"That was kind of you. It was really the most terrible thing."

"I'm so sorry."

"Did you know my husband?"

"Er, no. I have . . . other business associates, and I collect antiques in partnership with, er, a friend." It was going to be hard.

"And your friend . . .?" she filled in for me. I nodded.

"We were about to discuss some furniture with Mr. Field." I was sweating, wondering how long I could keep this up. If she knew anything at all about her husband's collecting I was done for.

"Was it a grandfather clock?" she asked, suddenly recalling.

I smiled gratefully, forgiving her the use of that dreadful incorrect term.

"Yes. William Porthouse, Penrith, made it. A lovely, beautiful example of a longcase clock, Mrs. Field. It's dated on the dial, 1738, and even though the—"

"Well," she interrupted firmly, "I wouldn't really know what my husband was about to buy, but in the circumstances . . ."

I was being given the heave-ho. I swallowed my impulse to preach about longcase clocks, but she was too stony-hearted and unwound her legs. Marvelous how women can twist them around each other.

"Of course!" I exclaimed, as if surprised. "We certainly wouldn't wish to raise the matter, quite, quite."

"Oh, then . . . ?"

"It's just . . ." I smiled as meekly as I could as I brought out the golden words. "Er, it's just the matter of the two pistols."

"Pistols?" She looked quite blank.

"Mr. Field said something about a case with two little pistols in." I shrugged, obviously hardly able to bother about this little detail I'd been forced to bring up. "It's not really important, but my friend said he and Mr. Field had . . . er . . ."

"Come to some arrangement?"

I blessed her feminine impulse to fill the gaps.

"Well, nothing quite changed hands, you understand," I said reluctantly. "But we were led to believe that Mr. Field was anxious for us to buy a small selection of items, including these pistol things." I shrugged again as best I could but was losing impetus fast. If any smattering of what Field had told me was remotely true, a pair of Durs flinters had actually resided under this very roof, been in this very room, even. I raised my head, which had bowed reverently at the thought. I felt as if I'd just happened on St. Peter's, Rome.

"As part exchange, I suppose?"

"Well, I suppose so. Something like that."

"I heard about them," she said, gradually fading into memory. Her eyes stared past me. "He showed me a couple of pistols, in a box. The police asked me about them, when George—"

"George?"

"My brother-in-law. Eric, my husband, phoned him the night before he . . . He was going to go over and show George the next morning. Then this terrible thing happened."

"Were you here, when . . . ?"

"No. I was in hospital."

"Oh. I'm sorry."

"We'd been abroad, Eric and I, a year ago. I'd been off color ever since, so I went in to have it cleared up. Eric insisted."

"So you knew nothing at all about it?"

"Until George came. I was convalescent by then. George and Patricia were marvelous. They arranged everything."

"Did you say the police asked about the pistols?"

"Yes. George thought whoever did it . . . used them to . . . to . . ."

"I suppose the police found them?" I said innocently. "They can trace guns these days."

"Hardly." Her face was almost wistful. "They were so old, only antiques, and they don't think he was . . . shot."

"What were they like?" I swallowed. The words were like sandpaper grating.

"Oh, about this long," she said absently, measuring about fifteen inches with hands suddenly beautiful with motion. "Dark, not at all pretty."

"My friend said something about gold decoration," I croaked in falsetto.

"Oh, that's all right, then," she said, relieved. "They must be different ones. These had nothing like that. Blackish and brown, really nothing special, except that little circle."

"Circles?" I shrilled. At least I wasn't screaming, but my jacket was drenched with sweat. She smiled at her hands.

"I remember Eric pulling my leg," she said. "I thought they were ugly and a shiny circle stuck in them made them look even worse. Eric laughed. Apparently they were pieces of platinum."

I realized I should be smiling, so I forced my face into a

54

gruesome ha-ha shape as near as I could. She smiled back.

"You see, Mr. Lovejoy, I never really . . . well, took to my husband's collecting. It seemed such a waste of time and money."

I gave my famous shrug, smiling understandingly. "I suppose one can overdo it," I lied. As if one could overdo collecting.

"Eric certainly did."

"Where did he get his items from, Mrs. Field? Of course, I know many of the places, but my friend didn't see very much of him."

"Through the post, mostly. I was always having to send down to the village post office. I think the case came from Norfolk."

"What?" I must have stared because she recoiled.

"The box. Weren't you asking about them?"

"Oh, *those*," I said, laughing lightly. "When you said 'case' I thought you meant the *cased* clock I mentioned." I forced another light chuckle. Stupid Lovejoy.

"The shiny pistols. I remember that because they were so heavy and the woman at the post office said she'd been there."

You have to pay for the pleasure of watching a beautiful woman. In kind, of course. Like struggling to understand her train of thought.

"Er, been where, Mrs. Field?"

"To the place in Norfolk. She said, 'Oh, that's where the bird sanctuary is, on the coast.' She'd been there with her family, you see. I tried to remember the name for the police, but they said it didn't really matter."

"Ah, yes. Well, I never get quite that far, so perhaps . . . er, one thing more." I was almost giddy with what she'd told me. "Yes?"

"What, er, happened to them? Only," I added hastily, "in case my friend asks."

"Well, I don't know." Any more questions would make her suspicious. "George asked, and the police asked, but that's the point. When I returned from hospital they were gone."

"And the rest of the antiques . . . ?"

"Oh, they were sold. I wasn't really interested, you see, and Eric always said to send them off to a respectable auction if anything happened. He was a very meticulous man," she informed me primly. I nodded.

He was also a very lucky man, I thought. For a while.

She was waiting for me to go. I racked my exhausted brain. How did the police and these detectives know what questions to ask, I wondered irritably. I knew that as soon as the door closed a hundred points would occur to me. I'm like that.

"Well, thank you, Mrs. Field," I said, rising. "I shouldn't really have called, but my friend was on at me about it."

"Not at all. I'm glad you did. It's always best to have these things sorted out, isn't it?"

"That's what my friend said."

She came with me to the door, and watched me away down the drive. A priest was walking up as I screeched away from the house, probably on some ghoulish errand. They're never far away from widows, I thought unkindly, but I was feeling somehow let down. I gave him a nod and got a glance back, free of charge. I had an impression of middle age, a keen, thin face, and eyes of an interrogator. Interesting, because I'd thought fire and brimstone weren't policy any more, though fashions do change. I didn't see his cash register.

She gave me a wave in the rearview mirror. I waved back, wondering even as I accelerated out of the landscaped gardens and back among the riffraff whether I could ask her out on some pretext. But I'd now blotted my copybook with all the pretending I'd done. Women don't like that sort of thing, being unreasonable from birth. Very few of them have any natural trust.

It's a terrible way to be.

5

Back at the cottage I summed things up, getting madder every minute at those slick so-and-so's on TV that make short work of any crime. I worked out a list in my mind of possible events as I made my tea, two eggs fried in margarine, baked beans with the tin standing in a pan of boiling water, and two of those yoghurt things for afters. I always like a lot of bread and make sandwiches of everything when I've not got company. A pint of tea, no sugar on alternate days because the quacks keep scaring the wits out of you about eating things you like, and I was off.

I sat down at the door to watch the birds fool around while I ate.

I'd learned the pistols were something vital, probably a really good pair, almost certainly Durs, as George said. Shiny, the lovely Muriel had said, and black. No decoration, but a platinum plug for the touchhole. And she'd indicated about fifteen inches long, not too far out. Shiny might mean not cross- or star-hatched, as Durs did his, but some of his early pieces were known unhatched, so that was still all right. Black, shiny, ugly . . . well, the poor lady was still probably slightly deranged after her shock. Cased. And Brother George had said there were

57

accessories in it. And bought by post from Norfolk, near a coastal bird resort.

All Eric's stuff had been sold, but George was certain the flinters weren't there when he discovered his brother. And if they'd been hidden anywhere in the house, presumably Muriel would have come across them by now.

I finished my meal and sat drinking tea. It was afternoon, and the sun threw oblique shadows across the grass. The birds, a fairly ragged lot with not much to do, trotted about the path and milled around after crumbs. My robin, an aggressive little charmer who seemed to dislike the rest, came on my arm and gave its sweet whistle. It was blowing a cool breeze, rising from the east. With the east coast so near, afternoons could take on a chill.

"Do people go to bird sanctuaries to look at things like you?" I asked the robin. He looked back, disgusted. "Well," I explained to him, "some people must. Know where it is?"

He dropped off and shooed some brownish things off his patch. You'd think robins were soft and angelic from all the free publicity they get around Christmas, but they're tough as nails. I've seen this one of mine take on rabbits as well as those big black birds that goose-step about after you've cut the grass. Tough, but means well. I'm just the opposite, weak and bad-intentioned.

"Margaret?"

"Lovejoy!" She sounded honestly pleased. "At last! Where are we to meet?"

"Cool it, babe," I said. "I'm after information."

"I'd hoped you were lusting force five at least." She heaved a sigh. "I suppose it's still that tart from London."

"Which tart?" I asked, all innocent.

"You know. The one you sent walking to the station on her own."

"O.K., Hawkeyes of the East," I said sardonically.

"I just happened to notice," she said sweetly, "seeing as I was dangling out of the pub window when you arrived."

I hadn't seen her. The thought crossed my mind that she might have overheard Tinker and George Field, but I hadn't time to hang about if a real genuine pair of flinters were in all this.

"She'd just been for a short . . . er . . . visit," I explained.

"How long's long, if three days is short?"

"Two," I snapped back, and could have bitten my tongue.

"Oh, two was it," she cooed. "You must be tired, sweetie, after all that entertaining."

See what I mean? They don't like each other really. I honestly believe that's what all that dressing up's all about. It doesn't matter what the bloke thinks, as long as they outdo any other birds in the vicinity. I often wonder how nuns get on, and whether they vie with each other for God in the convent. All the rest are fencing and machinating and circling warily, all for nothing. Frightening, if you let yourself dwell on it.

I once had this bird—the one I got the cottage from—and she found that I'd visited this other woman in the village. Honestly, it was quite innocent, really, but I'd had to stay away from the cottage for a night or two, only because I'd got pressing business, you see. My resident bird hit the roof—gave me hell—but was more eager to cripple this other woman for life than she was to tell me off.

I think they just like fighting each other, and I'd just given my bird an excuse for a scrap. How she found out I'll never know. They always assume the worst, don't they? Trust is not their strong point.

"I rang up to ask," I said with dignity, "about birds."

"How many do you want, sweetie?" she said coyly, putting barbs in.

"Birds that fly about," I reprimanded. "In the air."

"Oh, I beg your pardon, Lovejoy," she said, needling still. "I misunderstood. I thought—"

"Never mind what you thought."

"Stuffed?" she drooled.

"Now, look, Margaret," I snapped, and she relented.

"Sorry, old thing. What is it?"

"I have the offer of some glassed animals," I improvised. "Ten."

"Quite a collection."

"Well, the thing is, I haven't an idea."

"Want me to look at them for you?"

This was a blow, because Margaret was something of our local expert on such horrid monstrosities. Stuffed animals might be valuable antiques, rare as hen's teeth, but they still dampen my ardor.

"Er, well, you see . . ." I let it wait.

"All right, Lovejoy, I understand." She was smiling from her voice. "You don't trust me."

"Of course I do, Margaret," I said, fervor oozing down the phone. "It's just that I thought I'd rather learn a bit about suchlike myself. Anyway, I believe there are some bird sanctuaries further north along the coast which are pretty well known, so I thought—"

"Look, Lovejoy," she said, serious now, "I don't know what you plan to do, but if you're aiming to cart a load of stuffed birds into a bird sanctuary and ask them to help you identify them, you're going to be unpopular."

"Oh. Well, they might have some literature," I said weakly.

"I'll get the details. My nephew's in a club that comes out this way. Hang on." She left the phone a moment and then gave me a list of three bird sanctuaries, of which two were in Norfolk. I didn't say which one I was interested in, but said I'd probably go to the nearest.

Before she rang off, she asked if I was all right.

"Of course I am. Why?"

She hesitated. "Oh, nothing. It's just . . . Look, can I come and see you for a second?"

"Oh, Margaret." It was a bit transparent, after all, so I can be forgiven for being exasperated.

"Suit yourself, Lovejoy," she snapped angrily and slammed down the phone. Women don't like to give up, you see. Seen them with knitting? Yards, hours and hours, years even. And still they're there, soldiering on. Something pretty daunting about women sometimes, I often think. Anyway, it's change I like, and that's exactly what they resent.

While I went again through my records—locking up carefully as usual—there were two further phone calls. One was Sheila, who complained I hadn't rung. I said so what else is new, and she rang off telling me I was in a mood. Tinker interrupted me an hour later saying he'd had four possible tickles. Three were the same as I'd got from Dandy Jack and included the Yorkshire auction, plus one additional whisper of a man in Fulham who'd brought a load of stuff down from the north and had two cased sets among the items. That could have meant anything including percussion, so I took the address and said I'd speed off there in my speedster sometime.

There were numerous antique enthusiasts in Norfolk. Only a hundred lived near the coast. From the bird sanctuaries Margaret had given me I selected some five or six collectors, varying the narrow radius.

Cross-checking with the auction records I had, none of the six had bought within two years anything remotely resembling a Durs gun. Indeed, most of them seemed to be either furniture or porcelain people, though one particular chap, a clergyman called Lagrange, had purchased a revolving percussion long arm from a local auction not far from the Blakeney Point sanctuary. Adverts didn't help, except for a run of them from two Norfolk addresses in the *Exchange and Mart* some two years ago, wanting rather than offering flinters.

I emerged from my priest hole three hours later fairly satisfied that if Durs duellers had changed hands within the two years before Eric Field's death, it had been done so quietly nobody had known. Therefore the ones which came so innocently by post from Norfolk were a major find, something newly discovered to this century's cruel gaze.

My hands were shaking again, so I had my emergency beer. If it wasn't women it was antiques, or vice versa. I put the telly on and watched some little rag dolls talking to each other on a children's program. That did nothing for my disturbed state of mind.

I was getting closer to believing in the Judas pair.

Look about. That's all I have to say. Look about. Because *antique discoveries happen.* If in doubt read any book on local history. It'll set you thinking.

I've come across Minden *faïence jardinières*—posh pots for garden plants—being used as garage toolboxes. I've seen a set of Swiss miniature gold dominoes making up an infant's set of wooden building bricks, in the original gold case. I've seen a beautiful octagonal ruby-glass hallmarked silver-ended double scent bottle used as a doll's rolling pin. I can go on all night.

I've seen a Spencer and Perkins striking watch used as a weight on a plumb line. You still don't believe me? Don't, then. Go and ask the Colchester laborers who dug out an old bucket a couple of years ago—and found in it the lost Colchester hoard of thousands of medieval silver coins. Or go and ask the farmer who four years ago got so fed up with the old coffin handles he kept plowing up in his field that he took them to the authorities. They're the famous solid gold Celtic torques that museums the world over now beg to be allowed to *copy.* And while you're about it, you can also ask where the most valuable pot in the world was found. No, not in some sacred tomb. It was in somebody's porch, *being used as an umbrella stand.* Well, a Charles I silver communion cup is my own principal claim to fame. I bought it as an old tin shaving cup years ago. *And* kept the profits. None of this rubbish about "fair play," giving part of the proceeds up as conscience money. A sale is a sale is a sale.

My mind was edging further toward an uneasy belief.

I let the evening come nearer the cottage by having a small cigar. The darkness swung in, inch by inch. I swept the living room and got out some sausages for my supper. Those and chips, with a custard thing from our village shop to follow.

Though the cottage seemed cozy enough, this Judas business had taken the steam out of me for the moment. Perhaps it was just my turn to feel a bit down. I get that way.

As I listlessly tidied up I realized how really isolated the cottage was. Solitude is precious to me, but only when I want it.

I phoned Margaret, intending to say I'd perhaps been rather short with her on the blower. It rang and rang without answer.

While my grub was frying I stood at the darkening window and watched the road lights come on across the valley edge a mile away. The White Hart would be starting up. Harry, possibly Jane Felsham, Adrian, probably Tinker, and for absolute certain Dandy Jack—they'd all be there. Later would come the nightlies, the knocker dealers who touted door to door leaving cards or hoping housewives bored to torture would fall for their blue eyes enough to search their attics.

Then the pub dealing would start—cuts, rings, groups, fractional slices of profit, marginal gains, the entire lovely exhilarating game of nudges and nods. I pulled the curtains to.

Suppose I did find the thirteenth pair. What then? I hadn't asked Field. Whoever had them had murdered Eric Field. I was to tell George Field, probably, who would accuse the owner, whoever it was, to the police. So the police would then arrest the owner. Q.E.D.

I poked the sausages and chips onto a cold plate and margarined some slices of bread. The tea. I'd forgotten tea. I put the kettle on, but before sitting down tried to phone Margaret again. No luck. By then the kettle boiled. By the time the tea brewed the food was cold. I sighed and sat down to supper.

Having the telly on helped, but I kept wondering what they really do for a living during the day.

6

Next morning was just my sort, grayish but dry and promising a bit of sun. I had two eggs on bread, lashings of sauce to smother any taste that might linger on after my cooking, and a couple of Weetabix and powdered milk. Two apples and a pear for the journey, and the world was my oyster. My uneasy mood had vanished.

I rang George Field to summarize my progress, not mentioning my clue from Muriel, but saying I was following a couple of leads within the trade. He seemed disappointed, which was only to be expected. He was probably reared on Chandler's slick heroes.

The Armstrong didn't share my enthusiasm. Maybe it knew how far we had to go. I fed the robin, waiting for the engine to recover from an attempt to start it before half past nine. It usually functioned best about dinnertime. Oddly enough, it was also seasonal, preferring winters to summers and rain to sun.

I'm not a sentimental person. You can't be about a mere scrap heap, can you? But I have a liking for the old banger simply because it's the only time my bell's been wrong. I took the motor car in part exchange for a group of four small animal bronzes from a Carmarthen chap who, poor misguided soul, was interested in bronzes. Some people love them. Heaven knows why, as very few are attractive. Incidentally, always look underneath a bronze figure first. If it has a four-figure number, it may well be a "liberated" piece which arrived here after the war. "DEPOSE GESCHUTZT" or some such stamped in front of this number can lend weight to your suppositions. The value of most bronzes has increased eight times in the last couple of years among dealers alone.

I was on about my Armstrong. It is an open tourer with big squarish headlamps sticking out and a top that you pull over by hand. Nothing's automatic. The starter's a handle at the front, and you have to work a finger pump from the front seat before it will fire. The brake's outside, and a noisy exhaust runs like a portable tunnel from both sides of the long hood, which is held down by straps. It looks badly old-fashioned and clumsy, but it's sturdy as hell and safe as houses, which is the main thing. As I say, the fuel consumption is terrible. All along where the dashboard would be in a new car there are switches, handles, and a couple of mysterious gauges I've always been too scared to touch in case it stopped altogether. For such a huge car it is weak as a kitten, but once you get it going it is usually fine. The trouble is it seems to have only one gear, because there's no gear handle. Other motorists often blow their horns as they pass in annoyance at my slow speed. I only have a rubber bulb-type honker I never use.

It made a successful running start eventually. As I drove at maximum speed I worked my journey out. Margaret had given me the names of three places, Minsmere in Suffolk, Blakeney Point and Cley in Norfolk. I would say I'd been to Minsmere if anyone asked, and, engine willing, would look at the other two places in one go. I would reach home before opening time. I had the six significant addresses with me to consider one by one.

I was frankly disappointed with the bird sanctuaries, not that I knew what to expect. Quite a few cars were around when I drove up to Cley. A few folks, Rommelized by great binoculars and businesslike weatherproof hats, stood all forlorn in attitudes of endeavor staring toward acres of desolate muddy stuff where nothing was happening. Occasionally they murmured to each other and peered eastward. Perhaps they placed bets among themselves to make it interesting. As well as being disappointed I was puzzled. I've nothing against birds, feathered or not, but once you've seen one sparrow you've seen the lot, haven't you? Occasionally, one particular one might become sort of family just by sheer persistence, like some around the cottage. That's different. Unless you know them specifically it's a waste of time, like people. I asked one bloke what they were all looking at.

"Oyster catchers," he said. I stared about, but there wasn't a boat in sight.

"Oh," I replied, and honestly that was it.

There were no stalls, cafes, not even a fish-and-chip shop. As a resort it was a dead duck, if you'll pardon the expression. I talked the Armstrong into life and we creaked away on ye olde greate mysterie trail. I had more birds in my garden than they had on all that mud. I was frozen stiff.

Now brilliant Lovejoy had made a plan. Muriel's memory being what it was, I was down to guesswork—scintillating, cunning brainwork of the Sherlock type.

To post a case you need a post office, right? Sniggering at my shrewdness, I drove around trying to find one, lurching along country lanes where hedges waved in the gales and animals stooged about fields being patient as ever.

I eventually gave up and some time later drove through Wells into Blakeney, where there was a post office. I was dismayed. What do private eyes do now? I couldn't just bowl in and say "What ho! Who posted a heavy box about a year ago, give or take six months?" My plan hadn't got this far. I inspected it from a distance and then drove to the Point. More desolation, with some different shaped birds bumming around aimlessly, all watched eagerly by enthusiasts. No shops, no stalls, no real scene. I departed shivering.

All this countryside was dampening my earlier high spirits. It's nice from a distance. A few trees and a sparrow or two can be quite pleasant sometimes as a diversion. But you can't beat a good old town crammed full of people milling about on hard pavements, street after street of houses, shops, antique merchants, cinemas, pubs, the odd theater, and lots of man-made electricity. Bird sanctuaries are all very well, but why can't they share them with people?

I drove around Blakeney. In case you come from there, I'm not knocking it. Charming little joint, with the odd tasty antique shop and a place I had dinner near a tavern. But it's not a metropolis, is it? And it had no coastal holiday resorts nearby, either. From the way Muriel's postmistress had spoken, I wanted something like Clacton. That cold wind started up again. I decided there were no clues in bird sanctuaries and drove south. What dumps those places are, I thought, feeling a witticism coming. Those places, I sniggered to myself, are for the birds.

I like antique dealers. We may not be much to look at, but scratch us and we're nothing but pure unadulterated antique dealer all the way through. Everything else comes second. This means you've only to put us, blindfolded, anywhere on earth, and we home instinctively on the nearest fellow dealer. When I'm driving, I swear my banger guides itself along a route that has the highest number of dealers along it.

Trusting my Armstrong, I was at my ninth antique shop asking for nothing in particular, when the name "Lagrange" accidentally caught my eye. The shopowner, a doctor's wife, Mrs. Ellison, full of painting chat, had gone into the back to find a painting I'd heard of, alleged Norwich School, and to fill in time I was leafing through her invoice file. Lagrange had bought a pistol flask from her about a year before, and paid in groats from what I saw.

I was safely near the door hovering over a box of copper tokens when she returned with the painting. It was a water-color, not an oil, which was a measure of her knowledge. David Cox had signed it, so the name said. I held it. Good stuff, but not a single chime. I showed a carefully judged disappointment and turned to other things. David Cox taught a lot of pupils water-color painting, and had an annoying habit of helping them with little bits of their work, a daub here, a leaf there. If their final painting pleased him *he* would sign it, thereby messing up the whole antique business. Worse, his signature's dead easy to forge—so they say. Beware.

I bought a score of her copper tokens, to pay for my journey's expenses. They are cheap, rather like small coins. Merchants in the seventeenth and eighteenth centuries, times when copper change was in short supply owing to incompetence at the mint among other causes, made their own "coins" as tokens in cop-per. These were given for change, and you could spend them when you needed to go shopping again. It must have been a nightmare, because some shops would refuse all except their own tokens, so you might finish up with perhaps thirty *different* sets of copper "coinage" of this kind in your pocket, and still not be able to buy what you wanted from the thirty-first shop. The early seventeenth-century ones are about half the size of those from the next century—an important fact, as many are un-dated. I bought the "cleanest," that is those least worn, no matter how dirty. "Buy the best, *then* buy old," as we say. Of any two antiques, go for the one best preserved and remember that repairs or any other sort of restoration doesn't mean well preserved. Then consider the degree of rarity. *Then,* and only then, consider the degree of age. This is Lovejoy's Law for Collectors of Limited Means. Of course, if you have bags of money, head straight for a Turner seascape, a silver piece made by that astonishing old lady silversmith Hester Bateman, or a

Clementi (the London maker) square piano of about 1840, and two fingers to the rest of us. But for other poorer wayfarers, my advice is to have only these three general rules.

I paid up painfully and turned to go.

"Oh, one thing." I paused as if remembering. "You've not such a thing as a powder flask?"

"Powder? Oh, for *gun*powder?" I nodded.

"No," she said. "I had one a while ago, but it went very quickly." She'd probably had it on her hands for years.

"I'm trying to make one of those wretched sets up," I explained.

She was all sympathy. "Isn't it hard?"

I hesitated still. "No chance of you managing to pick one up, is there? I don't have much chance of getting one myself."

"Well . . ." I was obviously treading upon that sacred confidentiality.

"I'd be glad to pay a percentage on purchase," I offered, which made it less holy.

"I know," she said. "When you have money locked up in stock, trying to move stuff can be so difficult."

We commiserated for a minute in this style. She told me she'd sold the flash to a local collector. She gave me Lagrange's address, the one I already had. I expressed surprise and gratitude and handed her my card.

"He's a very pleasant padre," she informed me, smiling. "A real enthusiastic collector. I'm sure he'll be glad to see you."

"I'll either call back or phone," I promised, and set about finding the Reverend Lagrange, collector.

Mrs. Ellison had given me the usual obscure directions which I translated by a vintage RAC roadmap. He lived about fifteen miles off the trunk road, say thirty miles. I patted my speedster and swung the handle. I'd be there in an hour and a half with luck.

The trouble was I'd not had any feminine companionship for a couple of days. It blunts any shrewdness you might possess. Your brain goes astray. It's no state to be in.

I drove toward the Reverend Lagrange's place thinking of Sheila as a possible source of urgent companionship. No grand mansion here, my cerebral cortex registered at the sight of the grubby little semidetached house with its apron-sized plot of grass set among sixty others on a dull estate. Such trees as people had planted stood sparse and young, two thin branches and hardly a leaf to bless themselves with. I parked on the newly made road where there was a slope, a hundred yards away, and walked back among the houses. A curtain twitched along the estate, which pleased me as a sign that women hadn't changed even here in this desolation. But where was the Reverend's church? Maybe he was still only an apprentice and hadn't got one. I knocked.

Ever run into a patch of mistakes? My expectations were beginning to ruin my basic optimism. Just as Muriel had turned out to be half the age I'd anticipated, here was this padre who I had supposed couldn't be more than twenty-two. He was middle-aged. Worse still—much more upsetting—I'd seen him before, walking up Muriel Field's drive as I had left. All this might not matter to you, but to an antique dealer, it's his life-blood. First approaches are everything. I suppressed my flash of annoyance and gave my I'm-innocent-but-keen grin.

"Reverend Lagrange?"

"Yes?" He was a calm and judging sort, in clerical black and dog collar, not too tidy.

"I hope I'm not intruding." The thought occurred that it might be a feast day or Lent or something. Worse, he might be fasting. I eyed him cautiously. He seemed well nourished.

"Not at all. Can I help?"

"Er, I only called on the off chance."

"Do come in." He stood aside and in one stride I was in his living room. There was a cheap rolltop desk and a scatter of

Cooperative furniture. He had a one-bar electric fire for the chill winter evenings. My heart went out to him.

"It isn't anything to do with, er . . . the soul." I faltered. "I'm interested in antiques, Reverend. I was at a shop—"

His eyes lit up and he put his black Bible inside his desk, sliding the lid closed. "Do sit down, Mister . . . ?"

"Lovejoy."

"Splendid name," he said, smiling. I was beginning to quite like him. "The shop was—?" I told him and he raised his eyes heavenward.

"Ah, yes. I bought a pistol flash there, quite expensive it was," he said.

May heaven forgive you for *that*, I thought nastily. It was a steal. I would have asked five times what he paid.

"Er," I began, weighing out those grains of truth which gospel fables. "Don't I know you from somewhere?"

"Do you?" He seemed as careful as I was.

"You couldn't by any chance know the Fields?"

"Ah, yes." We unbent, full of reassuring noises. "My poor friend."

"I visited Mrs. Field. I *thought* I saw you arriving."

"And you're the gentleman in the long car. Of course. I *thought* I recognized you. Did you manage to get it seen to? I'm no mechanic myself, but I could tell from the noise and all that smoke—"

I wasn't taking that from any bloke. "You're a friend of Eric Field's?" I interrupted, peeved. My speedster might stutter a bit, but so did Caesar.

"An old friend." He went all pious like they do. "I try to visit Muriel—Mrs. Field, that is—as often as I can, to lend solace." He sighed. "It's been a very difficult time for her, seeking readjustments."

"I do appreciate that, Reverend," I said, considerably moved for a second or so.

It's pleasant being holy, but isn't it boring? Holy duty done with, I got down to business. "I know you'll think it a bit of a cheek, Reverend," I began apologetically, "but I'm trying to complete a set of accessories for a pistol I have, in a case."

"Oh." His eyes glinted. I was onto a real collector here, no mistake. "Any special variety?"

"Very expensive," I said with the famous Lovejoy mixture of pride and regret. "A pocket Adams revolver."

"Oh." His fire dampened. "Percussion."

"Yes, but almost mint." I let myself become eager. "There's one nipple replaced, and a trace of repair . . ."

His lip curled into an ill-concealed sneer. "Well, Mr. Lovejoy," he said, still polite, "I'm afraid percussion's not my first choice."

"Flinters?" I breathed in admiration.

"It so happens . . ." He controlled himself and said carefully, "I am interested. If you ever do hear of any flintlocks, I would be most happy to come to some arrangement."

"They're pretty hard to find these days, Reverend," I told him sadly. "And the prices are going mad. Never seen anything like it."

"You're a dealer, Mr. Lovejoy?" he asked, as if he hadn't guessed.

"Yes, but only in a small way." He would check up with the shop lady as soon as I was gone. Always admit what's going to be found out anyway. "I'm mainly interested in porcelains."

I got another smile for that. "I'm glad we're not flintlock rivals."

"I only wish I had the money to compete," I confessed. "What I came about—"

"The flask?"

"If you still have it," I said, carefully measuring my words in case this all turned into a real sale, "I'd like to make you an offer."

To my surprise he hesitated. "They're fairly expensive," he said, working out private sums.

I groaned and nodded. "Don't I know it?"

"And you'll require a flask more appropriate to a percussion—"

"Oh, that's a detail," I interrupted casually. "It doesn't matter too much. Anything goes these days."

I sank out of sight in his estimation. As far as he was concerned, I would forever be a tenth-rate dealer of the cheapest, nastiest, and most destructive kind. Even so, he still hung on, hesitating about selling me his flask. It was only after a visible effort that he steeled himself to go no further and courteously refused. I tried pushing him, offering a good market price, though it hurt. By then he was resolved.

We said nothing more. I didn't enlighten him about my visit to Muriel Field's. He'd be on to her soon enough. But, I wondered, had Eric told him about the Judas pair?

I went down the new road. This little estate miles from anywhere probably hadn't an antique from one end to the other. On the other hand, there were a few shapely birds here and there, but the sense of desolation was very real. I would phone Sheila and ask her to come back to Lovejoy's waiting arms in time for me to meet her off the London train in the romantic dusk. As I trotted around the corner I planned a superb meal for the luscious lady who would bring a little—maybe much—happiness into my humdrum existence. I would get three of those pork pies in transparent wrapping, a packet of frozen peas and carrots mixed, one of those gravy sachets, and two custard pies for afters. Lovely. How could any woman resist that?

I leapt into my chronic old speedster and started it by releasing the handbrake to set it rolling on the slope, wondering as I did so if I had any candles to make my supper party a really romantic seduction scene. I didn't give the sad new dwellings another glance. Give me bird sanctuaries any time.

7

I should own up about women.

It's a rough old world despite its odd flashes of sophistication. Women make it acceptable the same way antiques do. They bring pleasure and an element of wonderment, when oftener than not you'd only be thinking of the next struggle. There's nothing wrong in it all. It's just the way things are. Morality's no help. Keep cool, hang on to your common sense, and accept whatever's offered. Take what you can get from any woman that is willing to give it.

And before you even start to argue—no! I won't listen to all that junk about waiting for spontaneous out-of-the-blue "true love." Love is *made*. It is the product of many makings. A man and woman just don't fall in love at a glance, sighing and longing and whatever. They have to *make* love, build it up month after month, having sex and becoming loving toward each other. When they've made enough love and built it around themselves brick on brick, *then* they can be said to be in a state of love. Read those old religious characters. They knew all about love as a spiritual event. It didn't come to them by a casual notion as a sudden idea that sounds not too bad or from a weekly magazine. Love, that mystical magic stuff of a lifetime, came from working at the very idea of it, grieving and straining and suffering the making of it. Then, in possession of it, comes the joy and the ecstasy of knowledge in the substance of love.

Well, sorry about that.

I make it when and where I can. Any honest man will tell you that the main problem is where the next woman's coming from. Women often decry this truth. Cissie used to. For some reason women find it necessary to deny the obvious. Ever noticed how many phrases they have for that very purpose? "That's all you think about." "Men are like children." And so on, all wrong. I can't understand why women aren't more understanding.

Sheila was coming close to it. I'd known her a year, meeting her at one of those traction-engine rallies. She was there with her chap, a dedicated man who was so busy oiling things he didn't even notice when she left with me.

That isn't to say Sheila should go down as a cheap tart. These terms are as irrelevant as differences of racial color, engine pattern, weight, any nonessential of human behavior. Women like men, and men like women. It's only natural they tend to bump into each other now and again, sometimes accidentally, sometimes not. And if both parties wish to pretend it's more socially acceptable meeting properly introduced at the vicar's tea party drinking tea with little finger poised crookedly in the air, big deal. What difference does it make as long as the chance of making love emerges from the great masquerade?

I take love seriously. It's a serious business and doesn't deserve to be left to the tender mercies of penny-paper romances and demented Russian novelists griping at one set of commissars after another.

Her family keep a shop in Islington, clothes and that. She has a younger sister at school. She opted out of typing suddenly. "I read," she explained once, "they'd done experiments on a chimpanzee. It had learned to type. I ask you." That did it. She hitched up with this traction-engine chap, helping in his garage and generally doing paperwork while he played with plugs and valves.

I collected her at the station.

"Hello, Lovejoy," she said evenly.

"Hello, Sheila." I was standing there like a spare tool, holding these flowers.

"Pig."

She stood unmoving in the station foyer. It was the scene from "When did you last see your father?" all over again. I felt like the kid on the cushion.

"You know, love," I said lamely. "I was busy."

There were few people around. This was the last train in or out. She'd have to stay the night with me. Alf the porter used to stand and grin at these scenes years ago. Now all he wants to do is clear up, lock up, and push off before the White Hart shuts. We stood under the solitary lamp.

"You're not as thick as you pretend, you know that?"

I nodded. In this sort of mood you have to go along with them. She was wearing one of those fawn swingback coats that seem slightly unfashionable even when they're in, but never seem less than elegant. I'd never noticed before. Her clothes never quite matched the latest trends. She stood in a pool of light, smooth and blond. My heart melted.

"I'm not very nice, love," I admitted before I caught myself for a fool.

"I know."

"I rang because—"

"I know why."

"It was just that . . ." I petered out, holding the flowers toward her instead of explanation.

She gazed at me, making no move to take them. "It's just that you were taken short again."

"Beautifully expressed." I tried my clumsy jocularity act, which sometimes worked on the low graders. She evaded my attempt to thrust the bunch into her arms. I'd never seen her in this particular mood before.

"Lovejoy." Her voice was quite dispassionate.

"Yes, darling?"

"Stop that. I want to ask you something."

"Go on." The passengers were all gone. Two cars started up outside and purred away. I could hear Alf clattering buckets, encouraging us to leave.

"If I don't stay with you tonight," she said in that calm voice, "what will you do?"

"Have two suppers, hot bath, and bed," I lied.

She gave me that new calm look she'd learned during the last two days. I didn't care for it. "Liar."

I almost staggered. "Eh?"

"I said. liar."

"That's what I thought you said." Stalemate.

The platform lights suddenly plunged out behind her. The single overhead bulb gave her an uncanny radiance I'd never seen. Maybe it was just that I was wanting her so badly.

"You'll be out picking up some middle-aged tart," she said serenely.

"What, me?" I never can sound stern, though I tried. It came out weak as a blister.

"You, Lovejoy." She reached out and took the flowers. "And you'll lay her after three pink gins."

"Look, Sheila," I said, worried sick by all this.

"You'll give her the eye and the hi-baby act. I know you."

"Nothing's further—"

"From your mind? Perhaps not, because I'm dope enough to come." She sighed and scrutinized my shabby frame. "You'll get any flabby amateur tart from the nearest taproom and make love to her wherever she says, in the car, your cottage, her place if her husband's out."

"What's it all about?" I pleaded. "What did I do?"

"You can't help it, Lovejoy, can you?" she said.

I gave in, shrugging. "Sometimes it's not easy," I said.

She smiled and took my arm. "Come on, you poor fool," she said. "I'm famished." She climbed into the car and started to push the finger pump. As I said, she'd known me for a year. The motor responded. I saw Alf the porter thankfully closing up as we left the darkened station forecourt. We clanked through the silent village, my spirits on the mend.

"Not to worry, angel," I reassured her. "I've a repast fit for the Queen. One of my specials."

"I suppose that means your sawdust pies."

"Pork," I replied, narked.

"Custard tart for afters?"

"Of course."

"Beautiful."

I turned to say something and noticed she was laughing.

"What's the joke?" I snapped.

"Nothing." She was helpless with laughter.

"Look," I said roughly, "don't you like my grub? Because if so, you can bloody well—"

"N—no, Lovejoy," she gasped, still laughing.

"I've gone to a lot of trouble," I informed her with dignity. "I always do."

"I know, love," she managed to say, and held my arm as I drove. "It was just me. Don't take offense."

"All right, then."

She gave me a peck on the cheek. "Friends again?" she asked.

"Pals," I promised fervently, relieved her odd mood was over.

We held hands all the way home.

Next morning.

I was itching to have my priest hole open to enter up a few oddments of information I'd gathered on my journey the previous day, but with Sheila there I contented myself with cataloguing my tokens. One or two were quite good. I'd advertise those, priced high. The rest I'd sell through local dealers when the big tourist rush began.

She was watching me, turned on her side on the fold-out bed. "You love them," she said.

I sighed theatrically. "Don't come that soul stuff."

"It's obvious you do."

"It's also obvious that going all misty-eyed because we had it off is pretty corny."

She laughed again when she ought to have been put out. "Have you had breakfast, Lovejoy?"

"Yes, thanks."

"What time were you up?"

"Seven."

"Did you notice the bruise?"

"What bruise?" I felt guilty.

"When you belted me in the bathroom the other day."

"Oh. About that, love." I didn't look at her. "I've been meaning to say sorry. It was important, you see."

"A phone call?"

"Well, yes." I forced justification into my voice. "It turned out to be vital. I admit I was a wee bit on the nasty side—"

"Come here, Lovejoy," she said. I could tell she was smiling.

"No," I said, concentrating.

"Come here," she said again, so I did.

See what I mean about women, never giving up?

Muriel answered the door, still jumpy and drawn but as stylish as before.

"I'm sorry to bother you again so soon," I apologized.

"Why, Mr. Lovejoy."

"I just called—"

"Come in please."

"No, thank you." There was no sound of cutlery in the background this time. A gardener was shifting little plants from pots into a flower bed. "I thought they only did that on Easter Monday," I said. She looked and I saw her smile for the first time. It was enough to unsettle an honest dealer.

"Wait. I'll get my coat."

She emerged, putting a head scarf on over her coat collar.

"You'll remember me for ruining your day if nothing else." I shut the door behind her and we strolled to watch the gardener at work.

"These days I welcome an interruption," she said.

"Mrs. Field—"

"Muriel." She put her arm through mine. "Come this way and I'll show you the pond." We left the house path and went between a setting of shrubberies.

"I wish I could return the compliment." A woman's arm linked with yours does wonders for your ego. I felt like the local squire.

"Compliment?"

"Nobody calls me anything but Lovejoy."

She smiled and seemed glad to do it. "Me too?"

"You too. Oh, one thing more."

She looked at me, worried. "Yes?"

"Cheer up, love. Nothing's the end of the world."

"I suppose not." She was about to say more, but we came upon another elderly gardener tying those mysterious strings around plant stems. I must have looked exasperated, because she asked me what was wrong.

"Beats me why they do it," I said in an undertone.

"Do you mean the gardener?" she whispered back.

"Yes," I muttered. "Why can't they leave the blinking plants alone?" I was glad I'd said it, because it gave her a laugh.

The pond was a small lake, complete with steps and a boat. A heron, gray and contemplative, stood in the distance. I shivered.

"Cold?" she asked.

"No. Those things." I nodded to where the heron waited. "It's fishing, isn't it?"

"Why, yes." She seemed surprised.

"Can't you give it some bread instead?" I suggested, which made her laugh again and pull me around to see my face.

"Aren't you . . . soft!" she exclaimed.

"I'd like the countryside, but it's so bloody . . . *vicious.*"

"Don't you like my garden, Lovejoy?"

I stared around accusingly. "It's a county, not a garden." I flapped my hand but the heron wouldn't go. "Does it all belong to the house?"

"Of course. Eighty acres."

"It's lovely," I agreed. "But everything in it's hunting everything else. Either that or trying to escape."

She shivered this time and raised her head scarf. "You mustn't talk like that."

"It's true."

I watched her hands tidy her hair beneath the scarf's edge. They had a natural grace to set off their own gestures, doing hair, pulling on stockings, or smoking a cigarette. She saw me gaping at her. I looked back at the water.

"Lovejoy, what do you really do?"

"Oh, very little. I'm an antique dealer, really." I paused to let her load. Where the hell was all this kindness coming from? I wondered irritably. She said nothing. "I'm your actual scavenger. Nobody's sacred. I even winkled out your priestly collector friend, and he lives miles away."

"Reverend Lagrange?"

"Yes."

"He's been a good friend. He and Eric met years ago. I don't think he collects the same things Eric did."

Nobody else does, either, I thought enviously. We moved along a flowered walk with those trellises against a wall.

"I wasn't telling the truth the other day." Own up, Lovejoy. Never be only half stupid. Go broke. "You probably guessed."

"Yes."

I eyed her carefully. "Aren't you mad at me?"

"No." She pulled a leaf from some thorny plant that hadn't done her any harm. "You're not the first to have tried the same . . . thing."

"Trick," I said. "Be honest. We call it the box gambit in the trade."

"Box gambit?"

"I wish I hadn't started this," I said.

She put the leaf idly between her teeth and saw me wince. "What's the matter?"

"You wouldn't like it if you were that leaf." She looked at it and dropped it on the path. "It's not dead."

"But how on earth do you eat, Lovejoy?" she asked me.

"Like us all, but that's an essential."

"What's the box gambit?"

I told her, feeling rotten. Box as in coffin. Anybody dying leaves a house and antiques, if he's wealthy enough to get his name reported in the papers. Those who are missed by our ever-vigilant press are listed in the "Deceased" column by sorrowing relatives anxious to do the local antique dealers a favor. We read up the facts of the case. Within seconds, usually, and before the poor deceased is cold in his grave, we kindly dealers are around visiting the bereaved, claiming whatever we think we can get away with. And you'd be surprised how much that is.

"And do . . . widows fall for it?" She stopped, fascinated.

"More often than not."

"Do you really mean that?"

"Of course," I snapped, harshly. "Over ninety per cent of the time you come away with a snip, nothing less than useful information."

She seemed intrigued by the idea, part horrified and partly drawn to it. "But it's like . . . being . . ." She hesitated and looked back. The heron was still there.

I said it for her. "Predators."

"Well . . ."

"You mean yes," I said. "Which is what we are."

"But why do the wives give you—?"

"*Sell*. Not give. Never leave a box gambit unpaid." I quoted the trade's unwritten rule. "It's what makes it legal."

"And what if you're caught?"

She drew me to a bench seat and we sat. From there we faced the house beyond the water, trailing trees and sweeping grass studded with bushes. It was as charming as any scene on earth and made me draw breath.

"You think it's lovely," she said.

"Wonderful. They had a sense of elegance we've lost," I said. "It all comes down to judgment. They had it. Whatever shape or design or pattern was exactly right, they recognized it. You have to love it, don't you?"

"I know what you mean, Lovejoy." Her tone was cold. "I used to feel the same until Eric died."

"Will you stay here?"

"No, not now."

"Where will you go, Muriel?"

"Oh." She shrugged.

The heron stabbed, was erect and still before the drops fell from his beak.

"What if you *are* caught in the box gambit?" She shook my arm until I relaxed.

"You lie," I said. The ripples were extending toward us. "Lie like a trooper. You say that you, in all innocence, called at her house. The widow asks you in to see some heirloom because you'd asked particularly about antiques. You say she bargained like an old hand, and anyway you'd given her money for the object, hadn't you? She won't deny it."

"How do you know?"

I gazed into her eyes. "They never do."

"Have you done it, Lovejoy?" she asked as the first ripple lapped on the bank below us. I nodded.

"I don't believe you," she said candidly.

"You must."

"Why must I?"

"Because . . . because, that's all."

"Why, Lovejoy?"

"Look, Muriel." I rose and tipped earth with my shoe into the water, staring down. It seemed pretty deep. You could see a few pebbles, then a dark brown murkiness. "I don't know much about you, your family, who there is to give you a hand now . . . after your husband. But that mansion over there. These grounds. It's enough to bring every dealer and scrounger running from miles around."

"Are you trying to warn me?"

"Just listen." I tried to stop myself, but like a fool I talked on. "We dealers are pretty slick. Some are all right, but some are not. We're good and bad, mixed. There are grafters, crooks, conners, lifters, zangers, edgers, pullers, professional dummyers, clippers—every variety of bloke on the make. Some pretty boys, smart, handsome, looking wealthy. Cleverer than any artists, better than any actor. They'll pick your house clean any way they can and brag about it in the pub afterwards."

"Are you warning me, Lovejoy?" Womanlike she stuck to her question. I felt like shaking her.

"Never mind what I'm doing," I cried, exasperated. "Just be careful, that's all. Be suspicious and sharp, and don't let in everybody who comes knocking."

"I let you in, Lovejoy," she reminded, smiling.

I sat down and took her by the shoulders. "Can't you see the obvious?"

"What do you mean?"

I drew breath and tried to glare into her innocent eyes. "You're too damned trusting, Muriel. You should never have let me in the other day. It's too risky. Look," I said, maddened by her smile. "Look. In that house, that great mansion you live in, your husband Eric lost his life."

"I don't need reminding."

85

"You do." I was almost shouting, not knowing why I was so worked up. "Has it not dawned on you?"

"What?"

"Who killed him?"

She paled instantly. I could see the skin over her cheeks tauten. "Why . . . why are you asking me?" she said.

"Because somebody must have," I said. "Do the police know who? No. Does anyone else know? No. And not only that. Does anyone know *why* he was killed? Do you? No. The police? No."

"They . . . they said it must have been an attempted robbery," she said faintly.

"So they think," I said. "But is that reasonable? What was stolen?"

"Why, nothing," she faltered.

"Not even one or two of your husband's antiques?"

"No. At least, I don't think so."

"Did the police think so?"

"Practically everything was there, according to Eric's lists. They weren't complete, of course. He never did keep very tidy records."

"Think," I urged. "Was nothing at all missing?"

"The only thing is that my brother-in-law said a pair of pistols were gone. The ones you asked about. The police *did* go over the inventory when all Eric's antiques went to Seddon's afterwards, though. George had rather an argument with them about it, I recall. He seemed to blame them for not being concerned enough."

"That doesn't alter the fact," I put in, "that you're in this house, rich and with plenty of valuable stuff about, I guess."

She nodded. "There's the—" God help me if she wasn't going to give me a rundown of her valuables.

I clamped my hands over my ears. "Don't," I begged. "For heaven's sake, you're doing what I told you not to. Keep quiet about your things. Chain everything down. Change the locks. Treble the burglar alarms. Quadruple the dogs."

"I'll be all right, Lovejoy," she said, smiling. She pulled down my hands and kissed me. "I think you're sweet."

"How can I be sweet when I'm a hard nut?" I said angrily, pulling away. "You don't realize how versatile dealers, collectors can be. We'll do anything—any *thing*—to get what we want. It may only be a couple of old matchboxes, but if we collect matchboxes we'll do anything to get them."

Her face was back in its previous solemn, worried expression. "But that can't be true."

"It *is* true."

"It can't be," she said doggedly.

"It is."

"But, Lovejoy," she said, almost pleading, "that's so unreasonable."

"Of course it's unreasonable. All collecting's unreasonable. But it's real." I shrugged and beckoned her to her feet. We strolled on. "You're not really taking notice of me, are you?"

I could see I had upset her.

"You aren't telling me *all* collectors are like that, are you?" she said, hesitating beside a white-flowered bush set between large rocks.

"I am."

"All?"

"All," I said firmly. "That's what makes a collector special. Unique. Your husband must have been like that too."

"Well, yes," she said, "but he was—"

"Eccentric?" the sardonic note struck.

She swung on me. "How did you know I used to—?" she blazed, looking momentarily more frightened than angry.

I kissed her lightly. "All wives call their husbands that, Muriel, love," I said, smiling.

"Oh."

"Beware of collectors," I warned again.

She glanced obliquely at me as we walked. "And what about you, Lovejoy?"

I gave her my frankest avaricious leer. "I'm the worst dealer there ever was, as far as you're concerned," I said hoarsely.

"I doubt that."

"The greediest, the cleverest, and the randiest," I admitted, thinking, What am I doing? "So don't trust me, especially me."

"I don't believe that, either," she said. "But I'll do as you say."

"Right," I said with finality, disengaging my arm. "That's it, then. Madam, before I rape you under this elm tree, show me the door."

"I like you, Lovejoy," she said.

"Don't push your luck, Muriel." I watched the heron stab and crook in a swallow again. "You've only been safe so far."

She tried to laugh again, but something had gone from the day. We waited for the next ripple to reach the steps, then set off back toward the house as the boat slowly began to tug at its mooring.

Seddon's, I was thinking. They sent his antiques to Seddon's for auction.

8

Sheila said Dandy Jack had phoned but left no message, that Margaret had too but said not to bother.

"And a strange gentleman who seemed annoyed," she added.

"Pansy?"

"He had that . . . mannerism."

"Adrian."

"Will you call, please. And that's the lot." She made coffee better than I did, but only Yanks do it properly in my opinion. I drank it for appearance's sake. "What's she like?"

"Who?" On guard, Lovejoy.

Sheila curled on the divan. "Whoever it was you've been to see."

"Oh." A measure of truth was called for, I thought. Always dangerous stuff to handle. You know where you are with a good old fable, so much more adaptable.

"Pretty?"

"Yes. Her husband died in odd circumstances some time back."

"Was it a box gambit?"

"Sort of." I eyed her unkindly. "You're learning too much for your own good."

She blew a kiss. "I won't split." Dated slang, I noticed. Pity there's no market for it.

"Finish up," I told her. "We're going to the arcade, then Adrian's."

Instantly she was all about getting ready. Now, there's a difference for you. I knew a dealer in Manchester once who said that the only real difference between us and women was that they strike matches in an away direction, while men did it in a cupped hand toward themselves. But you can list a million things. Say to a chap, "Come on, I'll give you a lift. It's time to go," and he'll say, "Fine. Thanks," but not move for a while. A woman's immediately all bustle, hardly bothering to listen to the destination. Funny, that.

We pulled up near the arcade, doing the "Delivery" bit. I was proud of Sheila. She looked good enough to eat, as some of our local Romeos perceived. I went straight to Dandy Jack's. He was tilting a bottle.

"For my chest," he explained, grinning. "Hello, Lovejoy. Sit down, love."

His tiny shop was a ruin as usual. Everything lay under a coating of dust. He had two fire screens which would have been superb except that filth made them look like pieces of cladding, all that splendid granular coloring obscured.

"Why don't you spruce your place up, Dandy?" I couldn't help asking.

"Oh." He grinned. "Well, I would, but it takes time, doesn't it?"

Sheila sat gingerly on a Victorian piano stool, knees together and heels off the ground, with the air of a quack in an epidemic through no fault of his own.

"Bonny girl you got there, Lovejoy," he said.

"Thanks."

"Dandy Jack and Randy Lovejoy." He gave out a cackle and swigged again, wiping the bottle neck on his tattered sleeve.

"And they say wit is dead."

"No harm intended, love," he confided to Sheila, his hand on her shoulder.

"None taken," she said bravely without recoiling.

"You phoned," I reminded him. "But before you tell me why, have you still got those jades?"

"Of course." He delved into a pile of open trays and pulled one out. A jade tumbled off. He picked it up, rubbing it on his tatty pullover.

I snatched them all off him irritably and took them toward the light. It was still there, an unreal lustrous netsuke masquerading among jade and agate. I pulled off the ticket I'd written for it. A netsuke is a little carved figure of ivory, jade, or other decorative material. The Japanese made them for embellishing sword handles. We, of course, rip them out and ruin the entire setting.

"I've had second thoughts, Dandy." I tried not to feel guilty and avoided Sheila's eye.

He crowded close, stinking of rum. "It's not duff, is it, Lovejoy?" he asked anxiously.

"No. It's superb."

The bitterness in my growl made him cackle with glee. "You're too bloody soft for this game," he croaked.

"Don't keep saying that," I snapped. I wrote out a new ticket upping the price five hundred per cent. "Here. Now," I said ferociously, "move them, Dandy. Move them! They should be treated with velvet gloves, not rattled around this cesspit of yours, and sold fast."

He cackled again and offered me a swig, which I declined. He glanced toward Sheila as a caution, but I nodded.

"Well," he said, reassured. "Some geezer phones me early. He'd heard I was putting the whisper out for flinters and rings to ask what sort. Wouldn't leave a name."

"That's useless, Dandy."

"Wait. He asks after a Mr. Lovejoy, did I know if he'd anything for sale in that line."

"Eh? Are you serious?"

"Straight up."

There was nothing more. Now this smacked of some amateur sleuthing on somebody's part. No dealer would tackle A about B's intentions so directly. I cast about for Margaret on the way out of the arcade but didn't see her. Her small den across the shopping arcade was unlit and carried its "Closed" sign. I don't know what I'd done wrong.

We pushed down the High Street among buses and cars toward Adrian's. It's a cut above the arcade. He has a spruce display, tickets on everything. Today's offerings included a series of Adam-style chairs, good copies, a lush mahogany Pembroke table by Gillows—a great name—of Lancaster about 1820, and a run of Byzantine icons on the walls among English watercolors.

Incidentally, remember that the watercolor game is a characteristically English art. Continental light is too brilliant. It's the curious shifting lights in our countryside that imparted a spontaneity and skill to the art that made it a feature of this land as opposed to others. Praise where it's due.

Adrian had a Rowbotham (moderate value, great skill), a Samuel Palmer (much value, brilliant skill), an Edward Lear (moderate value, moderate skill) and a minute Turner that must have taken less than a minute to do. I touched the frame just to say I'd done so, not kneeling, and recoiled stunned by bells. Huge value plus the skill of genius.

"Now, dear boy," Adrian was saying when I could concentrate. "You're not going to tell me it's phony. Don't you dare."

"It's perfect, Adrian."

"Isn't he sweet?" he cooed at Sheila. She concurred while I looked daggers.

"You wouldn't by any chance have popped in one of the local auctions, Adrian?"

I waited, but he stayed cool. "All the time, sweetie."

"Seddon's." Still not a flicker.

"Fortnightly." He smiled. "To remind myself how low one

can sink, dear boy. They have rubbish and rubbishy rubbish, just those two sorts."

"You wouldn't have bought some gadgets about maybe a year ago? A collection of card cases, early nineteenth century . . . ?" My lies flowed with their usual serenity.

"No luck, love." He sat and thought. "Not heard of them either."

"Started out from a box job, so word is."

"Not even a whisper." He was sympathetic. "Ask Jane Felsham. It's more in her line. Got a buyer for them?"

I gave a rueful shrug. "I would have if I could find them."

"How many?"

"Ten—some mother of pearl, black lacquer, engraved silver, one silver filigree, and a couple chatelained."

He whistled. "I can understand your concern. Shall I ask about?"

"If you would, Adrian. Many thanks."

He cooed a farewell, waving a spotted cravat from his doorway as we went back to the car. I'd got a ticket from a cheerful traffic warden and grumbled at Sheila for not having reminded me about putting up my infallible "Delivering" notice.

Seddon's is one of those barnlike ground-floor places full of old furniture, mangles, mattresses, rotting wardrobes, and chairs. The public come to see these priceless articles auctioned. Dealers and collectors come to buy the odd Staffordshire piece, an occasional Bingham pot, or a set of old soldier's medals. The trouble is, the trade's nonseasonal at this level. To spot the public's deliberate mistake, as it were, you must go every week and never let up. Sooner or later there'll be a small precious item going for a song. It's not easy. To see how difficult it is, go to the auction near where you live. Go several times and you'll see what dross is offered for sale and *gets bought!* Now, in your half-dozen visits by the law of averages you could have bought for a few coppers at least one item worth a hundred times its auctioned price. The people who actually *did* buy it weren't simply lucky. They study, read, record, assemble information and a store of knowledge. It's that which pays off eventually. That, and flair—if you have any.

I stress "nonseasonal" because almost all of the antique business at the posher end is seasonal. It's too complex and full of idiosyncrasies to give it my full rip here, but in case you ever want to buy or sell anything even vaguely resembling an antique, follow Lovejoy's Law: All things being adjusted equally, sell in October or November to get the best auction price; buy between May and early September for the lowest prices.

It was viewing day, when you go around the day before the auction and moan at how terrible the junk is, and how there's cheaper and better stuff in the local market. That way, innocents hear your despair and go away never to return. Result—one less potential buyer. Also, it provides the auctioneer's assistants with an opportunity for lifting choice items out of the sale and flogging them in secret for a private undisclosed fee. We call it "melting down," and deplore it—unless *we* can get our hands on the stuff, in which case we keep quiet.

I took Sheila in and we milled around with a dozen housewives on the prowl and a handful of barkers. Tinker was there and came over.

"Any luck?"

"Yes, Lovejoy. Hello, miss."

Sheila said hello. We left her leafing through a shelf of drossy books and went among the furniture where nobody could listen in.

"I've got a cracker, Lovejoy," Tinker said. "You won't believe this, honest."

"You're having quite a run," I commented.

He got the barb and shook it off. "I know what you're thinking," he said, "but it's a whizzer. Listen. You're after a mint pair for that Field I put onto you—right?" I nodded. "I've found a cased set going."

"Where?" My mouth dried.

"Part exchange, though." This was Tinker creating tension. "Not a straight sale."

"What the hell does that matter?" I snarled. "Who the hell does a straight sale for the good stuff these days anyway? Get on with it."

"Keep your hair on." We chatted airily about mutual friends while an innocent housewife racked herself over a chest of drawers before marking it carefully on a list and pushed off steeling herself for tomorrow's auction.

Tinker drew me close. "You know that boatbuilder?"

"Used to buy off Brad down the creek?"

"Him. Going to sell a pair of Mortimers, cased."

"I don't believe it, Tinker."

"Cross my heart," he swore. "But he wants a revolving rifle in part exchange. Must be English."

I cursed in fury. Tinker maintained a respectful silence till I was worn out.

"Where the hell can I get one of those?" I muttered. "I've not seen one for years."

I actually happened to have one in my priest hole, by Adams of London Bridge, a five-chambered percussion long arm. There's bother with a spring I've never dared touch, but otherwise it's perfect. I cursed the boatbuilder and his parents and any possible offspring he might hope to have. Why can't people take the feelings of antique dealers into account before they indulge in their stupid bloody whimsies? Isn't that what all these useless sociologists are for? I came manfully out of my sulk.

Tinker was waiting patiently. "All right, Lovejoy?"

"Yes. Thanks, Tinker." I gave him a couple of notes. "When?"

"Any time," he answered. "It'll be first come first served, Lovejoy, so get your skates on. They say Brad's going down the waterside early tomorrow. Does he know—?"

"The whole bloody world knows it's me that's after flinters," I said with anguish.

When a punter puts money on a horse at two-to-one odds, as you will know, nothing happens at first. Then, as more and more punters back it, the odds will fall to maybe evens, which means you must risk two quid to win only two, instead of risking two to win four as formerly. In practically the same way, the more people want to buy a thing, the dearer it becomes. Naturally, merchants will explain that costs and heaven-knows-what factors have pushed the price up, but in fact that's a load of cobblers. Their prices go up *because* more people want a thing. They are simply more certain of selling, and who blames them for wanting to make a fortune?

Gambling is a massive industry. Selling spuds is too. Buying flintlocks or Geneva-cased chain-transmission Wikelman watches is not a great spectator sport, so the field is smaller. A whisper at one end therefore reverberates through the entire collecting world in a couple of weeks, with the effect that those already in possession of the desired item quickly learn they are in a position to call the tune. They can more or less name their terms. Hence the indispensable need of a cunning barker.

"I'll go and see him," I said. Nothing makes humanity more morose than an opportunity coming closer and closer as the risks of failure simultaneously grow larger.

A toddler gripped my calf crying, "Dadda! Dadda!" delightedly. I tried unsuccessfully to shake the little psychopath off and had to wait red-faced until its breathless mother arrived all apologetic to rescue me. The little maniac complained bitterly at having lost its new find as it was dragged back to its push chair. Sheila was helpless with laughter at the scene. The fact that I was embarrassed as hell of course proved even more highly diverting.

"Oh, Lovejoy!" she said, falling about.

"You can go off people, you know," I snarled. "Very funny. A spiffing jape."

"Oh, Lovejoy!"

"Mind that apothecary box!" I pushed her away just before she knocked it off a side table.

This gave her the opportunity to ask about it. I saw through her placatory maneuver, but for the life of me I couldn't resist. It gave me an excuse to fondle the box, a poor example it was true, but they are becoming fairly uncommon and you have to keep on the lookout.

Watch your words. Not an "apothecary's" box. It wasn't his, in the sense that he carried it about full of rectangular bottles and lovely nooky felt-lined compartments for pills and galenical "simples," as his preparations were called. It belonged usually to a household, and was made to stand on a bureau, a medicine cabinet if you like. You dosed yourself from it, or else hired an apothecary, forerunner of the general practitioner, to give advice on what to use from it. The current cheapness of these elegant little cabinets never ceases to amaze me. I wish they would really soar to a hundred times their present giveaway price, then maybe the morons who buy them and convert them into mini–cocktail cabinets would leave well alone and get lost.

You find all sorts of junk put in by unscrupulous dealers and auctioneers besides the bottles. This one had a deformed old hatched screwdriver thing with a flanged blade and a pair of old guinea scales imitating the original physic balance. I dropped them back in, snorting scornfully. Sheila heard my opinion with synthetic attention and nodded in all the right places.

"If I catch somebody doing it, darling, I'll smash it on his head," she promised as we strolled around.

"You'll do no such thing."

"No?"

"Smash a *brick* on his head, and bring the apothecary box to me."

"For you, Lovejoy, anything."

After an hour Sheila was protesting. Inspecting stuff's best done by osmosis. Don't rush, stroll. Be casual. Saunter, wander, learn.

"We keep going round and round, Lovejoy," she complained, sitting to take off a shoe to rub her foot like they do.

"Shut up," I said, wandering off.

Jim, one of the elderly attendants, guffawed. "Chivalrous as ever, eh, Lovejoy?" he said, and I was in with an excuse.

"This junk's enough to make a saint swear," I groused. "Never seen so much rubbish since Field's stuff came through."

He was aggrieved at that. Nobody likes their own stuff being recognized for the rubbish it is.

"We sold some good stuff that day," he said, quick as a flash. "If you hadn't gone to Cumberland you'd know better."

That explained why I'd missed it. I was beginning to feel better as things clicked into place.

"Nothing still around from it, is there?" I asked casually.

He grinned. "Do leave orf, Lovejoy. It was donkeys' years back."

"Oh, you never know," I said, hinting like mad.

He shook his head. "No, we played that one straight," he admitted ruefully. "Practically all of it went the same week we got it."

"Just a thought, Jim. Some things do get left behind occasionally."

"Pigs might fly," he said.

I played casual another minute, then collected Sheila and we made it back to the car.

We pulled out, rolling against protesting traffic to get started.

"We have one more call to make before home," I told her. "Game?"

She sighed. "These places always make me feel so grubby. I need a bath."

"Same here." I shrugged. The motor coughed into emphysematous life and we were under power. "What's that to do with anything?"

"Where are we going?"

"Down the creek."

"Is it a tip from Tinker?"

"You guessed, eh?"

"It was pathetically obvious, Lovejoy."

"You're making me uneasy."

And she was. Tinker was loyal, wasn't he? I paid him well by comparison with other dealers' barkers. I never disclosed a confidence. Twice I'd bailed him out. Once I'd rescued him from Old Bill, and once saved him getting done over by the Brighton lads. But you could never tell. Was it this suspicion that was worrying me? Something niggled in my memory, something I had seen.

We were out of town and down on the estuary in no time. It's not much of a place—four small boatbuilders in corrugated iron sheds, the usual paraphernalia of the pleasure-boating fraternity, and a few boats hauled up on the mud by the wharf. Those big Essex barges used to ply between here and Harwich in the old days, crossing to the Blackwater and even London, but the two that are left are only used for showing tourists the Colne estuary and racing once a year, a put-up job.

I found Barton planing wood. The lights were on inside his boathouse though outside was still broad daylight. You could see the town-hall clock in the distance some five miles off. I waited until he stopped. Well, what he was making could be a valuable antique in years to come. Never interrupt a craftsman.

"Hello, Lovejoy." He stopped eventually and nodded to Sheila as we sat on planks.

"When are you going to give this boat lark up, Dick?" I said. "You could go straight."

It gave him a grin as he lit his pipe. "Dealing in antiques?"

"Maybe," I offered. "I'd take you on as a substandard junior partner for a year's salary."

"I like a proper job," he countered, winking at Sheila. She was quite taken with him.

"On second thoughts, I couldn't see you standing the pace."

"Of course," he yakked on, "I can see the attraction. Nothing really matters in antiques, does it? Right or wrong, you get along."

"It's time for his tablet," I apologized to Sheila. "This feverish air down on the waterside, you understand. His blood's thin."

"I turn into a man after dark," he said solemnly to Sheila. "If ever you're thinking of ditching this goon, give me a tinkle."

"Flinters, Dick," I said gently. There was silence. A waterbird made a racket outside and something splashed with horrid brevity.

"Ah, well," he said.

These pipe smokers are one up on the rest of us. It might be worth taking up just for the social advantages. If you want a few moments peace, out it comes and you can spin out the whole ritual for as long as you feel inclined. The universe waited breathlessly until his pipe was chugging to his satisfaction.

"Launched?" I asked. "Better now?"

"Flinters," he said. "They're a problem, now, aren't they?"

"*You* are telling *me?*"

"And rare."

"And desirable. Go on, Dick. And costly."

"Ah, yes." He stared down the short slipway. "About a month ago I decided which pair I'd keep. I have two Sandwells and the Mortimers. The Mortimers can go, but I want exchange. A revolving rifle, English." Sandwell was an early brass-barrel specialist, lovely stuff.

"And cash adjustment."

"Something of the sort."

"And the Mortimers?" I could feel that old delicious greed swelling in my chest. Magic.

"Mint," he said.

"Really mint?"

"Not a blemish." He'd let his pipe doze. "Cased. Casehardening. I don't think," he said, winking at Sheila, "you'll be disappointed." The understatement of all time. Casehardening. Something scratched again at my memory, worrying me.

If you keep any metallic object in an unopened case for long enough, it acquires a curious characteristic. If the surface was originally made an acid-protected rust brown, it simply becomes shinier, almost oily in appearance. If previously made a fire-protected shiny blue ("gunmetal" blue), the surface develops an odd mother-of-pearl effect very like the sheen of gasoline on water. This casehardening is an especially desirable feature of anything metal having a protected surface, from coins to weapons. *On no account clean it off;* you will be doing posterity a cultural favor and yourself a financial one by leaving it intact.

"Look, Dick." I drew breath and launched. "I can lay my hands on one."

"Good?"

"A faulty spring I've not touched. Otherwise mint."

"Cased?"

"Come off it."

"Who by?"

"Adams, London Bridge. Five-chambered." I photographed it in my mind's eye. "It's beautiful."

He thought a second in a cloud of smoke. "How would we adjust?"

"Because you're a close relative," I said, in agony, "I'll pay the difference."

"Let's settle it tomorrow," he said, and we shook hands.

Sheila rose. "Is that all that happens?" She seemed peeved.

"What do you want, blood?" I demanded. I was drenched with sweat, as always. The excitement of the forthcoming deal was brewing in me. Tomorrow, with luck and good judgment and money, I would be in possession of a pair of casehardened flinters made by the most aristocratic and expensive of all the great London makers, Henry Walklate Mortimer.

"Thanks for coming, Lovejoy." Dick came to the door of his boatshed to see us out. "Still got your steamer, I see."

"Any more jokes about my motor and the deal's off," I shot back. "At least I've got a license for it. Have you, for that thing?" I pointed to his pipe.

"Bring your lovely lady again, Lovejoy," he called, and I replied with rudeness.

He was able to get his own back because my wretched banger refused to start despite all the cranking I could manage. Dick borrowed a trio of amused boatmen to push us off, to a chorus of catcalls and derision.

"Why don't you put an engine in, Lovejoy?" was Dick's final bellow as we pulled off the wharfside and escaped onto the road up from the village. I didn't reply because I was white-faced and my teeth were chattering.

"Love?" Sheila asked. "Are you ill?"

"Shut up," I hissed, foot flat on the accelerator. The needle flickered up to twenty and we pottered slowly upward past the church. It was almost time for lights.

"What is it?" She tried to pull me around, but I swore and jerked my face away.

"I've just remembered something."

"For God's sake, darling—"

"This bloody stupid car!" I almost screamed the words. "Why the hell don't I get a new one? What's the matter with it?"

"Darling, pull over to the side and I'll—"

"Shut up you stupid—" My hands were ice-cold and my scalp prickled with fear.

"Please, love. I'm frightened. What is it?"

"That frigging box!"

"What box?"

"That apothecary box! There's something in it. A . . . a . . ." The words wouldn't come.

"The bottles? Drugs?" I shook my head and strove to overtake the village bus, to the driver's annoyance. He hooted and pulled in as we crawled past toward the town. We were up to thirty. "Those little scales?"

"That other thing."

"You said it was junk the auctioneers put in to make it look complete. Wasn't it a screwdriver?"

"It was casehardened!" I snarled. "Who the hell puts a screwdriver away in a felt-lined case to preserve it for a whole bloody century?" I was practically demented, kicking and blaspheming at the decrepit motor, begging it for greater speed. "And its handle was hatched—*hatched like a Durs gun*. Oh, God almighty, please let them still be open. Please, please, please."

Sheila grabbed my arm. "Lovejoy, if we see a taxi, flag it down."

"Yes, yes, yes," I whimpered. "Please send a taxi. Please, please."

"What time do they close?"

"Half past five."

"It's twenty past."

"The swine will go early. They always do, those bloody attendants, the idle sods."

We reached the trunk road roundabout by the river bridge at twenty-five past five, and swung left away from the Ipswich road. East Hill was well into lighting-up time as we screeched to a graceful stop outside Seddon's. It was closed and dark.

"Knock," Sheila said, climbing out.

"They've gone." I was lost, defeated by the calamity.

She remained resolute and banged on the main door. I stepped down to join her just as one of the stewards opened the partition. My relief almost made me faint.

"What the hell—?"

"Jim," I said weakly. "It's me. Lovejoy."

"Closed till tomorrow."

"Not for me you're not." I pulled out a note. "A single question, Jim. Just one."

He eyed it and nodded. I gave it to him and asked, "The question is, Will you let me find my nail file? I dropped it in the showroom an hour or so back."

"Gawd." He hesitated. "Mr. St. John has the keys."

"And so have you, Jim."

"Well . . ." he was saying, when Sheila came to the rescue.

"It's actually *my* nail file," she broke in. "I was really careless. It's one of a set, you see, in a case."

"Well, miss, dealers aren't allowed—"

"I know exactly where it is, Jim," I said, calmer now. "I'll bet you five of those notes I could put my hand on it in three seconds flat." That was a mistake and scared him.

"Here, Lovejoy," he began, starting to close the door. "I don't want none of your fiddling—"

"You stay here, Lovejoy," Sheila said chidingly. She stepped into the doorway and turned to push me back. "You're always so abrupt. The gentleman said that dealers weren't allowed in after fixed hours so you'll have to wait here, that's all." On a tide of feminine assurance she swept past Jim, who humbly put the door to. I heard their footsteps recede along the passageway and keys rattle in the showroom door.

I hung about the sidewalk getting in people's way and generally prowling around for quite five minutes before Sheila reappeared. I was up with her in a flash.

"Thank you so much," she was saying to old Jim, who was smirking at all his extra gallantry. "I'm so sorry we delayed you. You've been so kind. Good night."

I honestly tried to grin at Jim, but he wasn't having any from me and banged the door.

Sheila walked to the car. "I've got it in my handbag," she said, swinging the strap to her other shoulder. "Don't grab, or Jim will see."

She was really quite smart at that. Old Jim would no doubt be lusting after her as we left. You could see virtually the whole hill from the office. With quivering fingers I set the handle and cranked. We rumbled up the hill and I pulled in by the park railings in town.

The cars pouring from the car park got in the way of this

maneuver. I'm sure they didn't really mind having to stop suddenly. Muriel Field was at the wheel of a gray Rover, but I'd no time for light chitchat. After all, she had no antiques any more. Not like Sheila, who had the device out. I carried it into the lights of the lamps on the war memorial. It was a Durs screw mechanism, the weirdest I'd ever seen, but authentic, star cross-hatched on the handle and casehardened, maybe in all five inches long.

"I'm afraid I have a confession, Lovejoy," Sheila said, beside me.

"Eh?"

"I'm afraid I . . . I stole it." She pulled away as I tried to embrace her, laughing. "Promise me."

"What? Anything."

"You'll pay for it tomorrow."

"You're off your head."

"Promise, Lovejoy."

I sighed at all this whimsey. "I promise." I gave her a rubbery kiss under the memorial's lamp despite the pedestrians. A car's horn sounded. Adrian and Jane sailed past signaling applause. He'd have some witticism ready next time. "Here. You can have the honor of carrying the find home."

"Is it important, Lovejoy?" I gave it to her and she slipped it into her handbag.

"Somewhat," I said, beginning to realize. "Somewhat."

A hurrying mother pulled her gawping child along the pavement to stop it from openly inspecting the couple kissing in the main street. I kept my eye on her as Sheila and I stepped apart to drive home, and sure enough she gave a swift glance back to see how we were managing. Aren't women sly?

9

I dropped Sheila at the station. She had to go to work, poor lady, on some crummy newspaper. We had a small scene outside.

"I'll be here on Sunday," she told me, and I nodded. She waited. "Well?"

"Well what?"

"Aren't you going to come onto the platform and see me off?"

"I daren't take my foot off this pedal or she'll never start again today," I explained. "Otherwise I'd come in with you like a shot."

She came around to my side and kissed me. "You know, Lovejoy," she said, "for the world's greatest antique dealer you're an awful dope."

"I keep telling you your slang's dated."

"No use trying to needle me," she said, cool as ever I'd seen her. "You're falling for me, Lovejoy."

"Look," I said testily. "This accelerator's down to the floor. It's costing the earth in gas just sitting here while you babble—"

She put her arms around me and hugged me tight. This, note, was about ten in broad daylight, with the paper man grinning and the kiosk lady enjoying the show.

"I have a secret to tell you, Lovejoy."

"You're not—?"

"Certainly not!" She reached under the dashboard in front of me. "Take your foot off the accelerator."

"I can't. The engine'll cut out."

"Please."

I did as she said. Just before the engine coughed to silence she twisted something near the steering rod. The engine muted instantly into a deep, steady thrum.

She stood back and dusted her hands. "There!"

I sat mesmerized.

"Now," she said casually, "care for a spin?"

"Er—"

"Push over." She came into the driver's seat and nudged me across. "Let the expert do it, honey," she said kindly, flicked a switch somewhere, and yanked on an angled rod-thing near her knee.

We took off. My spine nearly slipped from the force. The old Armstrong boomed easily around the station roundabout and Sheila put it onto the hill near the hospital at fifty. We zoomed onto the main A 12 about three minutes later, and Sheila crashed her slickly up into the seventies. Fields and trees flicked by. Wind pulled at my face and her hair streamed out flat against her temples. In a couple of breaths the signs to Kelvedon darted past. I sat in frozen disorientation while all this happened around me. Sheila pulled into the middle lane and did her mystery with the levers. We hummed alongside a column of slower cars, and as she overtook back into the inside the needle wobbled down to seventy. There was hardly a shudder. A couple more millisecs and we were at Witham. She brought us into the station and switched off. The motor breathed a sigh quieting into silence.

"Tea, guvnor?"

There was a tea stall within reach. I nodded and climbed shakily down. Let Sheila pay, I thought angrily. We stood in silence slurping tea from cracked cups. Sheila had this strange feminine knack of being able to drink scalding fluids without losing her esophagus. I was quite ten minutes finishing mine. I stared at the Armstrong while I sipped, thought, and wondered. I handed my cup onto the counter with a nod of thanks. The chap on the stall must have thought we'd had a row, because he studiously busied himself picking losers at Cheltenham and left the cup there.

"Is that what you were doing last night?" I managed to say finally.

"Yes, love. I'm so sorry." She held my hand.

"Was it . . . really obvious?"

"It was rather, Lovejoy," she said sadly. "A massive car like this, so old, supposedly only one gear, fantastic fuel consumption, no speed to speak of, weak as a kitten, all those gadgets within reach."

"When did you suspect?"

"Yesterday, when we were trying to hurry to Seddon's before it closed." She smiled. "It was ridiculous. And everywhere we go other motorists hoot at it, even when you're driving quite well. So, while you got our usual fantastic supper—"

"What's wrong with my suppers?" I said angrily.

"Nothing, love," she said quickly. "Nothing at all. Those pies are lovely, and I really look forward to those shop custards. But I had to do something while you, er, got it ready, didn't I?"

"I thought you were cleaning it," I said bitterly.

"It wasn't me, really," she pacified. "It was you. I remember you once told me the car was the only time your wretched bell proved itself wrong. That set me thinking. So I turned a few switches and—"

"Did you know all the time it was special?"

"No, love. Honestly." I looked askance at her. Sometimes women aren't quite truthful.

"I think you're lying in your teeth," I said.

She smiled. "I quite like a lie now and again," she said demurely, and I had to laugh.

"You know what?" I asked. She shook her head. "I think I'm starting to fall for you."

She inspected me for a few moments. "About time, Lovejoy," she said. "We're both suffering from malnutrition with those corny dinners you insist on serving up. I'll bring my things on Sunday to stay for as long as we last."

"I'll meet you at the station, seeing I'll be able to start the car now."

"There's a switch near the starting pump. Push it down, and she'll start with the first crank of the handle." She pulled me into the driver's seat and showed me an exotic circular gear wheel, five gears and one reverse. I sat like a beginner as she explained the controls.

"The London train, lady." The tea man knocked on his window to attract our attention.

"That's it, then, Lovejoy." She brushed her hair back and got her case out.

"I love you." I embraced her. "Give us a kiss, love."

The train came and took her away.

"Go easy in that monster," she called, her very last words to me. Go easy in that monster. Some exit line.

"I will. See you Sunday."

The tea man was out of his booth and examining the Armstrong as I came up. "You've a right bit of gorgeous stuff there," he said.

"Yes. I thought it was an Armstrong." I kicked a tire.

"Eh? Oh, no. I meant your young lady."

"Oh, yes. Her too."

I did the necessary and notched an intrepid forty-five on the trunk road back. The Armstrong—was it still an Armstrong?—didn't cough once and went like a bird.

I rolled up to George Field's house in style.

I was beginning to realize there was a lopsided distribution of wealth in the Field family. On the one hand was Eric, evidently wealthy, complete with mansion, eighty acres of manicured grass, and gardeners touching forelocks to the boss and his lady as they strolled out for a morning row on the two-acre pond. On the other was George, here in a two-bedroom farce on a small estate, with bicycles and wrecks of lawn mowers and old bits of wood bulging the garage. His little Ford, clean as a new pin, was parked in a drive barely long enough for it. Despite all this, he had dashed out a handful of notes, hired me as a would-be sleuth because of my knack of sniffing out antiques, and promised all those lovely D's for what could be a pipe dream.

He came to the door agog for news. It was obviously a major disappointment to him when I told him I'd only called to give him a progress report. We went into the living room and he asked his wife, a dumpier female version of himself, to bring some coffee. I told him some of the events but was careful when I said I'd visited Muriel.

"I'm so glad she's better now," Mrs. Field said. "She went through a very bad patch."

"She's still rather nervous," I agreed, setting her clucking at the tribulations all about. "Was she always?"

It seemed she was, but much worse since poor Eric's sudden end. I told George of my find in the apothecary box, mentally absolving myself of the payment I'd promised Sheila the day before.

"Do you recognize it?" I handed it over and he put on glasses.

"I wouldn't," he said. "I never touched the weapons, nor the screwdrivers. I wasn't much interested, as I said before."

I ran down the main events of the past couple of days for him and remembered to ask him if he had any details about the sale of Eric's stuff at the auctioneers, but without luck.

110

"It seems the cased weapons might have come from near a bird sanctuary near a coastal resort."

"There's a nice holiday place near Fellows Nab," Mrs. Field said. "Too many caravans there now, though. That's in Norfolk."

Mrs. Ellison's antique shop was a few miles from Fellows Nab. I'd seen the sign.

"You never saw the wrapping?" I asked George.

"No. You have to realize I only saw him and Muriel once a week on average, and he was always showing me this and that."

"You should have taken more notice, George," his wife said.

"Yes, dear," he said with infinite patience. I'd have to watch myself with Sheila, I thought uneasily, if this is marriage.

"I'm making a systematic study of every possible flinter transaction during the past two years." I was eager to show I was really trying. "It'll take a little time, though."

"But if you found out where they did come from, what then?" He was a shrewd nut.

"I don't honestly know," I said as calmly as I could. "But what else is there? They've vanished. The police are—"

"They've given it up," Mrs. Field said, lips thinned with disapproval. "I always said they would, didn't I, George?"

"I suppose what I'll do is find whoever sold them to your brother and ask who else knew where they were."

"Well, you know best, of course," he said, worried. "But poor Eric was a real talker. He wasn't the sort of person to conceal any of his finds in the antique world. He loved company and used to have his friends in."

"Friends?" I interrupted. "Collectors?"

"Oh, yes. And dealers."

"And dealers," Mrs. Field echoed. "Ever so many people thought highly of Eric's opinion. Very knowledgeable, he was, about practically everything. Old furniture as well."

"So it's probable a lot of people may have seen the Durs?"

"For certain."

I rose and thanked them. George came with me to the door.

"Look," I began hesitantly. "Please don't think I'm rude, Mr. Field, but—"

"Yes?"

"Well . . ."

Understanding began to dawn in his eyes. "You're wondering where I can get so much money from, Lovejoy," he observed with a smile.

"It's a lot of money," I said in embarrassment.

"Oh, I'm a careful man. Only thing I've ever done is run a shoe shop, and I didn't make good like Eric did in the property business." He was quite unabashed at my rudeness. "I have some savings, insurance. And the mortgage on the house is almost paid. I could take out a new one. You needn't be afraid the money would be forthcoming. After all, the Judas guns are the only real evidence, aren't they? If we can buy them back from whoever the . . . murderer . . . sold them to, they'll be proof, won't they?"

I listened as he rambled on about them for a moment, and chose my words with care.

"Mr. Field." I cleared my throat. "Do you mean to say that now, when you're comfortably settled and solvent at last, you'll chuck it all up and start working and paying all over again, just to—?"

"Don't say it, Lovejoy," he said gently. "Of course I would. And don't go looking at Eric's wealth for a reason, either. That just doesn't come into it. I approached you because somebody did Eric wrong. It shouldn't be allowed. It's wrong. It always was. Even these days, robbery and killing is still wrong."

I mumbled something I hoped sounded humble.

"You see, Lovejoy," he finished, "if you take away people, there's nothing else left, is there?"

I drove away. Ever feel you're beginning to lose your faith in human nature?

There was something wrong with the cottage. You get feelings like that even though there's nothing in particular you can detect consciously. I hadn't switched the alarm on that morning because I had planned only to run Sheila to the station, pop back to the cottage to collect my Adams revolving percussion gun, then drive to Dick Barton's boatshed and complete the deal, all this before going to George Field's. If Sheila hadn't been so knowledgeable about the car I'd have been back in time to prevent the robbery, for robbery it was. You can smell it.

Naturally I'd been done over before. Show me the antique dealer who hasn't. It's a hazard of the trade. Like injuries in motorcar racing, it comes with the job. Hence my usually meticulous concern for security. And the bloody alarm which had cost me the earth wasn't even switched on. Serves me right, I was thinking as I prowled about to make sure he'd gone. The place wasn't a complete shambles, but had suffered. Somebody in a hurry, obviously.

There were a couple of letters addressed to Sheila care of me on the doormat, so the post girl had called on time. Maybe her arrival had scared him off, I hoped, as nothing seemed out of place at first. The carpet hadn't been disturbed over my clever little priest hole, thank heavens, but I realized pretty quickly that my walnut-cased so-called carriage clock had gone.

I gave vent to every expletive I'd ever learned, ranting and fuming. I'd got the clock for a quid from a starving old widow —one of my kinder moments this, because if I'd been true to myself I'd have beaten her down to a few pence. The sheer effrontery of somebody having the gall to come in, finger anything of mine he wanted, then take a rare priceless antique was sickening. Literally, I felt physically sick. I phoned our ever-vigilant constable Geoffrey, who was mercifully in, probably still having his morning nap. He was ever so sympathetic.

"When you've stopped laughing," I snarled, "get my clock back."

"Estimate of value, please, Lovejoy."

"Six hundred," I said firmly. He was silent for once.

"Did— Did you say—?" And he laughed again, louder this time.

"Well, maybe three hundred."

"You mean about eighty."

"Ninety."

"As a friend, Lovejoy," he said sadly, "I can only make it eighty-five."

"But that's robbery."

He agreed. "You can argue it out with the insurance people, Lovejoy," he said. "Incidentally, how'd he get in?"

"I'll look. Hang on."

There was a cut around the window near its catch. The window looked right down the back garden and could be reached by anyone standing on the grass, which grows right up to the cottage. I told Geoffrey and he said it was typical, but how about my alarm system connected at great expense to a noisy little flashing light in his office? I explained I'd been in a rush that morning.

"Thanks, Lovejoy," he said cynically. "We love a bit of help from the public."

"Are you going to come and look for clues or aren't you?" I snapped and crashed the receiver.

I made some tea while I waited. Apart from scratches on the windowsill there was nothing. I moved about straightening things. The trouble is that you know where to look for antiques. Guns must be locked in an enclosed space, says the Firearms Act; porcelain will be in a fastened case; portabilia locked in a safe or drawer. He knew his stuff. Whoever had done this was neat, slick, and an opportunist dedicated to walnut carriage clocks. Now, two things worried me far more than the loss of the clock. One was that Geoffrey's guess about the clock's value wasn't too far out, which was important, because nobody robs for very little. The second thing stared back at me from the opposite wall as I lounged on the divan swilling tea. It was my Chien Lung plate, a lovely disk of hand-painted light pastel colors stenciled by a neat blue running-edge design. It stood in prominence on my desk on a three-leaved ebony hinge support of the sort the Chinese do so cleverly. Neither plate nor clock was unique, but of the two the plate was infinitely—well, ten times—more desirable in anybody's book, as well as being more valuable. So why pass it up?

That left two possibilities. Either my burglar was well informed enough to know that I had a carriage clock to suit him, or he hadn't come for the carriage clock at all. Which raised the question, Why take it if he didn't want it? Answer: To cause his intrusion to be written off as a simple uncomplicated robbery by a burglar who happened to have a casual eye for antiques.

It was starting to look as though I'd established contact with the owner of a very special pair of flinters.

The rest of the day's happenings I don't really want to talk about.

Geoffrey came on his bicycle and took notes. He examined the earth outside, searched patiently for heaven knows what sort of clues, and later went around the village asking who'd noticed what and when, with conspicuous failure. Left to my own devices, I retrieved my Adams from the priest hole before driving to Barton's on the estuary and settling with him for too much in part exchange, and bringing the cased Mortimers back home to gloat over despite the fact that I'd have to pay out to settle it before the month ended. I had my usual supper bought from the Bungalow Shop in the village, read a lot, and went to bed not knowing that by then Sheila was dead.

She had got on the London train, and apparently went home before reporting to work that same day. It was on the way home that evening that she was said to have stumbled and fallen beneath the wheels of an oncoming train.

The platform was crowded. In the friendly reliable way we

all have, nobody came forward to say who was even standing near her. To hear the witnesses at the inquest, the three thousand people must have clustered awkwardly along the platform leaving an open space for several yards all around Sheila as she waited for the train to come and kill her. Don't go trying to say people may not have noticed somebody pushing a woman off a platform because of the crowd. There's no excuse. Women notice a pretty woman because they're practically compelled to, and men notice because they're compelled to in a different way. People simply look away when they want to, and *they've no right*.

Later, a couple of days on, I remembered what George Field had said: If you take away people, there's nothing left. One can't be answerable for all mankind, no. But you can sure as hell stick up for the little chunks of mankind that are linked with you, no matter how that link came about—birth, relations, by adoption, love. It all counts. Podgy old George and his dumpy little wife knew the game of living, while I was just a beginner.

I learned about Sheila from Geoffrey the day after the burglary. I just said thank you and shut the door.

No jokes from now on, folks.

10

Somebody once said you get no choice in life, and none in memory either. Judging by what the Victorians left in the way of knickknacks, they made a valiant attempt to control memory by means of lockets for engravings, "likenesses" in all manner of materials ranging from hairs from the head of the beloved to diamonds, and a strange celebration of death through the oddest mixture of jubilation and grief. Their memory, they seemed to think, should be neatly ordered to provide the maximum nostalgia centered on the loved one. If it needed extra emotional work to achieve that reassuring state, then the labor would just have to be endured. You can't say the Victorians were scared of hard slogging.

I would have liked to have been as firm as they. You know what I mean, pick out especially fond moments from my friendship with Sheila and build up a satisfying mosaic of memories which would comfort me in my loss by giving assurance that all was really not wasted. Nice, but all really was wasted as far as Sheila was concerned. Finished. Done for. And for me Sheila was gone. Anyway, I'm not resolute enough to look inward for the purpose of emotional construction. Gone's gone.

So that terrible day I sat and sat and did nothing to my records, left letters unanswered, didn't pick up the phone. For some reason I made a coal fire, a dirty habit I thought I'd given up. I shifted my electric fire, put newspaper in a heap in the grate, chopped wood, and got it going first time. There was a residue of coal in the old coalbin by the back door so I set to burning that. The cottage became warm, snug, and the day wore on. I had no control over my memories of Sheila as I watched the flames gleam and flash in the fire.

She had this habit of watching me, not just glancing now and again to check I was still around and not up to no good, but actively and purposely inspecting me. I might be doing nothing; still she'd watch, smiling as if engaged in a private humorous conversation at my foibles. It made me mad with her at first, but you get used to a particular woman, don't you?

Another trick she had was reaching out and absently rubbing my neck for nothing while she was reading or watching TV in the cottage. I'd probably be searching through price data of antiques and she'd just put her hand on my neck. It distracted me at first and I'd shrug her off, but moments later back she would come caressing me. There was nothing to it, not her way of starting sex play or anything. It was just her preference. She used to do it for hours.

Then there was the business with the cheese. While I was studying she would suddenly put down her book, go across to the little kitchen, and bring back a piece of cheese so small it didn't matter, and push it in my mouth. Never said anything, never had any herself. It would happen maybe twice or three times in an evening. Often she'd not even stop reading; simply carried her book with her, reading as she went. As well she was tidy and neat, unlike most birds. They have this reputation, don't they, but most of them get fed up with the tidiness legend and chuck it in during their late teens. Sheila was really tidy by nature, almost to the point of being a bit too careful. Nothing of hers ever got in my way. I never fell over her shoes, for instance, because they were tidied out of sight, not like some I could mention.

And the fights. We scrapped a lot, sometimes because of sex, other times because stress is part of life and you let off steam. She was irritable sometimes. She'd announce it from the doorway on arrival, standing there. "I'm angry, Lovejoy," she'd say, blazing. "With me or without?" I'd say, and every time she'd fling back "With you, Lovejoy, who else?" and we'd argue for hours. I'd chucked her out before now because of her temper. Once women get their dander up, all you can do is send them packing, because there's no point in everybody getting in a rage to suit their need of a barney, is there? I've sloshed her too, sometimes when she'd got me mad and other times making love, but that's only the love sort of coming out, isn't it? Once I bruised her and got worried afterward, which made her laugh and call me silly. I don't follow their arguments, really, mostly because they make allowances for all sorts of wrong things yet go berserk over little matters you'd hardly notice.

The fire was hot on my face from staring at it. I needed one of Dandy Jack's embroidered fire screens but wanted to see the fire. Of course, a hundred years ago people had fire screens to protect their complexions from the heat, and to shield their eyes from the firelight while reading or sewing in a poorly lit room. A bright fire was a source of light. The complexion bit was the important thing, though. Only peasants and country women had ruddy complexions. Elegant ladies wanted lovely pale faces on the unmistakably correct assumption that though ruddy's only healthy, pale's interesting.

Natural light—fires, candles, oil lanterns—confers a special feeling in a room. One day a month when I feel like it I switch all electricity off and live by natural light. You'd be surprised at the effect it induces. Try it. Natural lights have sounds, small poppings and hissings betokening the fact that they have a life of their own. And that's another thing. Notice that word I just used, betokening? By natural light words you'd never even think of come back as it were from times before. Who uses words like that? See what even thinking of natural light can do for you. It teaches you a lot about times gone by too. Your eyes begin to sting sometimes if you use too many oil lamps in a room, so three is a maximum or you become uncomfortable.

One odd thing is that rooms which you'd think unduly cluttered become much more acceptable by natural light. You've seen mock-ups of Victorian drawing rooms in museums beautifully lit by bright inert-gas strip lights, and probably been dismayed by seeing practically every inch of wall space covered by pictures, every surface littered by ornaments and clocks, and the furniture draped with hangings so you wonder how they could stand it. The reason you're put off by all that congestion is that the museum's got the lighting wrong. Tell them to switch everything off and put a single oil lamp on the bureau and draw the curtains. *What a difference!* Those ornaments which *should* glow by natural light do so, while the rest merely set each other off in an easy, comfortable pattern of cozy acquaintanceship. Beautiful, really beautiful. The clutter becomes friendly and spaced out. Don't ridicule the Victorians when it's us that's being stupid and insensitive.

Sheila wouldn't rub my neck any more. No cheese would suddenly be pushed absent-mindedly into my mouth. No more fights. No more sex with her. No more being watched by her smile.

The fire kept in till dawn. Twice I put the radio on. A stupid woman was trying to be crisply incisive about domestic problems that really needed a kick up the backside instead of a psychiatrist. I told her my opinion in no uncertain terms and switched her off. Later I heard the television news about some Middle East catastrophe and switched that off as well. I managed half a cup of tea about midnight. My coal ran out about five-ish the next morning.

I cut up a piece of bread and some Wensleydale cheese to feed the robin. It was down to me within seconds, shooing competitors away from the door. You can't help waiting to see if they do different things from what you expect, or if they'll do exactly the same as they've done for years. In either case you're never disappointed.

"Sheila used to say I was too soft with you, Rob," I said to the robin. He came on my arm for his cheese. "You'll forget how to go marauding, she says-said." But that can't be bad, was my standard reply to her when she said that. If that's the worst we got up to, the world wouldn't be in such a mess. She'd insist the robin ought to go hunting worms to mangle them in the most unspeakable way because it was naturally what they did in searching for food. My cheese-feeding policy must pay off eventually, though, if you think about it. If you're crammed full of cake and cheese you can't fancy too many worms for at least an hour or two, can you? "Anyway, cheese is good for teeth and bones," I said to her. "You're foolish, Lovejoy," she used to say, falling about laughing. "Robins don't have a tooth between them." I used to say, So what, they'd got bones. It was a stupid argument, but she would never see sense.

Any sort of hunting is only very rarely necessary, it's always seemed to me. When the robin had surely eaten enough I scattered the remainder about on the path near the Armstrong for the sparrows and the big browny-black birds to share. Even so the robin wouldn't have any peace. He flew at them, making stabs with his beak and generally defending the crumbs against all comers. You can't help admiring a bird like that. I wondered if he was more of a hunter than I thought, but decided to stick to my pacification policy anyway. You have to stand by your theories because they're for that, otherwise there's no sense in making them up.

I left them all to it and rang Geoffrey.

"For God's sake," he said dozily. "Look at the time."

"Did Sheila's handbag turn up?" I asked him as he strove to

orient himself. He didn't know. I said to find out and let me know or I'd pester the life out of him. It took twenty minutes for him to ring back.

"She didn't have a handbag with her, your young lady," he reported.

"Then how," I asked evenly, "did they know to get in touch with me?"

"The station police. They asked . . . other passengers to try to recognize . . ."

I suppressed the terrible desire to imagine rush-hour queues being invited to file past.

"I suppose one of her workmates—"

"Eventually." Geoffrey was not enjoying this. "They went to her home. Your address was on the back of your photograph."

"Ta." I rang off, but he was back on the blower instantly.

"Lovejoy, anything up as well as this?"

"Clever old bobbies should mind their own business," I said, clicking him off.

I knew exactly what he would do. He'd sniff about the village uneasily for a day, then come around to pop the question, What was I up to? and warning me not to do anything silly. The answer he'd get would be a sort of mystified innocence: "But what on earth do you mean, Constable?" straight out of amateur rep, which would gall him still further.

You can't trust the law. Anybody in business will tell you that. As for me, the law is a consideration to be strictly avoided. Never mingle with it. If it's there in force, bow your head, agree like you meant it, and scarper. Then when it's gone for the moment, carry on as normal. It's not for people. I wonder where it all comes from sometimes. Think of it like weather; keep an eye on it and take sensible precautions when it proves intrusive.

The dawn had come. I stood at the door smoking a cigar. Red sky, streaks of crimson against blue and white. It was really average. You get the same blue-on-cream in those Portuguese vases, quite nice. I couldn't finish my smoke. The robin was singing, rolling up his feathery sleeves for the day's battles.

Indoors I ran a bath, thinking, This is where I clouted Sheila that time Tinker rang up about Field. I would do my favorite breakfast, fried cheese in margarine and an apple cut into three and fried in the same pan. Three slices of bread. Tea. Heaven knows how, but I managed to eat it all, with the radio going on about politics and me trying to sing with the interlude music like a fool. I banged the dishes with a spoon, pretending I was a drummer in a band. Don't people do daft things?

I'd never forget my alarm again. The doors locked, I repaired the window. Outside I ran some meshwire around the edge and put new bolts on the inside of all the windows. The day promised fine with a watery sun.

The bath water had cooled enough by the time that job was done. I soaked, working out my chain of suppositions.

Suppose somebody had killed Eric Field for the Judas pair. Suppose then he had learned that I'd managed to pick up the one possible gadget missing from the most costly unique set of flinters the antique world could ever dream of—a small case-hardened instrument with all the features of a Durs accessory. It had after all been probably chucked into the apothecary box from ignorance to up that particular crummy article's price, so it was definitely a hangover from Seddon's sale of Eric Field's effects. Continuing the idea, suppose then he'd seen me come from Seddon's, followed me here to the cottage. He'd have seen me give Sheila the instrument by the war memorial, seen her put it in her handbag. And the town war memorial's as private as Eros in Piccadilly. Adrian and Jane had passed, Muriel and her tame priest were there. It could be anybody, he or she, seen or unseen.

Maybe he'd waited outside all night.

Then, seeing us depart, he'd broken in, searching, failed to find the Durs instrument, taken the carriage clock as a blind, and, seeing Sheila's letters, guessed wrongly that she still had the instrument in her handbag. Perhaps he'd assumed I realized its importance and was too worried to have it about. So he'd sprinted off to London after her and pushed her under the train when perhaps she'd suddenly realized he was stealing her handbag. Or he'd just pushed her, and in the subsequent uproar picked up her handbag, escaping because of our splendid public's tradition of keeping out of trouble. Now she was dead. I had to say it, dead.

It was heavy in my hand, bulbous in my palm. It could have been a straight screwdriver except that it bent at right angles about the middle of the shaft. Two additional flanges served to catch on some projection, perhaps near a sear spring in the flintlock. I got the impression it slotted into rather than onto something, but it was like nothing I'd ever seen before. Despite my ignorance, I was certain it was the object for which Sheila had been killed.

I was dried and in my priest hole by nine o'clock. I was nervous, because I was going to kill somebody.

Who, I didn't know. Nor where, nor when, nor in what circumstances.

But I knew how.

He would get nothing but the best, the very best Lovejoy could manage. Price no object.

I had a small amount of black powder—smoky gunpowder—in a pistol flask belonging to the Barratt guns. They wouldn't do. Percussion, after all. Let's do it properly. I began to go over the contents of the shelves.

Now, Lovejoy's no killer. I love these flinters the way I love Bilston enamels and jades, as examples of supreme craftsmanship. I don't like weapons because they're weapons. Only maniacs love them because they kill. During one of these tiresome wars we used to have I was conscripted and put into uniform. We were stationed on a snowy hillside in the East and given some field guns to shoot. The trouble was, an army on the opposite hillside had guns of their own and kept trying to kill us by shooting back. For me, I'd just as soon we all kept quiet, but the general feeling was that we ought to keep firing. I couldn't see what it was all about. Our hillside had nothing but a few trees, and from what little I could see of their hillside they were just as badly off. It was a waste of time, in addition to which I was frightened to death. But now I began to wish I'd taken more notice of the bare essentials during training.

The Barratts wouldn't do, so could the Nocks? Samuel Nock had made special holster and pocket flinters swan-necked in the French manner, but occasionally deviated into singles made in a special utilitarian style. I had a pair of double-barreled side-by-side flinters of his making. They really were precious to me, so I included them as possibles. A Brown Bess, heavy as hell, wouldn't do. The space might be too confined when I came to it, and forty-odd inches of massive barrel might prove cumbersome. Also, he was going to die slowly if the opportunity offered a choice; the Land Pattern might help him on his way too precipitately. We had matters to discuss. Reluctantly I put it aside.

The Adams revolving long arm was gone to Dick. That left me with two Eastern jezail guns, flintlock of course, the Adams pocket weapon, an elegant gold-inlaid La Chaumette pinfire weapon with a folding trigger, a Durs air gun you have to pump up, a Cooper blunderbuss, an early Barbar flintlock brass-barreled blunderbuss good enough to eat, a lonely Henry Nock dueler I'd been trying to match with its missing partner for twelve years, and last but not least the beautiful Mortimer weapons acquired that terrible day from Dick's boatyard. The Mortimers it was.

I melted a piece of lead bar over a spirit lamp and poured it from the pan into the bullet mold, crushing the brass handles firmly to avoid pocking the bullet surface with bubbles. Twelve attempts it took before I got two perfect spheres of dulled lead. After cooling them, I polished both in a leather cloth until they were almost shiny.

The black powder I poured into the pistol flask. It was set correctly on the dispensing nozzle, so I cleaned inside the barrels with a swab of cloth screwed onto the wrong end of the ramrods. All this is easier said than done with white linen gloves on, but you must never leave fingerprints on a flinter. It ruins the browning after some years, and actually precipitates real rust even on the best Damascus barrel. The barrels cleaned, I poured the dose of powder into each, and forced the bullets in after tamping the powder down. It was hard work getting them to the bottom of the breech but I managed it. After that, a soft wad of cloth torn from a handkerchief down each barrel to keep the bullets in. Then a squirt of powder into each flashpan, bringing back the cocks to the half-cock position where the triggers wouldn't work them and clapping the steel closed, and all was lovely.

I replaced them in their mahogany case, pulling the safety catch into the halt position and dusting them off. They looked priceless, stylish, graceful, wondrous in their red-felted box-wood recesses among the accessories. Every item fitted snugly. Even the case itself was brilliantly designed, a product of an age of skilled thinkers.

There was one more thing they looked—lethal, maybe even murderous.

And that really pleased me, because I was going to blow some fucking bastard's brains out.

11

I'll be frank.

Before this the business had been a bit unreallike. You know the sort of thing—income tax rebates or these insurance benefits you get if ever you reach ninety. My attitude I suppose was one of blissful pretense. Sheila always said I pretended too much; "romancing," she called it. The Judas affair had previously been somehow at a distance, even though I'd been involved in setting up a search for the pistols through the trade. I suppose there was some excuse, since you can't believe in a Martian in Bloomsbury in quite the same way you might believe in the Yeti or Nessie. I'd paid lip service of sorts to the Judas pair idea. If they were mythical, well, O.K., I would spend time chasing a myth. If the bloke that had killed two people for those precious things believed in their existence, so would I. Funny, but my mind began to work clearer now I believed.

If he had searched and followed and then killed for a small accessory like my turnkey, it followed for certain that there could be no possible doubt about where the Judas pair were. *He had them.* I knew as sure as I breathed.

And I understood his anguish. Imagine the distress of scientists as they search for that one missing-link creature whose existence will finally prove a million theories. Imagine the shepherd's grief as he finds his prize sheep's gone absent. Double all those sorrows, and it comes somewhere near the anguish of a collector with a stupendous possession that is one vital component short. I would have felt compassion in other circumstances, even shared part of his grief. Now I cackled with evil laughter as I emerged from my priest hole and went about letting the light into the cottage and unlocking doors and windows. Let him suffer. He'd come again; somehow and sometime he'd come because I had the instrument he wanted.

From now on I would have to be ready every minute of every day. I therefore checked the garden from behind the curtains and decided to play the game to its fullest.

I telephoned George Field. His wife answered. George was out.

"I want a list from him, Mrs. Field," I explained. "Tell him I need u. gently—within the day—the names of all those people his brother was friendly with, known collectors or not. Dealers included." She was all set to chat, but I cut it short and then rang Geoffrey.

"Look, Lovejoy," he began wearily, but I wasn't being told off by any village bobby. I was going to do his job for him and he was getting paid from taxes I provided.

"Silence, Geoffrey old pal, and listen." He listened in astonishment while I said my piece. "I want the names, ranks, and stations of the people in charge of Sheila's . . . accident." Straightaway he began his spiel about not having the authority to divulge and all that. "Listen, Geoffrey, I'll say this once. You give me the names now, or I'll take your refusal as obfuscation and ring the Chief Constable, Scotland Yard, and my local M.P. I'll also ring the local newspaper, three London dailies, and the Prime Minister." I didn't know what obfuscation was, but it sounded good.

"What if I don't have the information you want?" he asked, a guarded police gambit.

"There you go again, obfuscating," I said pleasantly. "Goodbye, Geoffrey. You'll be hearing from the communications media and the politicians very shortly, if not sooner."

"Hang on."

They can be very helpful, these servants of our civic organizations, when they're persuaded in the right way. He gave me a number to ring and an address of a police station.

"What's got into you, Lovejoy?" he said, very uneasy.

"A rush of civic duty to the head," I explained.

"I don't like all this, I'll tell you straight."

"Meaning what?"

"Meaning I want to know what you're up to, Lovejoy."

"Geoffrey," I said sweetly.

"Yes?"

"Get stuffed, comrade," I cooed. "Go back to sleep."

I felt better now I was on the move.

Faith is a great prime mover. No wonder the distance to Jerusalem didn't daunt the early crusaders. With all that faith, the fact that they'd have to walk every inch of the way would have appeared a mere incidental. Faith gives a clarity of vision as well as thought, and I was reaping the benefit of the new believer. It gave me freedom. Apart from the law, I could tell anybody the truth, what I was after, and even say why. I could show my Durs turnkey to every collector or dealer I'd ever met, knowing sooner or later I'd strike oil. Word would spread like fat in a hot pan. Then, one fine day, my visitor would arrive at the cottage for his big farewell scene. He wouldn't be able to help it. He'd come back again.

I spent an hour on the blower. First to Adrian, explaining that a friend of mine, Eric Field, deceased, had had a pair of Durs flinters, now untraceable, and would he please keep an ear open for any whisper. I got derision back down the receiver but

129

persevered. In the way of his kind, he sensed swiftly there was something seriously wrong and went along with me, saying he'd put the word about.

No reply from Margaret Dainty, though I tried her number three times, and none from Dandy Jack either. He was probably sloshed still from last night, while Margaret was possibly up in the Smoke doing the street markets. Jane Felsham was in, coughing with the rasping breath of the morning smoker and asking what was the matter with me. She thought I was drunk.

"It's on, Jane," I said. "Don't muck me about, love, because I'm tough and nasty today. Just take the essentials down and spread it about. Tell anyone, bring anyone to see me any time. And I'll travel. There's a bonus in it. Keep thinking of all those pots you could buy with a bit of taxfree."

Harry was out too, also probably down on the market stalls the same as Margaret. I left a message at the White Hart for Tinker and Dandy Jack to contact me urgently. The barman was out on the village green with the pub's football team training for the Sunday League, but his wife Jenny was reliable.

I wrapped the turnkey in white tissue-paper hankies (always the best for carrying small antiques, even storing them for years) and put it in my jacket pocket, using a safety pin to fasten down the flap. That way, if he wanted it he'd have to get me first. Before locking up and leaving I phoned Dick Barton and asked him to sell me some black powder, as I wanted to try the Mortimers later on. He was surprised, knowing my antipathy to flinters as actual weapons, but promised me three-quarters of a pound.

I would collect it on my way back from Jim's, in case Geoffrey decided to finger my parked Armstrong to learn what I was up to. The sale of the black powder in this cavalier fashion is highly illegal, you see, and the law is especially vigilant in this matter. Terrible what some people will do. I chucked a handful of crumbs to the robin to keep it going and drove to Seddon's. On the way over I decided to park outside the showrooms, in accordance with my new plan of inviting my unknown enemy's attention. Old Jim lived in a neighboring street some four hundred yards down East Hill.

The town was almost empty of pedestrians and cars. One of those quiet days. Driving through in the dilute sun made a very pleasant change from the untidy scramble of the bad week. I parked, confidently facing uphill, and walked down to the street where Jim lived. Apart from a few folk pottering innocently off to shops and others strolling toward the riverside nursery gardens there wasn't a soul about. The terraced houses seemed cheerful and at ease.

I knocked. Jim came to the door, frowning when he saw my happy smiling face.

"Top of the morning, Jim."

"Morning." We stayed in an attitude of congenial distrust for a second. "No use coming here, Lovejoy," he said sourly. "All business must go through the firm, you know that."

"So I believe," I said, optimism all over.

"What you want then?"

"Now, Jim, you know me." I honestly felt benign toward him. "All for a quiet life." I let it sink in, then added, "You must be too."

"Aren't we all?"

"Some, only some, Jim." He was being careful.

"What's this about?"

"Your new job."

"Eh?"

"You start now." He started to close the door, but my foot was in the way. "No, Jim, leave the door open and don't go inside. Stay and listen."

"I want no trouble."

"And you'll get none, old pal." I beamed at him. "Remember the Field sale? Eric Field, deceased?"

"I *thought* you hinted a bit too much," he said. "Nothing wrong, was there?"

"Nothing," I said easily. "Your new job's trying to remember everything about it: sales lists, who the auctioneer was, who was there, who bought what, and how much they paid—"

"Confidential." Remarkable how self-important these pipsqueak clerks are.

I went all concerned. "What about your arm?" I asked anxiously.

"What about it? Nothing wrong with my arm."

I beamed into his eyes and winked. "There will be, Jim. It'll be broken in several places."

"Eh? You're mad—"

"Left or right, Jim?" I was really enjoying myself. No wonder people change when they get religion if this is what faith does for you. Faith's supposed to cancel doubt, isn't it? Marvelous how much calm conviction can bring. If Jim's four brothers had called about then I'd have said the same thing. Numbers are a detail when principle's the prime mover.

"Get the message?" I was so contented. "Don't get in my way when I'm moving. Now, you've got three seconds to agree, and by six tonight I'll have the invoices, the lists, the sales notes, and all essential details of the Field sale. You bring them around to my cottage and wait there until I come."

"You're off your bleeding head, Lovejoy," he moaned. "I've no car."

"Don't miss the bus from the station, then. Remember it's a rotten bus service."

"Get stuffed," he said, kicking at my foot.

My forehead felt white-hot. For a moment I struggled for control, then moved up into the doorway, pushing him back. I kneed him in the crotch and butted his nose with my head. Heaven knows where I learned it. I honestly am a peaceable chap. He tried to scramble away in terror and found an upright modern Jameson piano, only teak and 1930, to lean against. His face showed white above his two-day stubble.

"For Christ's sake—"

"Peace be unto you too, Jim," I said. "Now, be a good lad and get me the details."

"You've broken me ribs," he wailed. I nodded patiently. Some people just can't be hurried. Others must learn.

"And I'll break your arm at ten past six if you don't get me the answers, Jim."

"I've got to get to a doctor."

I shoved him down to his knees again and twisted his arm behind him.

"No doctors, Jim. No hospitals. You've a job to do, right?" He nodded through pain and fear. "Another word, Jim. I'm on the move. It's not a pretty sight. Now, you can call the law like any decent citizen and turn me in. I won't deny your allegations. But as God's my judge I'll came back and maim you for life if you do. You just do my little job like I ask and I'll leave you alone ever afterward."

I turned to go while he was sick all over his Afghanistan—he'd have said Persian—carpet, flower-fruit design with that rather displeasing russet margin they adopt far too often for my liking. I paused at the door. "Oh, and Jim."

"What?"

"Miss nothing out. All details complete, or you'll have to suffer the consequences. I must know everything about the Field sale. Understand?"

He managed a nod and I departed thinking of at least one task well done for a starter.

There wasn't a soul on East Hill except for a queue at the baker's and the car was quite untouched.

Black day. Traipsing from one cop shop to another making bother till they gave in. An inspector went over reports of Sheila's death word for word in the manner of his kind. Ever noticed how many people talk like union officials nowadays? Anonymous speech is everywhere—politicians, lawyers, priests in pulpits, auctioneers, the lot. Too many maybes. Listen to a political speech. I'll bet you a quid everything definite he says is canceled out by something else he says a moment later. Daft. As I sifted through the details I wondered where all the common sense had gone. It vanished about fifteen years ago, about the time those bone ships made by our French prisoners from the Napoleonic scraps vanished. You don't get either any more.

From the police I went to Camden Town, where Sheila's pal lived. Betty, fabulous for multicolored lipsticks, cleavage, and a legendary succession of loves, all with wealthy City men. Her husband, twice her age, kept model trains. I letched away as she gave her tale. She'd missed Sheila at home-time that day. Betty, all nineteen years of her, explained she'd had to work late. I pretended to believe her from politeness.

Seeing her old man was playing trains outside, I gave her my deep dark Lovejoy smolder. I only wished she'd been a customer. I swear I could have got rid of that tarty Dutch cutlery at last. You get no tax allowance for stock. Bloody Chancellor.

I held Betty's hand at the door. They measure you with their eyes, don't they? I said how I felt biological toward her. She liked biological and gave me the address of a little executive cottage she visited at certain times. These places can be a mine of antiques. What more pleasant than searching for antiques, up and down stairs with the help of a huge cleavage? Two birds per stone and that.

But no clues. Maybe the steam was going out of my crusade. It depressed me. I knocked about, saw the Bond Street arcade, did time in Fairclough's, did a few deals. The four-thirty train was on time from Liverpool Street.

I reached home at ten to six. Jim was waiting, gray-faced, hurting, obedient. I drove up with the now familiar knot of tension in my belly at the sight of him. It pleased me. My crusading zeal had only momentarily tired because of so many false leads. Here was one I relied on to give me a few more details.

He gave me a photocopied list of the Field sale and every

single invoice to do with it. In his own clumsy handwriting was a list of everybody who'd attended, the auctioneers, clerk, and his two mates who assisted.

"There's a good lad." I patted his head. "Look, Jim—"

"Yes?" He stood mournfully on the gravel.

"I don't want to hurry you, but the doctor's surgery closes at seven. You'll just make it on the bus."

"Aren't you going to give me a lift?" His spirits were on the mend. There was a faint hint of the old truculence.

I smiled. "Good night, Jim," I said and closed the door.

12

Some people kill me. You can invent a name for anything and it will be believed. Say anything and somebody'll cheer fit to burst. I'll give you an example. There was Dandy Jack looking for cracks on this piece of "cracked" porcelain—and him a dealer old enough to be my great-granddad. Of course, Dandy Jack was as indisposed as a newt, as one politician cleverly said of that minister who got sloshed and shot his mouth off on telly.

"Give it here, Dandy." I took it off him, exasperated. "Crack porcelain doesn't mean it's got cracks all over it." His bloodshot eyes gazed vaguely in my direction while I gave him the gory details.

"Kraak," not "cracked" porselain (note that "s"). Once upon a time, the Portuguese ship *Catherine* was sailing along in the Malacca Straits when up came a Dutch ship and captured it, there being no holds barred in 1603. Imagine the Dutchmen's astonishment when they found they'd bagged not treasure but a cargo of ceramics of a funny blue-white color. The *Catherine* was a carrack, or "Kraak." The nickname stuck. It looks rubbish, but folk scramble for it. I priced it for him and said I'd be back.

The town was jumping. I felt on top of the world without knowing why. A bad memory of something evil having hap-

pened recently was suppressed successfully in a wave of sun and
crowds. No dull weather, kids well behaved, trees waggling,
and people smiling, you know how pleasant things can look
sometimes. And the little arcade was thronged. Margaret
waved from her diminutive glass-fronted shop. Harry Bateman
was there with a good, really good, model compound steam
engine of brass and deep red copper, Robert Atkinson about
1864 or thereabouts, and shouting the odds about part exchange for a John Nash painting, modern of course, all those
greens and lavender watercolor shades. It would be close.

Several real collectors had turned up in the cafe and sat about
saying their antiques were honest. We were all in brilliant
humor, exchanging stories and gossip. Such a cheerful scene,
everybody entering into the act and taking risks in deals. It was
one of those marvelous times.

I told you I'm a believer in the gifts people have, and luck.
Luck is partly made by oneself. Go out feeling lucky, make
yourself behave lucky, and you will probably become lucky. Let
yourself slip into the opposite frame of mind and you'll lose your
shirt.

There'd been two flint collectors and one flint dealer in Jim's
papers, and both collectors were in my files. The dealer,
Froude, a pal of Harry's, wasn't bad, just cheap and useless, so
I could forget him. The collectors were different mettle. One,
a retired major called Lister, was a knowledgeable Rutland man
who ran a smallholding in that delectable county. He knew
what he was about. The second spelled even more trouble, had
an enviable record in my card system as a dedicated and lucky
collector given to sudden spurts of buying, often without rele-
vance to the seasonal state of the market. Brian Watson was by
all accounts one of those quiet-spoken northerners who seem
quite untypical of the usual image people have of cheerful,
noisy extroverts laughing and singing around pints in telly seri-
als. I had almost all Watson's purchases documented, but
though I'd never actually met him at sales, I'd heard he was

hesitant, not given to confidences but gravitating with a true collector's instinct toward the quality stuff. A good collector, Watson, who'd spend what seemed about two years' salary in an hour, then vanish for up to a year back to his native Walkden. Also on Jim's list were Harry, Adrian, and Jane together, Margaret, good old Dandy Jack, Muriel's Holy Joe Lagrange, Brad, Dick from the boatyard, and Tinker Dill, among the dross. And Muriel.

Now, of all those people, Brian Watson was significant because he already had one of the pairs of Durs duelers, and so was Major Lister of Rutland, because he'd been making offers to Watson for them ever since Eve dressed. The field was getting pretty big, but I was cock-a-hoop. The pace was quickening. And as I talked in the arcade I smiled to myself at my secret. At the finishing post lay my beautiful unpaid-for Mortimers—loaded. I left the cafe and wandered through the arcade.

Tinker Dill was at my elbow full of news. We pretended to examine a phony Persian astrolabe. It was described by Harry Bateman as "medieval" and priced accordingly. My sneer must have been practically audible. Don't overestimate their value, incidentally. Eighteenth-century Continental ones are usually more pricey, though they're all in vogue, and certain firms in Italy make excellent copies.

"You're getting busy, aren't you, Lovejoy?"

"Whatever can you mean?" I was all innocent.

"Bending Jim like that." He enjoyed the thought of Jim's injuries almost as much as a sale.

"I'm quite unrepentant." I put the astrolabe down, feeling it unclean, and took Tinker back into the nosh bar, where we could talk.

I told him of my developing interest in Watson and Lister. He whistled.

"They're First Division, Lovejoy."

"And Froude."

"He's rubbish."

"I have this about the Field sale."

"Eh?"

Over tea I showed him Jim's lists.

He slurped in his cup. "They're nicked!"

"On loan. Jim's good-hearted." I let him recover. "Heard anything special about any of these names?"

He flipped slowly through the lot, shaking his head each time. "Except the two big ones, that sale was a right load of heave-ho."

"You buy anything, Tinker?"

It hurt him. "You know me, Lovejoy. Antiques aren't my business."

I grinned in great good humor.

"Neither of those bought anything? Try to remember, Tinker." He would. It's like being a football fan. Just as they can recall incidents from games seen twenty years past, so we can tick off auctions as if they'd been yesterday.

You might wonder why I didn't just look at the purchasers' names on the invoices. Well. Invoices, however complete, never tell it all. I wish I had time to tell you what goes on in an auction. For every ten lots sold by the auctioneer, another ten are sold among dealers. We buy a lot from the auctioneer sometimes, and even before he's moved on we've sold it to a fellow dealer. All the time it goes on. "Ringing" you already know about, I'm sure, where dealers get together and do not bid for a choice item, say a lovely French commode. When it goes to Dealer A for a paltry sum—i.e., when it's been successfully "ringed"—he'll collect his cronies and they'll auction it again privately in a pub nearby, only on this occasion Dealer A's the auctioneer and his mates are the congregation, so to speak.

You'll probably think this is against the law. Correct, it is. And you may be feeling all smug thinking it is rightly so because whoever's selling her old auntie's precious French antique is being diddled out of the fair auction she's entitled to. Well, I for one disagree. Nobody actually *stops* the public from bidding, do they? It comes back again to greed, your greed. And why? Answer: You want that valuable commode for a couple of quid, and not a penny more. If you were really honest you'd bid honestly for it. But you won't. How do I know? Because you never do. You go stamping out of auctions grumbling at the price fetched by whatever it was you were after and failed to get. So don't blame the dealer. He's willing to risk his every penny for a bit of gain, while you want medieval Florentine silver caskets for the price of a bus ride. *You ring items by your greed.* We do it by arrangement. Why your hideous but dead-obvious greed should be quite legal and our honesty illegal beats me.

"That Bible pistol," Tinker remembered. "Not too bad. I did drop a note in at your cottage, Lovejoy."

"I passed it up."

"Watson bought it."

"In his usual style?"

Tinker's eyes glowed with religious fervor. "You bet." He rolled a damp fag and struggled to set it afire. "It was in one of his buying sprees. You know him, quiet and hurrying. I reckon he should have been a cop. Busy, busy, busy."

I wrote a mental tick against Watson's name. He'd attended six auctions that week, and the date matched no fewer than eight postal purchases, all after a ten-month gap. Phenomenal.

"Major Lister buy, did he?"

"Yes, a set of masonic jewels for some museum." I knew about those and the Stevens silk prints he'd bought as well.

"All in all," I asked, "a quiet, busy little auction with more than the average mixture of good stuff?"

"Sure. And not a bad word uttered," Tinker said, puffing triumphantly.

I let his little quip pass impatiently. "Is that list of people complete? Think."

He thought. "As ever was." He shrugged. "The odd house-wife, perhaps."

"Thanks, Tinker. Anything else?"

He told me of the Edwardian postcards from Clacton, the Regency furniture at Bishop's Stortford, that crummy load of silver being unloaded up in the Smoke, and the Admiralty autograph letters being put on offer in Sussex. I knew them all but slipped him a note.

"You got them Mortimers, then," he said as we parted.

"A hundred quid," I replied modestly. He was still laughing at the joke as I left to see Margaret's collection of English lace christening gowns.

"Sorry about everything, Lovejoy." She pecked my face and brewed up. There were a couple of customers hanging around, one after pottery, one after forgeries. (Don't laugh—collectors of forgeries will walk past a genuine Leonardo cartoon to go crazy over a forged Braque squiggle.) As they drifted out she hooked her "Closed" notice on the door.

"I've had a drink, Margaret, thanks."

"I saw you."

"Tinker reporting in," I explained, looking around. Her lace christening gowns were beautiful, but I always sneeze over them. "I can never understand why these things are so cheap. A few quid for such work, years of it in each case."

She smiled. "Keep plugging that attitude. Genuine?"

"Does it matter?" I said. "Any forger who does something so intricate deserves every groat he gets." I felt them. "Yes, all good."

"I thought you'd been neglecting me till I heard, Lovejoy." She brought tea over despite my refusal.

"No matter now." I took the Victorian Derby cup as a mark of friendship because her tea's notorious. "All over."

She sat facing. People outside in the arcade must have thought we were a set of large bookends for sale.

"Give, Lovejoy."

"Eh?"

"I've one thing you've not got, darling," she said in a way I didn't like. "Patience. What are you up to?"

"I'm going to find the bastard. And I'm going to finish him."

"You can't, Lovejoy." God help me, she was crying. There she sat, sipping her rotten tea with tears rolling onto her cheeks. "It'll be the end of you too."

"Cheap at the price, love."

"Leave it to the police."

"They're quite content with matters as they are." My bitterness began to show. "It's much more dramatic to rush about with sirens wailing than slogging quietly after the chap on foot."

"They know what to do—"

"But they don't do it." I pulled away as she reached a hand toward me. "I've no grouse with anybody, love. I just want help." Two people staring in turned quickly away at the sight of our tense faces.

"Supposing you *do* find him. Why not just turn him in?"

I had to laugh, almost. "And endure months or years of questions while he wheedles his way out?"

"But that's what law is for," she cried.

"I don't want law, nor justice," I said. "From me he'll get his just deserts, like in the books. I want what's fair."

"Please, Lovejoy."

"Please, Lovejoy," I mimicked in savage falsetto. "You're asking me to let him off with seven years in a cushy jail thoughtfully provided by the taxpayers? No. I'm going to spread his head on the nearest wall and giggle when it splashes."

She flapped her hands on her lap. "We used to be so . . ."

"Things have changed."

"You'll get yourself killed. Whoever it is must have heard you're spreading word about fancy Durs duelers. It's the talk of the trade. Half of them already think you're balmy." Good news.

"There's one person who knows I'm serious, love." I was actually grinning. "I'm going to needle and nudge till he has to come for me." I rose and replaced her cup safely.

"All right, Lovejoy." She was resigned. "Anything I can do?"

"Spread the word yourself. Tell people. Make promises. Invent. Tell people how strange I've become." I kissed her forehead. "And your tea's still lousy."

I phoned George Field from the kiosk. He agreed to send an advert to the trade journal whose address I gave him:

REWARD

A substantial reward will be paid by the undermentioned for information leading to the specific location (not necessarily the successful purchase) of the Durs flintlock weapons known to the antique trade as the Judas Pair.

I thought, Let's all come clean. He gasped at the sum mentioned but agreed when I said I'd waive any costs. I insisted he put his name and address to the notice, not mine, because he was in all day and I wasn't.

I called in at the cottage and then drove to see Major Lister, happy as a pig in muck. By the weekend the murderer would know I was raising stink and getting close, and he'd start sweating. Don't believe that revenge isn't sweet. It's beautiful, pure, unflawed pleasure. He was losing sleep already because I had the little Durs gadget. I slept the sleep of the just. My revenge had begun.

Major Lister turned out to be a fussy disappointment, a stocky, balding, talkative, twinkly chap who wouldn't hurt a fly. His vast house was full of miscellaneous children. Everybody there, including three women who seemed to be permanent residents, was smiling.

"I'll bet you're Lovejoy" were his first words to me. "Come and see my fuchsias." He drew me away from the front door toward a greenhouse, calling back into the house, "We'll have rum and ginger with the fuchsias."

"I like your system," I said. The nearest child, a toddler lick-

143

ing a dopey hedgehog clean in the hallway, cried out the rum message hardly missing a lick. The cry was taken up like on the Alps throughout the house until it faded into silence. A moment later a return cry approached and the hedgehog aficionado shouted after us, "Rum on its way, Dad."

"They like the system, not I." He twinkled again and began talking to his plants, saying hello and so on. A right nutter here, I thought. He chattered to each plant, nodding away and generally giving out encouragement.

Well, it's not really my scene, a load of sticks in dirt in pots. He evidently thought they were marvelous, but there wasn't an antique anything from one end of the greenhouse to the other that I could see. A waste of time. His sticks had different names.

"Same as birds, eh?" I said, getting to the point. "Identical, but each one's supposed to be distinct, is that the idea?"

"I see you're no gardener."

"Of course I am."

"What do you grow?"

"Grass, trees, and bushes."

"What sorts?"

"Oh, green," I told him. "Leaves and all that."

"Yes." He twinkled as a little girl entered carrying two glasses of rum yellowed by ginger. "Yes, you're Lovejoy all right."

"Seen me at auctions, I expect, eh?"

"No. Heard about your famous Braithwaite car."

"Braithwaite?"

He saw the shock in my eyes and sat me on a trestle. The little girl wanted to stay and sat on the trestle with me.

"Herbert Braithwaite, maker of experimental petrol engines early this century. Some o.h.v. cycles. Yours must be the only one extant. Didn't you know?"

"No. Well, almost."

"Drink up, lad." He settled himself and let me get breath. "Now, Lovejoy, what's all this word about a pair of Durs guns?"

I told him part of the story but omitted Sheila's death and the turnkey.

"And you came here, why?"

"You were at the Field sale."

"And Watson got the Bible pistol. Yes, I recollect." He took the little girl on his lap and gave her a sip of his rum. "Fierce man is Watson. One of those collectors you can't avoid."

"The Field sale," I persisted.

"Nothing very special for me, I'm afraid. Naturally," he added candidly, "if you're trying me for size as a suspect, ask yourself if I would dare risk this orphanage."

"Orphanage?" It hadn't struck me.

"I don't breed quite this effectively," he chided, laughing so much the little girl laughed too, and finally so did I.

"You saw Watson there?"

"Certainly. He'll be not far from here now, if indeed he's in one of his whirlwind buying sprees."

My heart caught. I put the glass down. "Near here?"

"Why, yes. Aren't you on your way there too? The Medway showrooms at Maltan Lees. It's about eleven miles . . ."

I left as politely and casually as I could. Nice chap, Major Lister. I mentally filed him away as I moved toward the village of Maltan Lees: Major Lister (retd.): collector flck dllrs; orphanage; plants; clean hedgehogs.

Then I remembered I'd not finished my rum. Never mind, that little girl could have it when she'd finished his.

Four o'clock, Maltan Lees, and the auctioneer in the plywood hall gasping for his tea. I had no difficulty finding the place, from the cars nearby. They were slogging through the remaining lots with fifty to go. The end of an auction is always the best, excitement coming with value. By then the main mob of bidders has gone and only the dealers and die-hard collectors are left to ogle the valuables. Medway's seemed to have sold miscellaneous furniture, including bicycles, mangles, a piano, and household sundries, leaving a few carpets, some pottery, a collection of books, and some paintings, one of which, a genuine Fielding watercolor, gave me a chime or two.

I milled about near the back peering at odd bits of junk. The auctioneer, a florid glassy sort, was trying unsuccessfully to increase bids by "accidentally" jumping increments, a common trick you shouldn't let them get away with at a charity shout. Among this load of cynics he didn't stand a chance. Twice he was stopped and fetched back, miserably compelled to start again and once having to withdraw an item, to my amusement. Another trick they have is inventing a nonexistent bidder, nodding as if they've been signaled a bid, then looking keenly to where the genuine bidder's bravely soldiering away. Of course, they can only get away with it if the bidder's really involved, all worked up. Therefore in an auction *keep calm*, keep *looking*, keep *listening*, and above all keep as *still* as you can. You don't want anybody else knowing who's bidding, do you? If you can do it with a flick of an eyebrow, use just that. Don't worry, the chap on the podium'll see you. A single muscle twitch is like a flag day when money's involved. Where was I?

You've only to stay mum and patterns emerge in a crowd. The old firms were there—Jane, Adrian, Brad, Harry, and Dandy Jack—and some collectors I knew—the Reverend Lagrange, the Mrs. Ellison from the antique shop where I'd bought the coin tokens while returning from the bird sanctuary, Dick Barton, among others.

A handful of traveling dealers had descended on lucky Maltan Lees. They smoked and talked noisily, moving about to disturb the general calm and occasionally calling across to each other, full of apparent good humor but in reality creating confusion. It's called "circusing," and is done to intimidate locals like us. They move from town to town, a happy band of brothers.

I watched a while. One of the traveling dealers paused near me.

" 'Ere," he growled. "Are you 'ere for the paintings or not?"
I gave him my two-watt beam free of charge. "I said," he repeated ferociously, "are you 'ere for the paintings?"

"Piss off, comrade," I raised my smile a watt. He rocked back and stared in astonishment at me before he recovered.

"You what?"

"Where I come from," I informed him loudly, "you circus chaps'd starve."

"Clever dick."

He barged past me, tripping over my foot and ending up among assorted chairs. His pals silenced.

I laughed aloud, nodding genially in their direction, and stepped toward their fallen companion. "Sorry," I apologized, because my foot had accidentally alighted on his hand. He cursed and tried to rise, but my knee had accidentally jerked into his groin, so he stayed down politely. I get annoyed with people sometimes, but I think I'd been a bit worse lately. I bent down and whispered, "Me and my mates got done for manslaughter in Liverpool—twice—so go gently with us, wacker. We're fragile."

"No harm meant, mate," he said.

As I say, a lie works wonders. I stepped away, embarrassed because people were watching. The auctioneer had kept going to keep the peace, and some fortunate chap got his missus a wardrobe for a song. It's an ill wind.

I settled down near the bookcases and all went gaily on. I fancy the auctioneer was rather pleased with my little diversion. I saw Adrian applaud silently and Jane nod approval. I noticed Brian Watson after another twenty minutes and knew instantly who he was.

Some blokes have this chameleonlike ability, don't they? My mate in the army was typical of the sort. The rest of us had only to breathe in deep for all the grenades on earth to come hurtling our way, but Tom, a great Cheshire bloke the size of a tram, could walk on stilts for all the notice the enemy took of him. It was the same everywhere. I've even seen blokes come into pubs, stand next to Tom, and say, "Anybody seen Tom?"

Brian Watson was standing a few feet away, virtually unseen. He stood there watching, quiet, listening, and I knew instantly he was as fully aware of me as I was of him. A careful chap, the sort you had to be careful of. I instinctively felt his capabilities. A real collector. If he starved to death he'd still collect. You know the sort. No matter what setbacks come, they weather them and plow on. I honestly admire their resilience. It's a bit unnerving, if you ask me, too straightforward for my liking.

I bought a catalogue. Now Harry and the rest were quite explicable in terms of attendance at any auction, virtually no matter what was on offer. But Watson? Every piece he had was known to me, apart from some I only suspected, bought by concealed postal bid but quite in the Watson pattern. A buyer not a seller. He very rarely sold anything, and when he did it was only to buy bigger still. A cool resilient man. Moreover, one who was now observing me with his collector's antennae.

All of which, I thought as the auctioneer chattered on, raised one central question: If everybody else was here with good reason, what good reason did Brian Watson have? There was nothing to interest him. I scanned the remaining lots but failed to find the answer. He was a pure flint man, never deviating into the mundaner fields of prints, pottery, and portabilia, which to my dismay seemed all that was left. There was no choice but to wait and see.

It came to lot 239, the small collection of portabilia. Watson was in character, waiting with the skill of an old hand until the bidding showed signs of ending, then he nodded gently and off we went. We, because I was in too, all common sense to the winds. People gradually became aware of the contest. You could have heard a pin drop.

While the bidding rose I racked my brains, wondering what the hell could be in the portabilia that could be so vital to Watson. On and on we went, him against me. Everyone else

dropped out. Portabilia are small instruments made especially
for carrying about. They included in this instance a sovereign
balance for testing gold coins, a common folding flintlock pistol
by Lacy of Regency London's Royal Exchange, a tin box with
a tiny candle, a collapsible pipe, a folding compass, a folding
sundial, a diminutive snuff horn, and other minutiae. It wasn't
bad, but you couldn't pay twice their value in open auction and
keep sane. I saw Adrian hide his face in his hands as we forged
inexorably on; and Jane, cool Jane, shook her head in my direction with a rueful smile. Many people crossed to the cabinet to
see what they'd missed. Still we drove the price upward until
my calculations caught up with me and I stopped abruptly,
white-hot and practically blind from impotent rage at missing
them.

"Going . . . going . . . gone. Watson. Now to lot two-forty," the
pleased auctioneer intoned.

I went outside to wait for Watson and, partly, to avoid the
others.

Jane followed me out. "Better now, Lovejoy?" She had style,
this woman with the smile that meant all sorts of business.

"No."

"What's it all about?"

"I don't know what you mean."

We crossed the road and sat near the window in the cafe
opposite the auction rooms. She ordered tea and faced me
across the daffodils. "Aren't you making a fool of yourself?"

"No."

"You're like a child without its toffee apple." She irritated me
with her bloody calm dispassionate air and I said so. "I heard
about Sheila," she went on. "Do you think it's what she'd want
you to be doing, going to pieces like this?"

"I'm not going to pieces." I wouldn't give in to this smarmy
woman who couldn't mind her own business.

"You look like it, Lovejoy." She should have been a teacher.
"We're all worried about you, everybody. Your business'll go

downhill next. Look at you. You haven't shaved, you're . . . soiled-looking."

That really hurt, because I'm not like that. I looked away in a temper because she was right. "Somebody killed her—the same character who killed Eric Field."

Another of her famous appraisals came my way. "Are you serious?"

I gave her an appraisal back. "You know I am."

"By God, Lovejoy," she breathed, "what are you up to? You're not seriously thinking—"

"I am."

"You don't think Watson—?"

"I'm not sure." The tea came. "He's a Durs collector, a clever one. I've eliminated most of the rest one way and another. It could be a dealer, of course, or somebody I don't know about, but I must try to follow the leads I've got."

"Was he at the Field sale you've been on about?"

"Yes."

"He may have nothing to do with it."

"And again," I said coldly, "he may."

For the next few minutes Jane quizzed me. I told her the whole story including the turnkey bit while she listened intently.

"Have you anything practical to go on?" she demanded. "So you found a posh screwdriver—big deal."

"Yes," I said after a minute, "there is something."

"What?"

"God knows." A few people drifted out of the doors across the way. It would end in five minutes. "I couldn't sleep last night for worrying. The answer's been given me, here in my hand, and for the life of me I can't think what makes me think so. I'd know who it is, but the bits of my mind won't connect."

"From Seddon's?"

"I feel helpless. I just can't think."

"Give it up, Lovejoy." She was less forbidding than I remembered. "It'll ruin you."

"I might." And I almost believed me, except that Watson came out of the auctioneer's that instant. I was up and out into the road darting between cars before I knew where I was.

He waited, casually looking through the window at a set of old seaside lantern slides that had gone dirt cheap. There's quite a market for them nowadays. It was decimalization that did it.

"Mr. Watson." We stood together, me somewhat breathless and aggressive, him a little reserved.

"Mr. Lovejoy."

"Right."

He smiled hesitantly. "I admired your, er, act with the circus crowd."

"Thanks."

"Could I ask"—I nodded and he went on—"er, if you, er, were very keen to have that group of portabilia?"

"No," I snapped.

"I thought not. May I ask then why you bid?"

"Never mind *me*, comrade," I said roughly. "Why did you?"

He was astonished. "Me? They belonged to my father."

"Eh?" I was saying as Jane strolled up.

"My brother put them up for sale," he explained, "somewhat against my wishes. Why do you want to know?"

"Well done, Lovejoy," Jane said sarcastically.

"Keep out of it," I said. "Why did you go to the Field sale?"

His memory clicked away for a moment, then his brow cleared. "After that collector was killed, you mean? Oh, the odd item."

"Never mind what you actually bought. What attracted you there?"

He glanced from Jane to me, but it was no use messing about at this stage.

"He gets like this periodically." Jane's casual excuse didn't calm me.

"It's my habit," Watson replied with dignity, "to do so. It's also my right."

"I couldn't agree more," Jane chipped in.

I looked about. People had gathered around. The windows of the auction rooms were full of faces, staring. Cars were slowing to see what the rumpus was about. My old aunts would have called it a "pavement scene."

"You're among friends, Lovejoy," Jane said kindly, and explained to Watson, "He's not like this normally. He's been under a strain lately, a bereavement, you know."

Murmurs of sympathy arose from a couple of old dears in the throng who quickly transmuted compassion into reminiscences of similar events in their own past. "Just like our Nelly's cousin when her Harry was took," etc., etc.

"Will he be all right?" Watson was asking anxiously of Jane. That more than anything shook me. When people talk over you as if you're not really there, you really might have vanished.

"His car's near here somewhere. Over there."

Watson and Jane frog-marched me to the Braithwaite. Rage shook me into a sweat, rage at Jane's smooth assumption of power and Watson's obvious concern. If I'd cast him in the role of murderer, why didn't the bastard behave like one?

"You'd better come to my sister's; it's a few miles." They discussed me while I trembled like a startled horse. My face was in my hands. I could hear their voices but not what they said, so sick did I feel from the stink of the leather upholstery and the extraordinary vertigo which took hold. Jane took my keys and we drove out of Maltan Lees in the wake of Watson's old white Traveller.

There's nothing much to say about the rest of that day except that I stayed at Watson's sister's house in a room the size of a matchbox full of toys. Children came to stare at me as I was given aspirin tablets and milk to swallow—heaven knows why

—and finally I dozed until dawn. Watson, my erstwhile villain, slept on a settee. Jane drove home in my old crate, saying she'd come back for me in the morning. When I woke I found one of the children had laid a toy rabbit on my bed for company, a nasty sight in the sunrise of a nervous breakdown. Still, thank God, it wasn't a hedgehog.

I can't remember much except Watson's kindness, his sister's concern, and Jane smiling too quickly at everything that was said as we departed.

"I feel a bloody fool" were my parting words, epitaph for a crusader. Amid a chorus of denials and invitations to return soon Jane ferried me away. I couldn't even remember what the house was like.

On the way back, Jane, a smart alert driver, told me she'd been summoned into Geoffrey's police station to explain what she'd done with me, because the cottage was raided again during the night. Our vigilant bobby, understandably narked by his ruined sleep, told her in aggrieved tones how he'd wakened to the sound of the alarm and arrived before entry was effected. The would-be intruder fled unseen.

I received the news with utter calm and stared at the ceiling.

13

Weeks of feeding my robin and watching weather, occasion-ally getting the odd visitor. Twice I found myself embarking on gardening expeditions armed with rusty shears and suchlike, but my heart was never in it. After all, grass does no harm growing and birds and bushes don't need mowing anyway, so there's not a lot you can do in a garden. Somewhere I'd cleared a patch for growing vegetables years ago, but it had reverted to jungle, as the herbaceous border had, and I couldn't find exactly where it was. I abandoned the attempt, taking the wise view that if vegetables had wanted to grow there they'd have done so whatever assistance they'd been given by me. There's a chap Brownlow in a bungalow not far from me who's never out of his garden. It beats me what he finds to do. Maybe he's got a blonde in the shrubbery.

Ever been stuck at home? You get up and make breakfast, put the radio on, and wash up. Then you mill about doing odd jobs like cleaning and washing, and that's the end of it. What house-wives keep moaning about heaven only knows, because I was up at seven-thirty and finished easily by ten, after which the rest of the day was waiting there—in my case, for nothing. Margaret called at first with provisions, and Jane dropped in with Adrian.

The itinerant dealer Jimmo called. Tinker came after the first day, but within a week all the visits had dwindled. I was pretty glad, because I was in no mood to talk and they were embarrassed. People are, where a nervous breakdown's concerned. It's posh and gallant to break your leg, and brave to have appendicitis, but a nervous breakdown's a plain embarrassment best avoided. You're better off with the plague. Maybe people think a breakdown's a sign of lack of moral fiber, that you ought to be pulling yourself together, putting your shoulder to that wheel, et cetera. It taught me one lesson at least, that any form of "weakness" is highly suspect. I wish I knew why.

I'd heard of breakdowns before, of course. Half my difficulty was that I didn't know what they actually were or where they came from, let alone what went on; yet there I was with all my anxieties gone, all my worries vanished, all interests evaporated. It would have been rather disturbing, if I'd been capable of being disturbed that is. As it was, I was utterly serene—dirty, unwashed, filthy, unshaven, unfed, and unkempt, but serene. Calm as a pond I was, uncaring. Worst of all, grief about Sheila had disappeared. Margaret came on a second then a third visit and discreetly left money on the mantelpiece, saying I was to be sure to remember to pay it back when I had a chance. I mumbled vacantly. Finally everyone had stopped coming. The letters lay in a heap by the door.

As days went into weeks I found myself stirring, not physically but something inside me. It really was an awakening. Instinctively my switched-off mind must have realized there was no point in trying to hurry things along and had stayed resting. My recovery was under way before I realized. The first event I can really recall is making myself some food—sausages and stale bread. Then I started feeding the birds again, sitting with them for a short while as usual, although I'd earlier automatically shunned their company as too intrusive, making too many demands on me.

About three days after starting eating I took conscious positive steps. I shaved. The next day I shaved and washed, then after that I bathed and got fresh clothes out. It was about sixteen days before I was presentable. The cottage was reasonable, and I started going down to the launderette. For some reason it was important to set myself a mental limit and stick rigidly to it, no matter how senseless that scheme actually was. Therefore, for four consecutive days I walked the garden's borders ten times every afternoon and counted all my trees and bushes assiduously after doing the washing up about nine o'clock; and for those four days I took my clothes, clean and soiled alike, to the launderette and washed them. Naturally I ran into practical difficulties such as coins for the slots, not knowing when the wretched machines were going to start or stop, what to do with that cup of powder and other details like losing socks. By the fourth day I was becoming quite intrigued by the system. You put in eight socks with your things and get out only five socks and one you've never seen before. Next day's the same. Unless you're careful you can finish up with an entirely different set of miscellaneous gear and all your own socks presumably transmuted into energy. I cut my losses on the fifth day and merely watched other sockless people's machines on the go.

My interest in antiques like everything else had suddenly vanished. Auctions had presumably taken place, the phone carried on unanswered, and Lovejoy was temporarily indisposed. Now, as I mended and consciousness returned, I took up a catalogue and read it in small stages during the course of an entire evening while the telly was on. It was an odd sensation, reading at a distance as it were, with details registering in the right places yet my own self somehow observing the whole process with caution and not a little distrust. Anyhow, I acted it out, feeling a flicker of interest here and there but suppressing it in case it got out of hand. It must have been the right thing to do, because the very next day I was answering letters and making decisions, about half speed. Injured animals go and lie quiet, don't they? Maybe that's what my mind had done.

The fourth week I faced the world again.

I began life by attending a sale in Colchester and after two more days another, this time in Bury St. Edmunds. As a starter, the tokens I'd bought in darkest East Anglia—easy material whose value you can always gauge by an hour's careful checking —were launched out in a coin mart we have not far away, and they went for a good profit. I was pleased *because* I was pleased. The cottage hadn't been assaulted while I was out. Cheered and feeling full of emotions that were no longer lying dormant, I whistled and sang and forayed into the garden for some flowers to put in a vase. I was unsuccessful, though, not because there weren't any but because you can't really go hacking plants' heads off just because you feel a bit bouncy. I seriously thought of planting one into a pot and bringing it inside the cottage but decided against that as well. There's no breeze inside a house like there is in a garden, is there, and plants might really depend on being pushed about by the wind, not being able to stretch themselves as we can. Also, you have to think of the proper sunshine outside instead of no real light indoors. And rain. And company. I don't know much about them, not like Major Lister would, for instance, but it stands to reason you're best not trying to dabble in what you don't understand. People do damage when they want things. If people didn't want things, hardly anything would go wrong with anybody's life. All bad's desire.

I temporarily shelved the notion that if it was true that all bad came from desire, then maybe all desire was bad too. Calm but feeling alive again now, I gently worked my way back to a proper behavior.

Six whole weeks after I'd gone up to Maltan Lees and met Watson I was well again.

Not that I was yet in the full circle of my usual life. I kept out of friends' way, didn't phone any of them, and only spoke when I was directly addressed if ever I ran into anyone I knew. Business picked up from nil, and a trickle of post came again. The phone calls started. It was a pleasure to be active and doing something useful, but I had to keep myself from regretting the lost opportunities during my holiday. There'd been an undeniable upsurge of deals in the antiques world during the previous weeks. I just had to accept that I'd done my business no good by chasing all over England looking for a needle in a haystack.

Finally, when I was really well and having to restrain myself hourly, I shook out the reins of my mind and took off.

I rang Field. He was very relieved.

"I'm sorry about your illness. What was it?"

"Oh, you know," I parried, "some virus I expect."

"Terrible, terrible things, those." After passing on some amateur therapy he told me of the replies to the advertisement.

"Were there many?"

"You've no idea!" He drew breath. "The wife nearly went off me. A mountain of letters, some really rather odd. I'd no idea people could be so extraordinary."

"Are they mostly cranks?"

"Some, but some I would say are worth your attention. You'd better come and have a look."

"I shall."

We fixed a time and I rang off. Feeling strong, I rang Tinker Dill at the White Hart.

"Tinker? Lovejoy," I greeted him. "What's new?"

"Christ!" he exclaimed in the background hubbub from the bar. "Am I glad to hear you!"

"I want ten buyers tomorrow, first thing." It was the best joke I could manage, feeling so embarrassed at his pleasure.

"Will do," he replied cheerfully. "I heard you was about again. O.K.?"

"Not bad, ta."

"When you coming into town again?"

"Oh, maybe tomorrow. I think I'll come into the arcade." I wasn't too keen on going, but I could always ring later and postpone it if I wanted.

"Everybody asks about you." I'll bet, I thought.

"Much stuff around?"

"Some," he said with sorrow in his voice. "You've missed quite a bit of rubbish, but there's been some interesting stock whizzing about."

"Ah, well."

"Tough, really, Lovejoy. A set of fairings went for nothing last week . . ." He resumed his job, pouring out details of everything important he could think of. It sounded lovely and I relished every word, stopping him only when his voice was becoming hoarse.

"Thanks, Tinker. Probably see you tomorrow, then."

"Right, Lovejoy. See you."

It was enough excitement for one day. I drew the curtains and gathered an armful of the sale lists that had arrived while I was ill. There was a lot of catching up to do.

As I read and lolled, lists began forming in my mind, of faces and where I'd seen them. I don't mean I stopped work, just studied on and let faces come as they wished. Tinker Dill seemed everywhere I'd ever been, practically, since the Judas pair business began. And Jane. And Adrian. Dandy Jack. And Watson, of course. And, oddly, the Reverend Lagrange, which for somebody who lived many miles north in darkest East Anglia was rather enterprising. But he said he went to Muriel Field's house, being such a close family friend and all that. Did priests get time off? Maybe he'd struck a patch of movable feasts and it was all coincidence. And then there was Margaret, Brad, Dick Barton who'd sold me the Mortimers. Plus a few incidental faces who appeared less frequently, so you barely noticed them at all.

But that's what murderers are supposed to be good at, isn't it?

That same afternoon I had a cup of tea ready for the post girl, a pleasant tubby lass who worked the village with her brother. He kept a smallholding and sold plants from a stall on the London road bypass.

"I brewed up, Rose. Come in."

"Whatever do you do with all these magazines, Lovejoy?" She propped her bicycle against the door and brought a handful of catalogues and two letters. She was a plain girl, long-haired and young. They seem so active these days and full of talk. "I've just had a terrible row with the Brownlows. Oh, you should have heard them going on at me! As if I have anything to do with how much stamps cost." She sank onto the divan thankfully.

"Been busy?" I knew she had two spoonfuls of sugar.

"Don't ask!" She grinned.

"What time do you start your round?"

"Five, but then there's the sorting."

"Do you do that as well?"

"Sort of. Get it?"

"Super pun," I agreed, stony-faced. She grinned and settled back. There's this shed in the middle of the village where the post comes.

"I was worried in case you had one of your birds in with you."

"You're too young to know about such matters."

"You're a hoot, Lovejoy, you really are." I tell you, youngsters nowadays must learn it from the day they're born.

"What's funny?"

"The whole village can hear you making . . . er, contact with your lady visitors some nights. And some mornings."

"They can?" That startled me.

"Of course." She giggled. "We're all terribly embarrassed, especially those of us who are still in our tender years and likely to be influenced by wicked designs of evil men." A laugh.

160

"Well the village shouldn't be listening."

"Face it, Lovejoy." She began to look around. "You've something of a reputation."

"That's news to me." And it was.

"Is it really?"

"Yes." She turned to eye me. "You're our most exotic resident."

"Pretty dull place."

"Pretty exotic character," she countered.

"I can't be more exotic than our musician." We have a man who makes an extraordinary musical instrument of a hitherto unknown pattern. Needless to add, it cannot be played—which for a musical instrument is some handicap.

"Compared with you he's a bore."

"Then there's the preacher." This is a chap who preaches somewhat spontaneously at odd hours of night and day. Very praiseworthy, you might say, to have deep religious convictions in this immoral world. Well, yes, but to preach to trees, fenceposts, and assorted bus stops is hardly the best way of setting a good example.

"Even the preacher."

"What's special about me?" I was fascinated. Rose seemed surprised at my astonishment.

"You collecting old pots."

"Thanks," I said ironically. So much for years of study.

"And that crazy old car. It's hilarious!"

"Go on."

"And your . . . lady visitors."

"Well," I said hesitantly, "they've diminished of late, apart from the odd dealer. I was ill, in a way. I expect you noticed."

"Yes." She poured herself another cup and stirred sugar in. "You had one special bird, didn't you?"

"Sheila."

"Better than that blousy brunette with all those teeth."

"Which was she?"

"About four months ago. You remember—she shared you with that unpleasant married lady with the nasty manners."

"You keep my score?"

She grinned. "Hard not to, when I'm coming here every day."

"I suppose so."

"Did she give you the sailor's farewell?" she asked sympathetically.

"Who?"

"Sheila."

"No, love." I drew slow breath. "She . . . died, unfortunately."

"Oh."

"It's all right."

"I'm so sorry. Was that why you . . . ?"

"Lost control, my grandma would have called it," I said to help her out. "Yes, it must have been."

"Was it over her you . . . ?" She hesitated.

"I what?"

"You were going to kill somebody?" Word had spread, then. Not really surprising, the way I'd behaved.

"How did you hear that?"

She leaned forward excitedly. "You mean you *are?*"

"Do I look in fit state to go on the prowl?"

She looked me up and down. "Yes, probably."

"Well you can think again." I offered biscuits while I got myself another cup.

"The whole village was talking about you."

"Even more than usual?" My sarcasm hardly touched her.

"We were all agog."

"Well you can de-gog then. I'm better."

"Oh." Her disappointment should have been a bright moral glow of relief at salvation from dastardly sin.

"Sometimes I wonder about you women."

She beamed roguishly. "Only sometimes?"

"I mean, you're all interested when you think I'm going to go ape and axe some poor unsuspecting innocent"—the word nearly choked me—"yet when I'm going straight again you're all let down."

"You must admit, Lovejoy," she was reprimanding, so help me, "it's more, well, thrilling."

"You read too many books for your own good. Or letters."

She accepted the jibe unabashed. "No need to read letters, the way some people carry on. You found quick consolation, Lovejoy."

"What do you mean?"

"I nearly saw her the other night, and her natty little blue pop-pop." She poked her tongue out at me.

I gave a special sheepish grin but shook my head. "I don't know what you mean."

"Oh, no," she mocked. "Just good friends, I suppose."

"It must have been the district nurse."

"Like heck it was. Nurse Patmore doesn't go shoving her bike in the hedge. It's been here twice. I saw it."

"One of the forestry men," I suggested easily.

"On a *woman's* bike?" She fell about laughing. "You're either kidding or you've some funny friends, Lovejoy. It's an old-fashioned bike, no crossbar."

"You're mistaken." Keeping up my smile was getting very hard.

"Can't she afford a car, Lovejoy? Or is it just that it's quieter in the dark and easier to hide?" She snorted in derision. "You must think we're dim around here."

I surrendered, grinning with her. "A little of what you fancy," I absolved myself.

"They run a book on you down at the pub."

"In what race?"

"The Marriage Stakes."

"Out!" I said threateningly, and she went giggling. "You're probably being raped, according to that nosy lot of Nosy Parkers."

"That an offer?"

"Don't be cheeky to your elders!"

"Any particular cheeks in mind?"

I waved her off, both of us laughing. She pedaled down the path and was gone. I went in to clear up.

Now, Rose starts her work about five, but her actual round only begins once the sorting is ended. That could take up to an hour. So she was around my place no later than six-fifteen in the morning. Her afternoon round was much more variable on account of the number of chats she had to have between the sorting shed and our lane. She must have glimpsed the woman's —if it was a woman—bike at the "ungodly hour" of six A.M. or so. How much light was there at that time? I couldn't remember whether the clocks had been put ahead an hour or whether we still had that to do.

Rose would be out of our lane by now. I locked up, chucked the robin some bread and cheese, and walked down to the lane. It's a curving road no more than twelve feet across, with high hedges of hawthorn and sloe on either side. My own length of it is two hundred feet, dipping slightly to the right as you look at it from the cottage. A house is opposite, set a fair way back from the lane like mine. I hardly ever see him, an ascetic chap interested in boats and lawn mowers, while she's a devotee of amateur opera. As I said, it takes all sorts. They have two grown-up children who periodically arrive with their respective families.

Down the lane is a copse, if that's the right word, a little wood joining my garden. For some reason old people once built a gate into the copse, perhaps to let pigs in to rummage for berries or acorns. Now it's derelict and falling apart. Up the lane but beyond another strip of hazels and birch is a cluster of a dozen houses centered on a well, then the lane gradually widens and levels off to join the main road at the chapel.

Since the lane leads down to a splash ford going to Fordleigh, the next village, not much traffic comes along it except for the milk float, sometimes a car risking the ford in exchange for rural scenic delights, and genuine visitors or people out for a walk or cycling. You can get to the village road again that way, but only with a bike or on foot. There's no way through for cars except by continuing on over the river.

Which sets you thinking.

The lane was empty as usual. You can hear cars approaching a couple of miles away. Nothing was coming, and with it being schooltime still, the children weren't yet out to raise hubbub at the chapel crossroads. Whoever intended to watch the cottage from a hidden position would have been wise to either come through the Fordleigh splash and appear in the lane at the copse, or pretend to be out for a quiet country stroll and walk down from the chapel toward the river. Whichever way they —she?—came, she could always duck into the copse and work her way near to the cottage among the trees. There was little likelihood of being seen so early anyway.

Yet there was one important proviso in all this. Does any *reasonable* morning stroller need a bike, and a motorized one at that? Answer: No. But my visitor did. And why? Because she was a stranger to the village, that's why. You don't go to a village miles away for a morning stroll.

All of which meant that my watcher was not a villager, and had come toward my place by crossing the river. She had used a motorized cycle of some sort to ride within walking distance of the copse and pushed the pop-pop into cover while slinking closer to the cottage. Then she'd watched me, presumably to nip in and steal the instrument when it was safe. *She?* But a forester or a farm laborer would never ride a bike without a reinforced crossbar.

I came to the copse gate. I'd not looked at it for years. You don't scrutinize what's familiar, though I must have passed it a hundred times. My hedge was only thick enough for conceal-ment in two places and they were undisturbed. It had to be here.

My scalp prickled. The gate seemed untouched, but behind the rotting post brambles and hawthorns were crushed. A few twigs were broken and one sloe twig was quite dead, hanging by a slip of bark. Deeper inside, the ground was grooved and clods of dried mud still showed above the vegetation. Some scooters have quite wide tires. Those of the more orthodox bicycle shape have tires thicker than for ordinary bikes but thinner than the tires of, say, a mini-sized car.

I entered the copse with as much care as I could and knelt to examine the ground. It must be a motorized pedal-cycle or something very similar, I thought. The grooves were of a tire fairly thin but of a probable radius about bike size.

There's something rather nasty about being spied on. I once knew this woman friend of mine. We'd been out for an evening and on reaching her home for a light chat and a drink—her husband was abroad—found the place had been ransacked by burglars, whereupon she'd been violently sick. It seemed odd to me at the time, but now I felt nausea rise at the image of a silent watcher here among the trees near the cottage. The intrusion was literally sickening. There wasn't exactly a beaten path through the undergrowth, but the path the watcher had taken was pretty obvious if one assumed the purpose was to get near to the cottage. It took me about an hour of careful searching to find out where she'd waited.

The ground was dry and had that beaten look it gets from being shadowed by trees. One edge of my garden runs adjacent to the copse and it was about midway along it that the watcher had established herself, having a broken stump to lean on. There was adequate protection from being observed. I leaned on the stump myself. You could just about see my front door and the near half of the gravel path. The car was in full view, plus the side window looking into my kitchenette and there was an oblique view of the front two windows. They're only small, so the chance of actually watching me move about inside was practically nil, especially as I'm not a lover of too much light.

And, considering how it's my usual practice to draw the curtains as soon as I switched on, that must make it more difficult. What really displeased me was the horrid sensation—I was having it now on the back of my neck as I imitated my silent watcher— of having somebody peering in. I actually shivered.

Moving further through the copse, I found that the nearest the ground cover approached the cottage was about a hundred feet, maybe a little more. The trouble was you could see both front and back entrances from the copse. I could neither leave nor enter without being in full view, unless she allowed her attention to lapse, which in view of the trouble she'd taken wasn't at all likely. That was the most worrying feature of the whole business.

Taking care not to displace the brambles, I stepped out of the thicket. One pace and I was on my grass in full view of the cottage window. There had been a fence in the old days, long since rotten. I couldn't help looking back, seeing the copse and hedge in a completely new way. Before, everything had been almost innocent and protective, if not exactly neat. Now, even the odd bush in my lawn was somehow too near the cottage for comfort. And as if that wasn't enough, no sooner was I indoors than I began imagining odd noises, actually hearing them, which is most unlike me. The number of creaking sounds in an old cottage is really very few, but there I was like an apprehensive child full of imagination left alone for the night.

I examined the entire place minutely. The walls were wattle-and-daub, a common construction in East Anglia. These dwellings have been standing hundreds of years. In this ancient method you put sticks in wattle fashion as your main wall structure and slap mud between, adding more and more until it's a wall. Then a bit of plaster and you're home, providing you've a few beams and thatch for a roof. It's cool in summer, dry in winter, and offers the best environment for the preservation of antiques known. Not all the best preservation happens in museums and centrally heated splendor. In fact that environment's a hell of a sight worse for the really good stuff.

Like a fool I found myself peering at the copse from every conceivable angle. What I'd seen of the cottage from the murderer's stump told me it would be impossible, without the help of artificial light, for him/her to see much of me unless I was actually close to the window. The trouble was, whoever stood inside the cottage was equally blinded, because the copse formed a dark opaque barrier at the edge of the grass. Worse, there were two sides of the cottage I couldn't look out from.

I couldn't grumble, though I felt peeved at the mess I was in. I'd told Geoffrey the constable to get lost, alienated all my acquaintances, found myself discredited and scorned and regarded as a mentally sick buffoon without sense or judgment. To undo this would be the work of a lifetime. And it was no good grumbling that the cottage was an awkward shape, remote and rather vulnerable, because what I now regarded as its defects I'd always thought of as marvelous attributes, exactly the sort I needed for my antiques. And my hidden priest hole—now seeming so useless because it could have been made into a lovely airy cellar with a cellar door I could get out of—had seemed in my palmy days a perfect boon. It was private, hidden, and ventilated. Whoever had built the cottage had been wise in the way of country crafts. Two small ventilation shafts each about six inches wide ran from the priest hole to a point about a foot from the outside of the wall, ending in an earthenware grid set in the grass and partly overgrown. I kept the grids clear of too many weeds so the air could circulate. That way there was no risk of undue humidity, the great destroyer of antiques of all kinds.

The chiming clock struck four-thirty, which meant the village shop was still open. Suddenly in a hurry, I collected some money and rushed out to the car, remembering and cursing the locks and alarms for holding me up. I made it with about five minutes to spare. Mrs. Weddell judged me with an expert eye to list any grim details about me suggesting further decadence, but I wasn't having any. Knowing the dour insistence of the Essex villager upon gossip of the most doom-ridden kind, I gave her a ten-watt beam of exuberance and demanded information about her health. That put her off her stride. She was rather sad I wasn't at death's door and became quite miserable when I kept smiling. Added to that I bought enough provisions to feed a battalion and managed to find the right change with many a quip and merry jest, which was one more in her eye. "I've decided that a plump man's a happy one, Mrs. Weddell," I told her. "I'm going to put some pounds on." Exit laughing.

One of the hardest things I've ever done was to drive up to the cottage and not search the copse for the intruder. Whistling flat and nonchalantly, I unloaded the three carrier bags, making myself do it one bag at a time and deliberately controlling the urge to sneak a glance.

The night fell quicker than I'd realized that evening. I couldn't help leaving the curtains alone just to get a good look in the direction of the thicket without risk to myself, but finally had to draw them to keep things seeming normal. I sat with the telly and radio silent all evening, listening, and made a supper by the quietest possible means, though I'd usually have a noisy fry-up. A million times I heard somebody outside. Worse, a million times I didn't hear anything at all. It reminded me of the story about the students' hostel where a studious lad had complained of his neighbor who entertained a girl friend in the next room: "It's not the noise, it's the silences I can't stand!"

The distance across the grass grew shorter in my imagination. You could shoot somebody with fair ease from the cover provided by the bushes, especially if killing was getting to be a habit and you had the unique advantage of possessing a priceless flintlock that could kill without leaving the slightest trace of evidence. Still, no matter what else he tried I was fairly secure. I had enough food, milk, and water to last well over a week, and there was always the phone.

And the loaded Mortimers, waiting patiently and still motionless beneath the flagstone floor.

The phone suddenly rang, making me jump a mile. It was Margaret. She'd heard I was on the mend and chatted a full minute about antiques real and imaginary. It was kind of her and I urged her to ring again when finally we'd run out of things to say.

"I miss you around the arcade," she said. "Are you really better, Lovejoy?"

"Yes, love," I said. "Thanks. I appreciate the phone call."

"Pop around here whenever you want." She lives at Fordleigh. I promised I would, but I wanted friends checking up on *me* to make sure I was in the pink, not invitations to go visiting. I invented a couple of false promises to entice Adrian, Tinker, and Harry to phone in, knowing Margaret would pass the messages on.

The rest of the night was quite uneventful.

I only wish I'd rested and harbored my strength.

14

I didn't sleep a wink. Long before dawn I was up being brave. Today was going to be my round of people. Today the old debonair impeccable Lovejoy would hit the road as politicians do to show how young and thrusting they actually are behind that comfortable rotund shape. It was really something of a confidence trick, but I was going through with it anyway. The night had taught me how alone I was.

Further reflection had increased my nervousness. Despite having the phone and living so near other people, there was one major problem. Whereas I didn't know who'd killed Sheila, the murderer certainly knew who I was. Collecting's a small world. Sooner or later I would come across him, and whether *I* recognized him or not was irrelevant. The risk I represented was still there.

I drove to George Field's house and collected the replies to his advertisement, some twenty replies, with one catalogue from an overseas dealer casting bread hopefully on distant waters. The ones Field thought most likely turned out dud. Disappointed, I promised to read them with enthusiasm and left.

Muriel Field was next. I enjoyed the drive, but exactly how many times I caught myself looking carefully into the rearview mirror I'll never know. The one blue scooter I did see turned out to be ridden by a district nurse. She's probably wondering yet why a complete stranger gave her a glare for nothing when she was in the opposite lane. I didn't recover for miles.

Muriel was glad to see me. I honestly mean that, really pleased. That whole morning was brilliant; every cloud seemed effervescent and the sky a deeper blue than it had ever been. She was radiant, dressed maybe somewhat younger than her age, and looked as though the party was soon to begin. The difference between the anxious, hesitant woman she'd been some weeks before and the scintillating beauty I now saw was remarkable. I was coerced into drinking coffee.

"If that heron keeps its distance," I warned.

She laughed. "I promise I'll protect you."

We sat on the patio and made small talk while a crone fetched coffee, Sheffield plate of some distinction, and Spode. The sugar bowl's fluted design didn't quite match but could be passed off as the right thing with luck in a nooky antique shop. My pleasure made me careless.

"I'll remember you above everything else for elegance," I said playfully, and saw her face change.

"Don't talk like that."

"It was a compliment."

"It sounded . . . so final."

"A joke," I said.

She wouldn't be appeased and set about pouring for us both. "Everything needn't be bad or sad." I felt out of my depth and said so. "I just don't like it when people talk about going away or changing things," she said. "It happens too often without anyone wanting it."

"I was only admiring your coffee set. It would have been terrible if you'd spoiled the effect with a spoon made out of Georgian silver coins." I took my cup and stirred. "Have I put my foot in it?"

"No." She shook her hair, head back and face toward the air, as they do.

"I'll be careful in future." That was better. She raised her cup to toast me.

I asked about her upbringing. As she talked I absorbed security and ease all around. No chance of being spied on here, with the two loyal gardeners busy interrupting plants and keeping an eye on the mistress. Inside the house stalwart ancient ladies —infinitely more formidable than any gardeners—creaked and bustled vigilantly. So many things came down to money. Wealth is safety. Muriel chatted on about her father, her many aunts, her mother's concern with spiritualism ("But, then, it was all the fashion in her day, wasn't it?"), and her inherited wealth. Husband Eric had been as wealthy as she, it appeared, when they met.

"Will you stay on here, Muriel?" I asked.

She glanced away. "It depends."

"On . . . ?"

"Oh, just things." Her vagueness was deliberate, yet there was a hint of a reflective smile in her expression. Oh-ho. I began to ask about Eric.

Society's cynicism clouds our minds sometimes. When a younger woman marries or cohabits with a much older man, it's supposed to be only for money. Conversely, when an old woman takes up with a much younger man, she's blamed for wanting physical gratification and is condemned on those grounds. This is one of the few occasions women come off worst. Society says they're cheap chiselers or sex-crazed. On the other hand the old chap's regarded as a sly old dog, and the young chap's seen simply as having just struck lucky getting sex and a steady income together in one parcel, as it were. So as Muriel chatted happily on about her elderly husband, I found my treacherous mind wondering what possible motive she'd dreamed up for marrying Eric Field in the first place. Naturally under the influence of Muriel's undoubted attractiveness and charm I was stern with myself and forced these unbecoming suspicions out as best I could.

"He had a real sense of fun," she was saying, smiling.

"I suppose it's a lot quieter now," I put in.

"Oh . . ." For some reason she was hesitant.

"I mean, fewer visitors," I hurried to explain. She seemed to become upset at the slightest thing. "You won't have dealers and collectors bothering you quite so much, seeing we only go for antiques."

"No." She saw my cup was empty and rose a little too quickly. "You haven't really seen the house, have you?"

"Er . . . no, but—" I was taken a little by surprise.

"Come on. I'll show you." Mystified by these sudden changes of course, I followed her in from the terrace.

The house wasn't quite the age I'd expected. Despite that, it was only just beginning to feel lived-in. Muriel had taste. Flowers matched the house colors and weren't too obtrusive the way some people have them, though you couldn't help thinking what a terrible fate it was to be scythed off in your prime and stuck in a pot to decay.

"Could I please . . . ?"

"Yes?" We were on the stairs, apparently about to tour upstairs.

"Would you mind very much if I asked to see where Eric was found?" To my surprise she was unperturbed.

"Not at all." We descended together. "I thought you might."

The room led off the marble-floored hall and was beautifully oak-paneled, done about 1860 or so at a quick guess. Muriel's unfaltering taste had enabled it to be exposed to more daylight than others could have allowed. She'd used long heavy velvet curtains drawn well back from the tall windows to draw attention to their height.

"I like it."

"Eric used it for a collecting room and his study. I never came

174

in much when he was alive." She wandered about touching things rather absently, a book, the desk, adjusting a reading lamp. The carpet was Afghan but pleasing for all that. A small Wilson oil, the right size for that missing Italian waterfall painting he did, hung facing the desk, setting my chest clanging. However, care was needed, so I filed the facts and said nothing.

"I warned you about interlopers," I said.

"I know what you collectors are like. All Eric's things have gone, as I said, so I've no reason to fear."

"Do you see any of Eric's acquaintances still?"

"No," she said firmly.

"No collectors?" She paused at that, then again told me no. I shrugged mentally. It was none of my business. "If one does turn up," I said, chancing my arm, "tell him I'd rather like to see him."

We gazed at the lawns and admired the sweeping landscaped gardens. Muriel was eager to explain her plans for the coming flower show. I let her prattle on and, adopting an idiot smile, stared toward the flower beds.

In the window was the reflection of a small occasional table, mahogany drop-leaf with a single stem leg, quite good but Victorian. I couldn't see the top surface because it was covered with a neat new tablecloth. On it were mats and the essentials for starting the inevitable tea ceremony. *I never came in it much when Eric was alive* were her words. Therefore she did use it now, and fairly frequently from the way she had spoken. And whoever the visitor was must be a fairly regular customer. He rated the cozy intimacy of a sophisticated room from which all sour memories had been happily erased. I only rated the terrace. Hey-ho.

That would account for her reflective smile when I'd asked if she would keep the house on. It depended on *just things,* she'd said. Maybe it would also explain her displeasure when my miscued remark had suggested that collectors were hardly interested in people. *Was he therefore a collector?* I wondered about her holy friend. Older, but age doesn't really matter. Never mind what people say.

Still, where was the harm? It was quite some time ago since her husband had died. Sooner or later she was going to meet somebody new, as the song says. You couldn't blame her—or him, come to that. I honestly felt a twinge of jealousy. I couldn't help starting to work out how much I could buy with Muriel's wealth. I'd start with a group of Wedgwood jaspers. Then I'd— No good, Lovejoy.

"Come and see me off," I asked.

She agreed. "I'll get my coat and ride with you to the gate."

I strolled out onto the drive. The gardeners were grumbling with the endurance of their kind. As I approached I heard one saying, "That swine never grew those leeks himself. The bastard bought them, I'll bet." And I grinned inwardly at the politics of village competitions. At that moment his companion, detecting the presence of an observer, made a cautionary gesture, at which both turned to greet me with rearranged faces. Seeing my slipshod frame, they relaxed and grinned. I nodded affably and strolled on. They'd thought perhaps I was Muriel. Or Lagrange?

She was in the car when I returned. I'd get no kiss today. You can tell a woman enraptured by someone else. The delight isn't delight with you. Her vivacity's pleasure at what's to come, and in case you miss the point it's you that's departing. The minute it took to drive her to the gate I used to good effect, being as secure and companionable as other characters of the landscape. She blew me a kiss from the gate.

A child, I thought, just a child. Everything must be kind and happy for her. And in her protective shell of opulence she would instinctively make the whole world appear so. Lucky bloke, whoever he was.

The White Hart quietened a bit as I entered, but when a raving nut goes anywhere people behave circumspectly no matter how hard they try to look normal. Tinker bravely came along the bar for a chat, but Jimmo and Harry Bateman were obviously preoccupied and couldn't manage a nod. I was calm, easily innocent, and merely eager to talk about antiques. Jane, cautious on her stool, was relaxed enough to offer me a couple of rare book bindings—though I wouldn't normally touch them with a barge pole and she knew it—and Adrian gave me welcome only a little less effusive than usual.

Tinker had a source of antique violins—no, don't laugh, they're not the trick they used to be—for me, owned by a costermonger of all things. He had found as well a collector of old bicycles who was in the market for price-adjusted swaps, wanting assorted domestic Victoriana, poor misguided soul; and his third offer was some collector after old barrows. You know, the sort you use in gardens. At a pinch this last character would buy antique shovels if the antique wheelbarrow market was a little weak.

"An exotic crew, Tinker," I commented over my pale ale.

"It's the way it's happening, Lovejoy," he said. "I don't know whether I'm coming or going these days, honest. No two alike."

"Good."

"I wish it was." Drummers like Tinker are notorious moaners, worse than farmers.

"Better for business when tastes vary," I said, nodding to Dick, who'd just come in with traces of the boatyard still on him. Dick waved and gave me the thumbs-up sign.

"I like things tidy," said Tinker, except for Dandy Jack the untidiest man I knew.

"I like collectors," I answered just to goad him and get a mouthful of invective for my trouble.

A couple of new dealers were in from the West Country and, unaware of my recent history, latched affably on to me and we did a couple of provisional deals after a while. I earmarked for them a small folio of antiquary data, drawings of excavations in Asia Minor and suchlike, done by an industrious clergyman from York about 1820. It was supported by abstracts from the modern literature, photographs, and articles, plus the diary of a late-Victorian lady who'd spent a lengthy sojourn near the excavations and described them in detail. All good desirable script. They in their turn came up with a Forsyth scent-bottle lock, which they showed me there and then, an early set of theodolites they'd bring to the pub next day, and what sounded a weird collection of early sports equipment I'd have to travel to see. Knowing nothing about early sports gear, I fell back on my thoughtful introverted expression and said I was definitely interested but I'd have to think about it. They asked after a Pauly air gun, but I said how difficult it was to find such rarities and I'd see what I could do. I might let them have a Durs air gun in part exchange.

Ted the barman, pleased at my appearance of complete normality, was only too glad to serve me when I asked for pie, pickle, and cheese. "Nice to see you up and about again, Lovejoy." He beamed.

"Thanks, Ted."

"Completely well now, eh?"

"A bit shaky on my pins now and again," I said.

With transparent relief he said it was understandable. "The girl friend had one of these viruses too," he said. "She was off work a month. Time them researchers got onto things like that and left smoking alone."

Back in my old surroundings with Dandy Jack and the rest popping in and out for the odd deal, I passed the time in utter contentment. I honestly admire antique dealers, like me. They are the last cavaliers, surviving as an extraordinary clone against fantastic odds by a mixture of devotion, philosophy, and greed. The enemy, it practically goes without saying, is the succession of malevolent governments who urbanely introduce prohibitive measures aimed at first controlling and then finally exterminating us. We don't bow to them. We don't fit neatly into their lunatic schemes for controlling even the air everyone breathes. The inevitable result is hatred, of us and of our freedom. It includes the freedom to starve, and this we do gladly when it's necessary. But we are still free, to be interested in what we do, to love what we practice and to work as and when we choose. And we work on average a good twelve hours a day every day, our every possession totally at risk every minute we live. And these poor duck eggs in the civil service actually believe they can bring us to heel! It's pathetic, honestly. Our ingenuity will always be too profound for a gaggle of twerps—I hope.

Listening to the banter going on hour after hour in the bar, my troubles receded and my fears vanished. We ranged over subjects as far apart as Venetian gondoliers' Renaissance clothing to Kikuyu carvings, from eighteenth-century Eskimo gaming counters to relics from the early days of the American wild west. It was lovely, warm, and comfortable.

Then I noticed it was dark outside.

15

I rose and left amid a chorus of good nights, quite like old times. The two strangers promised they'd be back about noon the next day, same place, and I promised I'd fetch my stuff.

The road to the cottage seemed endless. Worse still, it was quiet in a degree I'd never before experienced. My old car seemed very noisy. Its engine throbbed a beat out into the dark on either side of the road only to have it pulsed back to reintensify the next chug. In the center of a growing nucleus of contained deep pulsation, the motor moved on between high hedges behind its great rods of beamed headlight. A moon ducked its one eye in and out of static cloud at me. It was one of those nights where moon shadows either gather in disquieting clusters or spread across moon-bright lanes making sinister pools where the ground you have to tread is invisible.

The probing lights turned across the hedges down by the chapel. Unfortunately nobody was about, or I could have bolstered my courage by giving them a lift. With a sinking heart I swung into the path and curved to a stop outside my door. The silence, no longer held back by the throb of the great engine, rushed close and paused nearby in the darkness. I switched my door alarm off, using the key, and went in.

Even the cottage seemed worried. The electric light had a wan air about it as if it too was affected by concern. I examined the miniature hallway for marks but found no signs of intrusion. My unease persisted. I pulled the curtains to and flicked on the living-room lamps to make it seem cozier. Putting the TV on seemed a wise move until I realized that I would be deaf to the sound of anyone approaching as well as blinded by the darkness. Easy meat for whoever was watching out there.

To encourage what resolution I had left, I made a rough meal I didn't want. I hit on the idea of putting the radio on for a few moments. That way, when I eventually switched it off it might seem as though I had begun preparations for bed. With another stroke of genius I turned the hall light out and cautiously opened the front door a chink, just enough to get my arm out and insert the alarm key in the raised box on the door alcove. I usually didn't bother to set the alarm when I was indoors, but it might prove one more thing to lessen my many disadvantages. With the door safely closed and barred again I felt pleased at my inventiveness. Nobody could now pierce my perimeter, so to speak, without Geoffrey being roused at his police house. It would admittedly take some while for him to come hurtling over on his pedal-cycle, but I could hold the chap until he came.

A braver man would have decided to be bold, perhaps take a weapon and stalk the blighter out there in all that darkness. I'm not that courageous, nor that daft. Whoever was outside would see me leave from either door, while I would be treading into the unknown. Let the cops pinch him if he tried any funny stuff, I thought. They get paid for looking after us. Geoffrey had had my break-in and two chickens with fowl pest, and that had been his lot since Michaelmas. Big deal.

I've never really believed very much in all this subliminal learning stuff they talk about nowadays. You know the sort of thing—showing a one-second glimpse of a complex map in semidarkness and getting psychiatrists to see if you can remember its details twenty years later. Nor do I go in for this extrasensory perception and/or psychomotive force, spoon bending, and thought transference. Yet as I forced my food down and swilled tea, my discomfiture began to grow from an energy outside myself. It was almost as if the cottage had been reluctantly forced into the role of an unwelcome spectator to a crime about to be committed. That energy was, I became certain, generated by the watcher in the copse. Either I was acting as a sort of receiver of hate impulses or I was imagining the whole thing and he was at home laughing his head off, knowing I was bound to be getting hysterical. My plan to flush him out by the advertisement and my inquiries had backfired. He was now forewarned, and I was set up for reprisal.

Humming an octave shriller than usual, I went about my chores, finished the food, and washed up. It was important not to vary my routine. I got my bed ready in the adjoining room, leaving the bedside lamp on for about half an hour to simulate my usual reading time. Then I switched it off together with the radio, and the whole place was in darkness.

Living so far from other people—a few hundred yards seemed miles now—the cottage always had alternative lighting about: candles, a torch, two or three oil lamps. It would be safe to use the torch only if I hooded it well, say with a handkerchief or a dishcloth, and was careful to keep the beam directed downward. There was no need of it indoors, because I knew every inch of every room, but there might come an opportunity to catch him in its illumination like a plane in a searchlight. I'd get a good glimpse of him and just phone the police. Notice that my erstwhile determination and rage had now been transmuted through fear into a desire for an army of policemen to show up and enforce the established law—another instance of Lovejoy's iron will.

The curtains were pale cream, a bad mistake. Anything pale is picked out by the moon's special radiance, even a stone paler than its fellows being visible at a considerable distance. Were I to pull them back from the kitchen window, the movement would be seen by even the most idle watcher. Still, it had to be risked.

I got the torch ready in my right hand and moved stealthily toward the window. Do everything slowly if you want your movements to go unnoticed, was what they used to tell us in the army. Not fast and slick, but silent and slow. Feeling a fool, I tiptoed toward the sink. By reaching across I could pull the curtain aside. There was no way to step to one side close against the wall because of the clutter in the corner. A derelict ironing board stood there with other useless impedimenta. The slightest nudge would raise the roof.

Holding my breath, I gently edged the curtain aside. The copse, set jet-black above a milky sheen of grass, seemed uncomfortably close. I hadn't realized it was so short a gap, not even pacing it out the previous day. Nothing moved. *But I knew he was there.* Exactly in the way I was peering out at him, so he was staring at me. Could he see the curtain? I'd moved it without squeaking its noisy runners, but there was the danger of the moonlight exposing a dark slit between pale material. I let the edges meet and exhaled noiselessly.

To my surprise I was damp with sweat. Peering eyeball-to-eyeball with a murderer was no job for a growing lad. Maybe the best course would be to telephone Old Bill. Then what if Scotland Yard arrived in force only to discover an empty copse without any trace of a lurking murderer? Imagine their annoyance when discovering they'd been summoned by a frightened idiot with a recent history of a nervous breakdown. That would be crying wolf with a vengeance. I'd have to wait until I had proof he was there.

The view from the other windows was the same quiet—too-quiet—scene. No breeze moved the trees, and shadows stayed put. I began to feel somewhat better, a little more certain of myself. No matter what he tried I was certainly a match for him. He was only one bloke. If he had a gun along with him, well I had a few too. On the other hand, if he was waiting for me to

183

make another mistake, such as going out for a nocturnal car ride without remembering to set the alarm or something making another burglary easier, he was going to be sadly disappointed.

I waited another thirty minutes. Let him think I was sound asleep. My one bonus was my conviction he was out there. He, on the contrary, knew I was in the cottage but he had no way of knowing I was certain he was sitting on the tree stump and waiting. Sweat broke over me like a wave. What the hell *was* he waiting for? What point was there in watching a silent cottage when I was supposed to have retired for the night? Nothing could possibly happen until dawn when I awoke—or could it? My increasing nervousness took hold. It was ridiculous to let it, but I could not withstand the rush of adrenaline.

Shading the torch, I read the time on the wall clock. Ten minutes to twelve. A plan evolved in my mind. I would wait until dawn, when he was probably dozing, then rush outside, down the path to the lane, sprint across into my neighbor's drive, and hide deep in the laurel hedge. Of course I'd have a gun with me, maybe my Durs air weapon, which could shoot three, possibly four, spherical bullets without needing a further pumping up. With that relatively silent weapon I could prevent him leaving the copse from the far side. His bike would be useless.

This cunning plan had an undoubted risk, but there were two advantages. One was that it postponed any action at all, true Lovejoy style, so I needn't do anything dangerous just yet and maybe by dawn he would be gone. The second advantage was that in rushing out I'd set off the police alarm. He'd be trapped. All I'd have to do would be to sit tight and threaten him with the air weapon. He'd recognize it, collector that he was, with its great bulbous copper ball dangling beneath the stock. No mistake about that. Unfortunately, though, he might guess I would try a morning sprint and simply move toward my path. I wouldn't care to meet him face to face with him sitting ready and me disarrayed and running.

184

The front doorbell rang.

I dropped the torch from cold shock. A strange echo emitted from the walls about me, taking some seconds to die away. Fumbling along the carpet, I found the torch again and dithered, really dithered. Holding it in fear now, I peered out of the dark living room toward the door. The moon was shading the front of the cottage. Anyone could be there. My heart seemed to boom at every beat. Why does sweat come when you are cold from terror? The shelling I'd endured years ago had been nothing to this. It was somehow worse because whoever waited now at my door was in a sense unknown.

It could be Margaret. She might have sensed my fright and come to make sure I was all right. Why not telephone instead? Surely she'd do that, a far more sensible approach. Maybe she'd wanted to see for herself. I was on my way down the hall toward the door when the obvious flaw came to my mind—the cottage had been still as death. I'd been listening for the slightest sound for nearly an hour now and had not heard a thing. And the path outside was gravel. You could even hear a rabbit cross it. But not a clever, oh-so-clever, murderer. Nobody creeps up to a door, then rings the bell.

Sweat trickled from my armpits. It dripped from my forehead and stung the corners of my eyes. Should I call out, asking who was there? Not if he had the Judas guns with him, which might be used to shoot me down as soon as he located me.

I didn't dare creep closer to the door, in case he fired through. And if I crept back to the telephone for the police he'd hear the receiver go and me dialing. Would he honestly dare to break in? Panicking now, I slithered out of the hall and pulled the carpet back from over the priest hole. I needed no light to find the iron ring in its recess. Astride the flag, I hauled it upward and rested it against the armchair as I usually did. Cursing myself for a stupid unthinking fool, I clambered down the steps into the chamber. By feel alone I found the Mortimer case and extracted the duelers. The Durs air weapon might have been more useful,

185

but I'd relied too much on having the upper hand. Positions were bitterly reversed now.

The slab lowered in place, I covered it with the carpet. Where was he now? Would he still be there at the front door, or was that a mere bluff to draw attention while he crept around the side and gained entrance there? I stood, armed but irresolute, in the living room. Waves of malevolence washed through me—all from the external source he represented. He was there outside, watching and waiting. It was all part of his game. His hate emanated toward me through the walls. I could practically touch it, feel it as a live, squirming, tangible thing. The pathetic unpreparedness of my position was apparent to him as well as to me.

Something drew me toward the kitchen window. Had he given up lurking by the front door and gone back to his place in the copse? I tried turning myself this way and that, stupidly hoping my mental receivers would act like a direction finder and tell me exactly where he was. Perhaps my fear was blunting the effect. If he was in the process of moving through the copse I might see his form. It seemed worth a try. If only it wasn't so utterly dark in the shadows from that treacherous moon.

The difficulty was holding the torch and the Mortimers. I finally settled for gripping one dueler beneath my arm and holding the torch with my left hand. Leaning across the sink, I slowly pulled the curtain aside.

For one instant I stood there, stunned by sudden activity. The glass exploded before my eyes. A horrendous crackling sound from glass splinters all about held me frozen. Behind me inside the living room a terrific thump sounded which made even the floor shudder. The curtain was snapped aside and upward, flicked as if it had been whipped by some huge force. I stared for quite three or four seconds, aghast at the immensity of this abrupt destruction, before my early training pulled me to the floor. There was blood on my face, warm and salty.

Something dripped from my chin onto my hands as I crawled

on all fours back to the living room. I had lost one of the Mortimers but still held the torch. Broken glass shredded my hands and knees as I moved, a small incidental compared to the noise I was making. I rolled onto the divan to get my breath and see how much damage I'd sustained.

My face and hands were bleeding from cuts. They'd prove a handicap because they might dampen the black powder if I had to reload, but for the moment they were a detail. My handkerchief I tied around my left hand, which seemed in the gloom to look the darker of the two and was therefore probably bleeding more profusely. To my astonishment I was becoming calmer every second. The situation was not in hand but at least clearly defined. Even a dullard like me could tell black from white. The issue couldn't be clearer. He was outside shooting at me, and there was to be no quarter. Simple.

I crawled messily toward the telephone. Even as I jerked the receiver into my bandaged hand I knew it would be dead. The sod had somehow cut the wire. O.K., I told myself glibly, I'd wait until morning when the post girl would happen by and bring help. She came every day—rain, snow, hail, or blow.

Except Sunday, Lovejoy.

And tomorrow was Sunday. And my neighbors opposite drove to Walton-on-Sea every Saturday for the weekend.

Depressed by that, I set to working out the trajectory of his missile. Naturally, in my misconceived confidence I'd not drawn a plan showing the position of his stump relative to the window. That would have helped. Knowing it roughly, however, I peered through the gloom at the corner farthest from the kitchen alcove and finally found it sticking half buried in the wall. A bolt, from an arbalest.

Bows and arrows are sophisticated engines, not the simple little toys we like to imagine. An arrow from a longbow can pierce armor at a short distance, and Lovejoy at any distance you care to mention. But for real unsophisticated piercing power at short range you want that horrid weapon called the arbalest, the crossbow. Often wood, they are as often made of stone, complete with trigger beneath the stock. Their only drawback was comparative slowness of reloading. By now though he'd have it ready for a second go.

He was a bright lad. No flashes, no noise, no explosions, even if they'd been audible to any neighboring houses. And I was still no nearer guessing where he might be. My assets were that I was alive, was armed, and had enough food to last out the weekend and more. But I'd need to keep awake, whereas he could doze with impunity. I felt like shouting out that he could have the wretched turnkey.

At that moment I knew I was defeated. He had me trapped. And as far as I was concerned he could move about as he pleased, even go home for a bath, knowing I would be too scared to make a run for it in case he was still at his post. How the hell had I got into this mess? I questioned myself savagely.

Half past twelve, maybe something like five hours till daylight. Then what? I still wouldn't be able to see into the copse. And I would be that much more at risk.

I sat upright on the divan in the living room. The side window was paler than the rest, showing the moon was shining from that direction. I opened the hall door wide and, keeping my head down, pulled back the kitchen alcove's curtains as far as they would go. That way I'd be as central as I could possibly be, and he'd get the Mortimer first twitch if he tried to break in.

My spirits were starting to rise when I heard a faint noise. It was practically constant, a shushing sound like a wind in trees, not sounding at all like someone moving across a gravel path or wading through tall grass. Maybe, I thought hopefully, a breeze was springing up. If it started to rain he might just go home and leave me alone.

The noise increased, hooshing like a distant crowd. Perhaps the villagers had somehow become alarmed and were coming in a group to investigate. Even as the idea came I rejected it. People were not that concerned. Worried, I forgot caution and crept toward each of the windows to listen. The sound was as loud at each. I even risked approaching the front door, then the side door, but learned nothing except that the noise was ever so slightly intensifying as moments passed.

It was several puzzling minutes before I noticed the odd appearance of the side window. Shadows from it seemed to move in an odd way I hadn't seen before. The other window, illuminated blandly by moonlight diffusing through the curtains, cast stationary shadows within the room. My sense of unknowing returned again to frighten me. I couldn't even risk trying to glance out with that arbalest outside waiting to send another bolt trying for my brain.

Then I smelled smoke.

The shushing sound was the pooled noise of a million crackles. My thatched roof had been fired, probably by means of a lighted arrow. A kid could have done it. A hundred ways to have prevented all this rose to mind, all of them now useless. I was stuck in the cottage, which was burning. Thatch and wattle-and-daub.

Madness came over me for a second. I actually ran about yelling and dashed to the kitchen window. Recklessly I pulled the curtain aside and fired into the darkness through the broken pane. I shouted derision and abuse. The copse, vaguely lit by a strangely erratic rose-colored glow, remained silent. I heard the slap of the lead ball on its way among the leaves. Maddened, I tried filling a pan with water and throwing it upward. It left a patch on the ceiling. Hopeless.

I had to think. Smoke was beginning to drift in ominous columns vertically downward. Reflected firelight from each window showed me more of the living room than I'd seen for some time. I was going to choke to death before the flames finally got me. The beams would set alight, the walls would catch fire, and the fire would extend downward until the entire cottage was ablaze. I'd heard that glass exploded in fires. There would be a cascade of glass fragments from every possible direction ricocheting about the place. Those, and the flames, but first the asphyxiating smoke would do for me.

It would have to be the door. I'd make a dash for it. He'd be there, knowing my plight. He'd let me have it as soon as I opened the door to step outside. And it would have to be the front. Going out of the side door, I'd just have farther to run to get out of my blind garden. Unless I ran toward the copse. But once in there, assuming I reached it, what then? He knew it intimately. Maybe he would even stay there, confident of his marksmanship and having me silhouetted against the fire. You couldn't ask for an easier target.

The smoke intensified. I started to cough. The walls began creaking as if anticipating their engulfment. Above, a beam crackled unpleasantly and a few flakes of ash began to drift downward. So far I couldn't see the flames, but their din was beginning to shake the cottage. Faint tremors ran through the solid paving beneath my feet. You die from asphyxiation in a fire, I'd heard somewhere, probably in pub talk. Then, dead and at the mercy of the encroaching fire, your body becomes charred and immutably fixed in the terrible "boxer's stance" of the cindered corpse. I'd seen enough of the sickening war pictures to know. Tears were in my eyes from the smoke.

"You bastard," I howled at the side door. "Murderer!"

If I was to dash toward possible safety with all guns blazing I would need guns to blaze. Spluttering and now hardly able to see as the cottage began to fill with curling belches of smoke, I dragged the carpet aside and lifted the flagstone of the priest hole. As I did the idea hit me.

For certain I was practically as good as dead. No matter which way I jumped he'd kill me. I had enough proof of his intentions to know he was going to leave me dead. There was no escape. So what if I hid in the priest hole?

I dashed back for my torch, finding it easily in the flickering window glow. The shaded light showed the cavity at which I looked anew. Could fire ever penetrate paving stones? Maybe heat could. On the other hand, how long would a cottage like mine burn? And how long would the heat take to cook me alive in there?

The sink. I raced back, filled two pans full of water at the tap, and hurried back. The smoke was making it practically impossible to see. I was coughing constantly. The carpet had to be soaked to keep the flags as cool as possible. If they were damp, though they might eventually burn, they would perhaps act as a heat barrier for a while. I poured the water over the carpet and dashed into the kitchen alcove again.

By plugging the sink and turning both taps on at full blast I might eventually manage to flood the cottage floor. I'd actually done it once by accident. I wedged a dishcloth into the overflow at the back of the sink, which was the best I could do. It broke my heart to leave the Mortimers, but since he knew I'd fired at him they were going to be evidence of my doom. Quickly filling two milk bottles with water, I grabbed a loaf and a big piece of cheese which would have to last me. I remembered the torch at the last minute.

The idea was to have the flag in place covering the priest hole with me in it and the wet carpet covering that neatly. Under a mound of ash and fallen debris there'd be little sense in searching the ground unless they knew of my priest hole, and nobody else did. But how to do it? I stood on the steps with my shoulders bracing back the flag while my fingers inched the carpet forward until it touched the floor. Then I lowered the flag by edging my way down step by step. The last step was done with the heavy paving stone actually supported by my head. Twice I had to repeat the maneuver because the carpet somehow folded inside and wedged the stone open a fraction. I couldn't risk that. I stepped down inch by inch. The stone finally clicked into place without a hitch. Now it was covered by the carpet, and above me the cottage was roaring like a furnace.

I was entombed. Ovened.

The vents showed a hazy glimpse of orange redness to either side. Fine, but there was smoke starting to drift in from the direction of the back garden. My water and food I placed for safety on the lowest shelf, where I couldn't possibly knock them over. I swiftly took stock of what I had to fight with. First, his ignorance of my priest hole. Second, the weapons I had available.

There were the powder guns, but black powder is notoriously unstable. Even the modern version such as I had got from Dick Barton could not be completely free from capricious behavior. Weapons already loaded could easily explode in heat. I'd heard of it happening. Still, if I loaded a couple of pistols and left them cased and carefully pointing along one of the vents, there might not be too much risk, and they'd be cooler. I stuffed my shirt into a vent and shielded the other with my body. I switched on the torch.

I decided on the Barratt pair although they were percussion. The sight of my bloodstained hands frightened me almost to death. I was glad I hadn't got a mirror, because my face was probably in a worse state still. Shakily, taking twice as long as usual, I loaded the pair of twin barrels and slipped valuable original Eley percussion caps over the four nipples. Half-cock. Then I loaded the Samuel Nock pair. They were more of a danger in this growing heat, being flintlock, as the powder in the flashpan was external to the breech and so more easily ignited. For what it was worth I laid them flashpan downward in one of the vents.

The heat was greater now. Smoke was still drifting from one vent. I must find some means of creating an increased draft from one vent to the other, perhaps bringing in cooler fresh air from outside to dilute this hot dry air inside the priest hole.

Barrels. Barrels are tubes. The longest barrels I had were on the Brown Bess and the Arab jezails. Perhaps, I reasoned, if I drew in a deep breath facing one vent and blew it out down a barrel lying along the other vent I would be all right with the faint draft it was bound to create. But I'd need to take the breech plugs out. The tools were handy, which was one blessing.

As I worked I stripped naked. The heat was almost intolerable now. I used up a whole bottle of water wetting my shirt and using it to cover my head. The barrels together would reach about half way down one vent, so they'd have to be bound in sequence. I did this with an old duster soaked in my urine, binding the rag around the junction of the two barrels to make it as air tight as possible. Because the priest hole was so narrow I had to complete the job standing on the steps with one barrel already poked inside the vent's shaft and the other sticking out past my face. By the time it was done I was quivering from exhaustion.

I tried my idea of blowing but the heat was beginning to defeat me. The air entering my lungs was already searingly hot. From above my head came frantic gushing sounds, creakings, and occasional ponderous crashes, which terrified me more than anything. The walls would be burning now, and the beams would be tumbling through the living-room ceiling. Twice I heard loud reports as the glass windows went. It must be an inferno. I was worn out and dying from heat. Too clever by far, I'd got myself into the reverse of the usual position. I was safe from smoke and being cooked in an oven. If only I could bring air in.

I forced myself to think as the blaze above my head reached a crescendo. What could make air move? Propellers, windmills, waterwheels? A fan. A jet engine. A ship's screw. A paddle device. What had they used in prisoner-of-war camps when digging those tunnels? Bellows, conveyors of buckets, paddle engines? Bellows.

Below me, on the shelf near my precious bottle of water, was the air gun. I had a pump for it, but at what rate did it actually pump air? It usually needed about four minutes to fill the gun's copper globe going full pelt, and that was tiring enough. I took the implement and gave a couple of trial puffs. The force was considerable, as it indeed would need to be, seeing that the eventual ball pressure was enough to propel a fourteen-bore lead sphere some thousand yards or so. I clasped it to me and put the screw nozzle against the open gun breech projecting from the vent. With some difficulty I began pumping. Almost immediately I felt a marvelous gentle breeze against my back from the opposite vent, but there came an unpleasant inrush of smoke with it. I would need to blow air out in the opposite direction. There might be less smoke that side.

The barrels were easy to swap over as the vents were of a height. I simply slotted them in, having to mend the junction on the way across. That way around it was easier to use the pump, because I found I could use the wall as a support and one of the shelves as a fulcrum for my elbow. This time I was rewarded by the cool air on my shoulders without very much smoke. I guessed that a faint breeze must be blowing the fire and smoke in the direction I was facing.

There was a certain amount of squeaking from the air pump, and its leather bellows flapped noisily, but in the cacophony from the fire above nothing I was doing could possibly be distinguished from the other noise. My only worry was if he saw a steady current of air somehow piercing the slanting smoke from somewhere in the grass. The shifting firelight would help.

As minutes went by I improved on the system. Once it became obvious the system was working, I started settling down to a less frantic rate. I might, I reasoned, have to do this forever. You see fires still burning days after they've started, don't you? I counted my rate at about twenty pumps a minute. By stuffing my shirt into the vent around the jezail barrel I improved the motion still further by preventing any back draft. All incoming air was from the opposite side. Occasional gusts of smoke frightened me now and again, but they weren't too bad.

I tried pausing for two consecutive beats to listen. Was there shouting from above? I dreamed—Was it a dream?—I heard a big vehicle revving, followed crazily by a sound of splashing of water. But the bastard might be trying to pretend the firemen had arrived. Twice I was near screaming for help. Drenched and demented, I resisted and pumped on, haunted by the memory of the stables which had burned down behind the old rectory. Submerged by the low evening mist, horses and stables were found as just ashes a full day later. And worse still I had no way out whether it was friends or foe on the other side, except through the flames.

For some daft reason it seemed vital to suppress hopes of people like Margaret and Tinker Dill, those smug bastards in comfort somewhere who were believing I wasn't dying. The smarmy pigs, all of them. I sobbed and sobbed, pumping crazily on amid the lunatic noise.

One really monumental crash interrupted me about an hour or two after my life-supporting system had been started. That would be the central longitudinal beam, I thought. The whole cottage was down now, with the exception of maybe part of a wall here and there.

After that, nothing but the faint shushing roar, the ponderous crumblings and tremors all about me, and the steady slap-click-pat-hiss of the ancient bellows pump wafting beautiful cool air over my shoulders and out through the old barrels.

Nothing but my arms moving, the pump handle slippery from sweat and spurts of blood as a cut reopened briefly. Nothing but leaning one way for a hundred pumps and another way for another hundred to ease my tiredness, nothing but the hiss of outgoing and the gentle coolness of incoming air. The question of survival receded. I became an automaton.

There was nothing in my mind, no thought, no reasoning, no plans, virtually no consciousness, nothing but to continue pumping forever and ever and ever and ever.

16

It must have rained about ten o'clock that Sunday morning as far as I was able to tell. All that did was make the wretched ashes cool a little faster than they'd otherwise have done.

As time went on the noises above lessened somewhat, though the intolerable heat reached a peak some hours after the sounds of the fire had faded. The first improvement I noticed was that smoke wasn't coming in anything like as frequently as it had. My breathing was difficult from the heat, though, and once I cried out in pain when, shifting my cramped position on the steps, I inadvertently touched the flagstone above my head. It burned my arm, and stinging blisters rose swiftly on my skin. As I resumed my pumping they burst and serum washed warm patches down my arm and onto my knee. I'd been going some eight hours at a guess when I finally decided to chance a minute's rest.

Numbly, I forced myself to work out the time by counting. The vent was showing that daylight glow. I could actually hear the cracklings of the settling ash mixed incongruously with faint twitters of the birds. No sound of revving engines now, no faint shouts either real or imaginary. If the firemen had come at all, they were gone now. And a wise murderer returns to see his job's properly done. Maybe he was already sifting through the embers for the turnkey. I know I would have done just that. God knows, I thought wearily, what the robin thinks of all this. I drank about a third of my water and endured the discomfort as the heat rose while I sat down. The ache was almost pleasurable. Sitting and eating dry bread and cheese seemed almost bliss after the horrible efforts I'd expended at the old bellows. Within two or three minutes, however, the heat rose again and I had to resume my action with the air pump to cool the cell down and allow me to breathe properly.

Throughout the morning I drove myself into forming a scheme. I would pump for about five minutes, then rest for as long as I could tolerate the heat, upon which I'd resume pumping. Limping along in this fashion for a while, I soon realized I'd overestimated the rate at which the incoming air cooled my prison. I reluctantly had to increase pumping time to about half an hour or so, which gave me sufficient coolth for about five minutes. There was an additional danger here, in that I was tempted to fall asleep while resting. I had to prevent this by standing up.

With time to think I became bitter. Where the hell were the fire people? And the police? And my lazy, swarmy, self-satisfied bloody friends? Why weren't they calling frantically for me, digging through the ash with their bare hands? I would. For them. But Lovejoy's nearest and dearest let him have a private bloody holocaust. The swine had all assumed I was shacked up elsewhere with some crummy bird. Could life be so outrageous that I'd been trapped by an armed maniac and so-say roasted alive by him in my own bloody home, and the entire country was just not caring enough? I wept from frustrated anger at the insult. All life in that moment seemed utterly mad. No wonder people just set out determined to simply get what they could. Who could blame them? The proof was here, in ashes above me. And I, honest, God-fearing Lovejoy, finished up buried underneath the smoking ruins of my own bloody house, cut, filthy, bleeding, weary, and as naked as the day I was born.

My elbows were like balloons full of fluid, swollen and soggy. My wrists were more painful still but not so swollen. Despite them and the blisters I had to resume at the bellows.

As time wore wearily on I became aware of lessening temperature. In rest periods I could hear rain on grass and a faint drumming. Could it be rain on the old Armstrong? My rest periods were becoming longer and safer and the need of cool air was not so absolute. I was able to risk sitting down and having a rough meal.

Eventually there came a time when I felt it would not be risking total extinction to fall asleep. I lodged myself upright on the steps and was into oblivion within seconds.

You'd never seen such a sight. The cottage was a pile of smoking cinders and ash. In the dusk the garden seemed so small without the cottage to make the plot seem a little more imposing. The whole scene was pathetic. Where the kitchen alcove had been the ash was knee deep, perhaps the result of my water trap. Water was seeping from below, there, probably from a damaged rising main.

The rain had ceased. Smoke still rose from the debris in places. You can't help wondering at the curious consequences of physical events, almost as much as at biological goings-on. Why, I wondered, had that particular crossbeam, lying half charred among the ruins, not burned all the way through as the rest appeared to have done? And why was part of the wattle-and-daub wall still standing to a height of about three feet close to where the front door stood, with the rest in ashes?

It had taken me a full hour to extricate myself from the hole. The weight of smoldering debris had made the slab difficult to lift. Still, I thought grimly, the murderer can't push even his phenomenal luck too far. Quick-to-burn stuff makes light ash.

I placed the time at about nine o'clock Sunday night. The grass was wet from the rain. I had the sense to kick ashes back onto the paving over the priest hole to obscure signs of my escape, and I skipped swiftly onto the damp grass because my trousers were smoldering. With the same facility of the previous night I knew he'd gone. I had the Nock with me and slipped it to half-cock for safety.

The car was a wreck, the tires shreds of charred rubber, the paint gone, the metal twisted, and the trimmings burned to blazes. I hadn't a bean. Except for the few items down in the priest hole I was bust. Dizziness forced me to rest a few minutes. I sat in the darkness beneath the hedge to recover and bathed my face with wet grass. There was nothing for it but to ask for help, but from whom?

My neighbors didn't get back until Monday as a rule, so they weren't about yet, assuming I'd guessed right about it being Sunday evening. Other people up the lane couldn't be approached. I knew hardly any of them, and anyway I would send them into screaming fits by heaving out of the darkness like a charred scarecrow. I would have to phone somebody. Muriel? Margaret? Jane? Tinker? Dick or Brad? Who was safe?

There were signs people had come. Great marks were gouged in the gravel path. Several bushes were crushed. A fire engine, probably. Foot hollows in the grass were filled with rainwater already. A small crowd of well-wishers, half disappointed at not seeing Lovejoy crisped, the rest busy speculating which bird it was that had luckily seduced me away from the danger. Friendship's a great restorative.

The idea of a telephone seemed bizarre. You just pick up the receiver, dial, and have a perfectly normal conversation with whoever's at the other end. After a night such as I'd spent? I'd heard somewhere that people rescued from bizarre episodes full of danger—like sailors on a raft for days—weren't allowed back to normal life immediately but were put into solitude until the idea of rescue became a tangible reality. Maybe human brains can't accept too much relief all at one go. Not knowing if I was doing right or not, I compelled myself to sit there beneath the darkening hedge watching the ruins smolder, trying to keep my relief from dominating my thoughts.

The proper thing to do would be to walk through the gathering dusk to the policeman's house. It was only about a half-mile. Nobody would see what a state I was in. He might lend me some clothes. I was wearing socks, shoes, trousers, and a shirt, all filthy and torn. Caked as I was with grime, ashes, and dried blood, I couldn't be a pretty sight, cut and blistered. Or perhaps the telephone booth? Our one public phone was always lit and stood by the village pond in front of the Queen's Head. We have no street lamps, but the place was too prominent.

After some two hours or so tasting fresh damp air, I rose creakily, holding on to the hedge to keep myself upright. It proved difficult even to walk, to my surprise. I kept to the verge of the gravel path so as to make no noise and examined the lane before limping quickly across, carrying the two-barreled pistol now at full cock should my premonitions let me down.

My neighbor has two cottages knocked into one and extended to the rear. Like me he has a curving gravel path up to the front. I ignored this and crept slowly through his garden to the rear of the house. To help in harvesting his apple trees, he has two extending ladders in an open shed there. I laboriously carried one to the house and climbed to an upstairs window. Anybody can get in modern catch windows. Within minutes I was blundering about downstairs in the darkness and on the phone.

I dialed Margaret. Mercifully she was in.

"Thank God!"

"What's He done to earn gratitude?" I snapped. "Look. Have you your car?"

"Yes. Did you know—?" she began.

"I know. I'm still in it."

"*What?*"

"Come and get me, please." I rang off.

I'd cleared away any trace of my trespass in the house as best I could and was back in the shelter of my own hedge by the time her Morris approached. Funny how bright the headlights seemed.

"Lovejoy?" Her voice was almost a scream as she slithered to a halt on the gravel. The cottage really did look like something from a nightmare.

"Here."

I stepped from the hedge and she really did scream before I could calm her.

"It's only me, Margaret."

"My God! Are you—?"

"Sorry about the fancy dress," I said wearily. "Calm down."

"What's happened to you? The police phoned me. I came around. We've looked everywhere. The fire brigade was here. It was terrible. Somebody said you'd gone off with—"

"Turn the headlights off, there's a good girl."

With her help I got in and leaned back feeling almost safe. She slid behind the wheel. I could see her white face in the dashboard's glow.

"Shouldn't I phone Geoffrey, or—"

"Disturb him at this hour?" She didn't miss the bitterness. "I'll take you around to the doctor's."

"No," I snapped. "Are you on your own at home?" She nodded. "Then can I come there, to clean up?"

"Yes." She started the engine and backed us down to the lane. "Did you manage to save anything?"

"One thing." I said, lying back, eyes closed. "Me."

Bathed and in some clothes Margaret happened to have handy—perhaps from the estranged husband—I examined myself in the bathroom mirror. I'd have been wiser to stay filthy. My face was cut in a dozen places. An enormous bruise protruded from my temple. My left eye was black, a beautiful shiner. I'd lost a tooth. My hands were blistered balloons.

She gave me a razor to shave with, a messy job with more blood than whiskers.

"Your husband's?" I asked.

"Mind your own business," she said.

She made a light meal and I went to sleep on her couch with the television on. I couldn't get enough of normality. She sat in an armchair close by to watch the play.

"Let me take that."

I hugged the Nock close and refused to give it to her. "I'm, trying to make the pair," I said, a standard antique dealer's joke.

She didn't smile.

17

The day dawned bright and brittle. For an hour I could hardly move a joint and tottered about Margaret's house like a kitten. A bath loosened me up. I felt relatively fresh after that. Just as well, I thought, as it was going to be a hard week.

The telephone rang about eleven, Tinker Dill asking if I'd been located. I told Margaret to say I'd gone to London for a couple of days with a friend. She didn't like this but went along with it. The story was that the post girl had seen the cottage afire. She'd called the police, the fire brigade, and an ambulance —a thorough girl. I made Margaret ring Dandy Jack to say she wouldn't be in to the arcade for a few days and to let prospective customers know she'd be back soon.

I also got her to ring Muriel and say there'd been an accident of some description. She told her about the cottage and what she'd heard over the phone. Muriel seemed dismayed, Margaret reported to me. Real tears, as far as one could judge.

"Well, some people love me anyway," I cracked, leering with my gappy grin.

"God knows why," she said.

They gave me a column and a picture—of the burned cottage, not me—in the local paper on Tuesday evening. Police, it said, were making inquiries. Arson could not be ruled out. My own whereabouts were not known, but speculation was that, in the throes of a depressive illness, I had accidentally started a fire and died, or else I was staying with friends. It was made to sound fifty-fifty, and who cared anyway. Too bloody casual by far. The ruins were being searched for clues. It was widely known that I was mentally disturbed after the unfortunate accidental death of a close friend. By Thursday I was written off from public awareness, which suited me. The local paper went back to the more important foot-and-mouth disease.

On Friday I asked Margaret to take me for an evening drive.

I felt absolutely calm. The Nock just fitted the glove compartment, wrapped in a dry duster to prevent scratches. All anxieties and fears vanished in the calm that certainty brings.

Margaret had been marvelous during the week. We'd chatted about antiques and I'd been pleasantly surprised at how stable my thoughts were, and how I enjoyed her company. She'd taken the full account of my escapades at the cottage quite well. The only point where I differed from the truth was the invention of a hidden tunnel beneath the sink out to the back of the copse. After all, the honor among dealers is bendable, and my remaining stuff was still down there. I'd partly paid my keep by authenticating some musical seals of about 1790 for her, lovely they were too.

"You're not going to do anything silly, Lovejoy?" she asked as she drove.

"People keep asking me that."

"And what do you answer?"

"Women do keep on, don't they?" I grumbled.

"I'm waiting, Lovejoy."

"Of course I won't do anything silly."

"Then why the gun?"

"Because he'll have two, and a crossbow."

The car slowed and she pulled in, angry as hell. "Who?"

"The murderer."

"Is that where we're going?"

"Yes." There was a prolonged silence. For a moment I thought she was going to make me get out and walk.

"Does she know?" she asked after a while.

"No."

"Certain?"

"No." I paused. "But she might have guessed. You know how people guess the truth sometimes."

We resumed the journey.

"Aren't you going to tell me?" she said.

"Lagrange, the Reverend gentleman from near the wrong bird sanctuary."

"So that's what all those lies were about stuffed birds?"

"Well, the odd white lie," I mumbled.

"You mean it was him? The shooting? The . . . Sheila's accident? Everything?"

"And poor Eric Field."

"And you?"

"And *nearly* me," I corrected.

"But he's a . . . a reverend."

"Borgia was a pope."

I told her how my suspicions gradually rose about Lagrange. Who had the best opportunity of learning of Eric Field's find? Who couldn't afford a car yet would need a small put-put for frequent local visits in a rural community? And what was more natural than a woman's bike for somebody who occasionally had to wear priestly garb? An authentic collector-friend of Eric Field's, he'd started revisiting Muriel's house. Collectors, like all addicts, need money. He was with Muriel in her posh gray Rover when Sheila gave me the turnkey at the war memorial. Muriel had blossomed with his feet under her table, and he'd started watching me from then on, using Muriel's place as a base. Not a lot of trouble with a small motorized bike and only a narrow valley to cross.

I'd stirred things up and reaped the consequences.

It fitted together.

"Are you . . . fond of this Muriel?" Margaret wanted to know.

"I suppose so."

"More than that?"

"I'm always more than that where women are concerned," I said starchily, then added, "She's just a child, gormless and bright."

"Poor Lovejoy," Margaret commented in a way that told me I'd had my lot. You can tell from how they say things, can't you?

She asked if Lagrange would be at Muriel's. I said I couldn't be sure.

"He's her boyfriend, though," I said sardonically. "The gardeners set me off thinking the other day, by being embarrassed at the odd innocent cussword. Thought I was him for a moment. He's a cool customer. Insists on having tea in the same room where he killed poor Eric Field stone dead. A right nutter."

"Couldn't we get the police—?"

"Not just yet."

After that I got a dose of the thick silence they give you as corrective when you've transgressed. Nothing short of a miracle would make her smile on me again.

There was a small blue motorized bike to one side of the Field drive, no surprise. We rolled to a stop.

"Lovejoy?"

I paused, already at the door.

"Is there no . . . jealousy in this?"

"Jealousy?"

"You. Of him."

"No." Nothing had ever seemed so true. She accepted it and came with me.

"Good heavens!" Muriel, open-mouthed, was in the doorway. Her reaction was a disappointment to me. They are supposed to faint or at least go white, but then she hadn't felt quite so gone over me when I was alive, so I couldn't really expect too much.

"You remember me, Muriel?" I'd planned a much cuter entrance line and forgotten it like a fool.

"Why of course, Lovejoy!" She drew me in. "We heard the most dreadful things about you. The papers said you'd had a frightful accident! Do come in."

"I'm Margaret."

"I'm Muriel Field— Oh, you telephoned. I remember. Please come in. What a perfect nuisance the newspapers are!"

"Aren't they!" The bastard would be in the study glugging tea from the Spode. Hearing my name would have made him slurp.

"What's happened to your face?"

"The odd crossbolt," I said airily. "Nothing much."

"Look, Mrs. Field," Margaret started to say, but I cut in sharply.

"Where's Lagrange?"

Muriel looked blank. "How did you know he was here?"

"His scooter, and a good guess."

"Hello, Lovejoy."

He was standing in the doorway to the study, pale but polite as ever. For some strange reason he was actually glad to see me.

"You bastard," I said. "You killed Sheila."

"Have you brought the police?"

"No. They'll have to wait their turn."

"Just one witness." He nodded at Margaret.

"Don't fret," I snapped.

"This is the man, Lovejoy," Margaret said to me quietly.

"Eh? What man?"

"He came to the arcade asking about you some time ago. I tried to tell you but didn't see you for days." The phone message to ring Margaret I'd not followed up.

"Darling what is this?" Muriel went to stand by Lagrange.

He shook her from his arm impatiently. "Nothing of any

importance, my dear." He was even beginning to talk like a squire.

"He killed your husband, Muriel," I said. "He used the Judas guns your Eric had found. Some 'accident' while Eric was showing them to him, probably. Then he stole them for himself, only he couldn't quite make up the set. The turnkey was missing. I got it from the auctioneers. He saw me and Sheila. You remember coming out of the car park and seeing us by the war memorial. Then he killed her and tried to do the same for me."

"That set of sharks—incompetent sharks!"

I understood his anguish and rejoiced. "You'll never get it now, Lagrange."

His eyes blazed. "Won't I?"

"Lovejoy, what did you mean?" Muriel glanced from me to Lagrange. "What does he mean?"

"He killed Eric," I explained. "Then he realized your brother-in-law had asked me to find the Judas pair. He assumed Sheila'd kept the turnkey in her handbag for safety when his burglary at my cottage proved fruitless. So he snatched it and he pushed her under the train."

"No!" Muriel stood facing me practically spitting defiance. No compassion for Sheila now, I observed.

"Yes," I said calmly.

The pig was smiling. "Well, yes," he admitted, shrugging.

"You must recognize the truth, love," I told Muriel gently. "He's mad, a killer. He tried to kill me with a crossbow, and he burned my cottage down."

"I knew you'd get out," he said regretfully. "There wasn't a trace of you. I had a suspicion you were still around, an odd feeling you were *there*. Know what I mean?"

"Oh, yes," I said bitterly. "I know."

"Lovejoy," Muriel said.

"What?"

"He is my husband."

"Eh?"

"We were married three days ago." I swallowed but it was too late to change things.

"Don't be tiresome, my dear," Lagrange said to her. "You'd all better come into the study. No use standing in the hall."

I uncovered the Nock and brought both flints to full cock. "Stay where you are."

He gave me an amused glance. "Don't you be tiresome, either," he said, and walked ahead of us all into the study. That's the trouble with conviction. It can be as crackpot as anything, like the great political capers throughout history, but if it's utterly complete even sane people become meek in its presence. We three followed obediently. He paused at the desk and gestured us to be seated. I remained standing as an act of defiance. The swine actually smiled at that. "Now, Lovejoy," he said conversationally. "What to do about all these goings-on, eh?"

"Police," I said.

"Rubbish. Act your age."

"I'm going for them now. And I'd advise Muriel to come with us for her own safety."

"You're getting more fantastical every minute." He put his fingertips together, a thin burning little guy intense as hate, certain of success. How the hell had he got Muriel under his thumb? "I shall simply deny everything. And you, Lovejoy, aren't exactly the most convincing witness, are you?"

"You'll never get away with it."

He snorted with disgust. "That the best you can do, Lovejoy —a line from a third-rate play?" He grinned. "I already *have*, you see."

"I . . . I don't understand." Child Muriel was at it again.

"I'll explain everything to you later," he said calmly. "Well, Lovejoy?"

"Margaret," I said desperately. "We're both witnesses. We heard you admit it."

"Certainly," he said. "A man forces himself into my house

carrying a loaded gun and accuses me of murders, burnings, robberies I'd never heard of—wouldn't anyone try to humor him into reasonable behavior? Especially as he's known to be . . . mentally unstable?"

"Lovejoy," Margaret said gently, "come on home. He's right."

"Then I'd better kill you now," I said.

"Alternatively . . ." Lagrange said, and pulled out from his desk a case. He placed it on the leather writing surface with pure love shining from his eyes. "Alternatively, Lovejoy, there's a means here to settle your obsessions once and for all."

"Is that . . .?" My voice choked and my chest clanged and clanged.

"Oh." He feigned surprise. "Would you care to see them?" He turned the case so the keyhole faced the room and gently opened the lid.

Never in all my life. I mean it, never, never. They lay dark and low, glowing with strength. Their sheer lines were hymnal, the red felt imparting on their solemn shading a ruby quality setting them off to perfection. I practically reeled at the class, the dour elegance of the pair of flintlocks embedded in the shaped recesses. Not an atom of embellishment or decoration marred their design, not a hatch on either butt, yet there was the great maker's name engraved in the flickering luminescence of the casehardened locks. A silver escutcheon plate was set into each stock, but no monogram had been engraved on either. The only jarring feature was the empty recess for the turnkey. Murderer or no murderer, I thought, reverently taking out the missing item from my handkerchief and passing it over. For once he lost his composure.

"Thank you, Lovejoy," he said, moved. "Thank you. I'll remember that."

The set was complete.

"What are you going to do?" Muriel was shaking me.

I emerged irritably from my reverie to hear Lagrange say,

"Do, my dear? Why, we're going to resolve poor Lovejoy's delusions permanently."

"How?" I asked, knowing already.

"Duel," he replied. "We have the perfect means here already to hand. And the motivation."

"You can't!" It hurt me to hear Muriel's cry for him. "You might be—"

"Not I," he said calmly. "Impossible."

"Is it really?" my voice asked from a distance away.

"Oh, yes. I'm afraid so."

"Lovejoy, come away!" Margaret dragged at me, but I couldn't take my eyes off the Judas pair.

"He won't, my dear," Lagrange said gently. "He has to know, you see. Don't you, Lovejoy? Also, let's all four contemplate the benefits of a duel—no loose ends for a start. Either way, I'll gain by knowing Lovejoy won't one day lose his composure and come to kill me with that rather splendid Samuel Nock he's waving, and should matters inexplicably go right for him he'll have the satisfaction of knowing justice was done. And nobody can be blamed afterward, can they? I'll explain to the police I was made to fight a duel by this maniac here, and alternatively Lovejoy will have the proof of the means of poor Eric's death."

"Please, Lovejoy!"

"No, Margaret." That was me speaking, wanting to duel with a monster. I could hardly stand from fear at what I was doing.

"There's no choice," Lagrange said kindly to her.

"But—"

"No, Muriel." He pointed to a chair and she crossed meekly to sit down. "There's absolutely no danger. It will all come right. Now." He shut the case and carefully lifted it. "If you will excuse me."

"Where are you going with that?" I demanded. He looked pained.

"For black powder," he said. "I have it in another room. Surely you don't expect me to leave these in your tender care?"

"You might . . ." I dried, not knowing what he might.

He smiled. "I'll bring the powder back, dear boy," he said. "You can load them any way you like, I promise."

His bloody certainty dehydrated my tongue and throat. I could feel my forehead dampen with sweat.

The door closed.

"Muriel, you have to stop this." Margaret shook her shoulder roughly.

"Will he be all right?" was all she could say.

"You stupid woman!" Margaret cried. "Don't you care that he killed your husband? And Sheila? He's going to do the same to *him!*"

Even paralytic with fear I felt a twinge of resentment that everybody was speaking of me as if I was an odd chair. I spent the few minutes waiting, while Margaret went on at Muriel and me alternately, trying to think and failing hopelessly. The terrible idea emerged that it would happen too quickly for me to understand. I might—would—never know.

"Everyone all agog?" He came in smiling, as though to one of his little tea parties. "You'll find everything in order, Lovejoy. Oh, and I thought we shouldn't put too many finger marks on such lovely surfaces. Here's two pair of white gloves."

"I know."

"I'm phoning the police." Margaret rose, but Lagrange stepped between her and the door.

"No, my dear. Lovejoy?"

"Er, no," I managed to croak.

"Lovejoy!" she pleaded once, but I already had the gloves on. He offered me a piece of green velvet to rest the flinters on as I loaded.

I became engrossed. Their sensual balance, vigorous and gentle, almost brought them to life. Their quality sent tremors up my fingers as I poured black powder from the spring-loaded flask. Tamp down. Then bullet, then wadding. Test the vicious Suffolk flints for secure holding in the screwed jaws of each weapon, flick the steel over the powder-filled pan only after ensuring the touchholes were completely patent. Interestingly, I noticed one had gold stock pins and the other silver. I'd never even heard of that before.

Ready. Lagrange was waiting at the desk. Throughout the loading he had watched intently. I'd been stupid. Only now it dawned on me that I'd fallen for every gambit he'd played. Being so distrustful of him fetching the powder I'd been tricked into loading. Now here I was with the obligation of having to offer both to him for his choice under the rules. No wonder the bastard kept smiling.

"Ready, Lovejoy?" If only he didn't sound so bloody compassionate. I nodded.

"No!"

"Get away with you!" I snarled at Margaret, and offered both weapons to Lagrange after making a clumsy effort to swap them from hand to hand to confuse him.

"Thank you. This one, I think." He took one and weighted it in his hand. "The study's not quite sixty feet, Lovejoy, I'm afraid."

"That's all right."

All this stuff about ten paces is rubbish. It was usually ten yards each way, carefully measured, making twenty yards in all.

"Where would you like to stand?" he asked pleasantly.

"I want both of us to sit at the desk."

His eyebrows raised. "Isn't that a trifle unusual?"

"There are precedents."

"So there are." He wasn't disconcerted in the least.

I brought a chair and sat as close as I could, opening my legs wide for balance. He sat opposite.

"Closer, please."

"As you wish." He hitched forward until his chest touched the rosewood. We leaned elbows on the top and waited.

"We need your assistance, Muriel," he said calmly. "Over here, please, with your handkerchief."

She came and stood by the desk.

"Hold your handkerchief up above us," he told her, watching me. "When Lovejoy tells you, let it fall."

"But—"

"Do as you're told, my dear," he said patiently. "It won't take a moment. You'll be quite safe. Do you understand?"

"Yes," she quavered.

It was now. No matter what I did, how fast I was, how good my aim, I would die the instant I pulled the trigger. He needn't fire at all. Yet I'd loaded both meticulously. There couldn't possibly be any trick.

I pointed the beautiful Damascus barrel. His gaped back at me. Behind the cavernous muzzle his calm, smiling face gazed into my eyes. We held position, brains and barrels inches apart, me sweating in terror and him enjoying the last few moments of my life. In a blur I saw the single line of awareness—his eyes, his barrel, the black muzzle, then my own ribbed barrel and, in a blur nearest me, the blank silver escutcheon plate just showing above my hand gripping the stock. The silver plate set in the stock. All in a line, from his mad hating brain to my terror-stricken consciousness. Eye to eye, in a line. And, nearest of all to my eye, the silver escutcheon plate. In line with my eye.

"Now," I said.

The handkerchief fluttered down. I turned my flinter around as the handkerchief fell, *pointed the muzzle of my own gun against my forehead, and pulled the trigger*.

There was no explosion, but the recoil snapped the barrel *forward* against my skull and nearly stunned me from the force of the blow. As if in a dream I saw Lagrange's eye splash red and gelatinous over his face. His head jerked back. He uttered a small sound like a cough as he died and the flinter in his hand clumped heavily down onto the desk, firing off as the hair trigger was hauled back by his convulsing hand. The ball sent glass flying from a shattered window. I was missed by a foot or so.

It seemed an hour before the echoes died away and the

screaming began. My senses slowly came creeping back.

It was logical. Your eye's in line with the barrel. So if it's your own gun that shoots you through your right eye, aiming it frontward at your own right eye will shoot your opponent. But how?

Amid the moanings and the tears, as poor Muriel wailed and screamed on Lagrange and Margaret tried some hopeless first aid, I examined the pistol I held. It was the one with the silver stock pins—that was probably how to tell them apart. Lagrange had picked the gold-pinned one. Yet mine was still loaded.

I got the green velvet and the case and set to work while somebody phoned the police. It's always important to unload a gun first, no matter how old it is. This I did safely, then dismantled the lock. Any flinter enthusiast lifts the lock out to look. It does the piece no harm and the mechanism's everything.

It was exquisite, delicate as a lady's hand. There were not two lock mechanisms inside as I'd guessed. The standard firing mechanism was actually unworkable. The trigger activated a small air chamber which worked by propelling a missile along a reverse concealed barrel toward the eye of the person holding the weapon. The missile pushed up the silver escutcheon plate on a minute hinge unlocked by the trigger. Highly ingenious. The better your aim the more likely you were to shoot your eye out.

But what was the missile? What exploded into his eye with such force? Clutching the parts, I went out into the hall. An old crone—the one I'd seen on my previous visit—was sobbing information into the telephone.

"Excuse me," I said politely, taking the phone from her to calm her down. "When the Reverend came out of the study a few minutes ago, where did he go?"

"Into the kitchen for some ice," she said, red-eyed, and at last I knew.

You crushed a piece of ice into a sphere in the bullet mold, inserted it into the concealed chamber, and made sure your opponent got the silver-pinned pistol. No wonder the pathologist had never found the bullet. The ice had pierced Eric Field's eye, penetrated his brain from there, and instantly melted away from his body heat, just as the ice ball was now doing in Lagrange's silent skull.

Yet . . . I sat at the hall table examining the weapon further. Who on earth had had the gall, not to mention the authority, to compel the world's greatest gunsmith to make a treacherous pair of weapons like this so long ago? Dueling was crackers, but it *was* supposed to be an affair of honor. Somebody had wanted to be bold and dashing around the Regency clubs but was unwilling to run any actual risk while going about it. I inserted the turnkey and rotated gently against the spring's weight.

The locks came out and showed their secret beneath the recess. There, engraved in gold was my revelation: REX ME FECIT. *The King made me.*

It brought tears to my eyes. I had a vision of the old gunsmith in his darkened workshop, all his assistants and apprentices sent away for the night, as in obedience to royal command he fashioned the brilliant device alone. Yet he was determined his complaint should be recorded for others to realize in later years. The old genius *had* made the Judas pair. They bore all the characteristic features of his consummate skills. But he cleverly recorded the customary Latin inscription to tell the despairing truth *why* he had: the King had made him. That deranged sick man George the Third, or the Prince Regent, wencher and gambler? Probably the latter.

Before the police arrived I'd substituted a pair of officer's pistols, Joseph Heylin of London, quite well preserved in an altered cutlery box, for the Judas pair. Lagrange's small collection in the morning-room cabinet was easy to find and he'd left the key in. I whisked the Heylin pair outside, where I burned a little black powder in one and loaded the other. Amid the general alarms and excursions nobody took much notice of me wandering about. I swapped both pairs. Going out to wait for the police to arrive, I tucked the Durs case on top of the engine of Margaret's Morris beneath the hood—carefully wrapped, of course, and wedged in good and proper.

And when the pathologist couldn't find the bullet? I was suddenly unutterably weary. I decided to let them all guess till they got tired, as they had of old Eric Field and Sheila. When the Old Bills came hurtling up I was back in the study wringing my hands with the others. I was clearly very upset.

Three weeks later Margaret was quizzing me again. I was just back from George Field's.

"What did he say when you told him you'd found the Judas guns?"

There'd been no mention of Margaret's husband. We'd just taken up together, going into her arcade shop daily and scratching a living. Naturally, the inevitable had happened, as it always does when a man and a woman live in one dwelling, but that was all to the good and it was long overdue anyway, as we both knew.

The trouble was this conversion gimmick they have. That I was quite content to drop in to my old garden and still hadn't started clearing away the cottage's ruins obviously niggled her. She'd let several hints drop, asking what plans I had for rebuilding and suchlike. You have to watch it.

"Lovejoy!" she complained. "You're dreaming again."

"Oh. He said he didn't want anything to do with them, said it was poetic justice."

"And then?" she pressed.

"He shut the door."

"I don't think he likes your instincts very much, Lovejoy."

"I'm surprised," I said. "I'm really quite lovable."

"Won't you offer them back to Muriel?" was her next gem. Sometimes I think women have no sense at all.

"Of course," I said, thinking, That's not poetic justice.

"When?"

"Well," I said after a long, long pause. "Well, maybe later."

217

"Lovejoy!"

"No, look, honestly," I began, searching desperately for some way out. "It's honestly a question of time and personal values."

"Lovejoy! How *could* you! It's stealing!"

"Honestly, love, judgment comes into it," I said. "I'd take them back this very minute but—"

"You've absolutely no excuse!" She started banging things about.

"Maybe in time, honestly," I said. "I'm only thinking of her."

Women have no tact, no tact at all. Ever noticed that?